To Rye and many a happy hour spent there

Chapter One

Lahore, October 1879

**He was acutely aware of her warm body sitting snug beside him and of the slightest trace of jasmine filling the air.**

There was no space in his life for a woman— for any woman. From a young age he had steered clear of entanglement despite others' best efforts, and he was not about to let a girl he had met by chance destroy his peace of mind.

She had given him no clear answer as to why she was wandering in the grounds of Chelwood and he had the uncomfortable suspicion that she had come looking for him. If so, alarm bells should be ringing very loudly. Her physical attractions were manifold, and they were dangerous. He was quite aware of that. If that was all… But he knew it was more than that—there was an ardent soul behind those deep brown eyes, and even in the small time he had been with her he'd found himself tumbling towards its bright sun.

**Isabelle Goddard** was born into an army family and spent her childhood moving around the UK and abroad. Unsurprisingly it gave her itchy feet, and in her twenties she escaped from an unloved secretarial career to work as cabin crew and see the world.

The arrival of marriage, children and cats meant a more settled life in the south of England, where she's lived ever since. It also gave her the opportunity to go back to 'school' and eventually teach at university. Isabelle loves the nineteenth century, and grew up reading Georgette Heyer, so when she plucked up the courage to begin writing herself the novels had to be Regency romances.

**Previous novels by this author:**

REPROBATE LORD, RUNAWAY LADY
THE EARL PLAYS WITH FIRE
SOCIETY'S MOST SCANDALOUS RAKE
UNMASKING MISS LACEY

# THE MAJOR'S
# GUARDED HEART

Isabelle Goddard

First published in Great Britain 2013
by Mills & Boon, an imprint of Harlequin (UK) Limited.
Harlequin (UK) Limited, Eton House, 18-24 Paradise Road, Richmond, Surrey TW9 1SR

© Isabelle Goddard 2013

ISBN: 978 0 263 89860 6

Harlequin (UK) policy is to use papers that are natural, renewable and recyclable products and made from wood grown in sustainable forests. The logging and manufacturing process conform to the legal environmental regulations of the country of origin.

Printed and bound in Spain
by Blackprint CPI, Barcelona

# Chapter One

Sussex—Autumn 1813

'I am the resurrection and the life. He who believes in me will live even though he dies.'

Lizzie tried to arrange herself more comfortably on the hard pew. She had never attended a funeral before and it was proving a sombre affair. She'd hoped for a large congregation and her wish had certainly been granted—the church was packed to overflowing. But the gathering of the fashionable that she'd envisaged had not materialised. Her eyes travelled over the crowded rows as the vicar continued to intone the burial service. Not one bonnet worth a second glance, she thought, then chided herself for her flippancy.

She had never met Sir Lucien Delacourt but it seemed the whole of Rye had turned out to mourn his sudden passing. It was a measure of her dawdling existence that she had looked forward to this event. Mrs Croft was kind enough but in the three weeks Lizzie had been at Brede House there had been few visitors under the age of sixty, and her days had been filled with a wearisome round of fetching and carrying.

A flutter of white handkerchiefs amid the unrelieved black of the congregation reinforced the sadness of the occasion. Adding to the gloom was the church itself for it was vast and beneath its dark and lofty beams, even such a large gathering as this appeared puny. Stained glass paraded along two entire walls of the building, but on a day of gathering cloud the images seemed flat and opaque. Only the flowers, vase after vase of them filling the altar steps, breathed light. But they were lilies with a perfume so intense that Lizzie began to feel nauseous. And though she tried hard to stop herself fidgeting, the bonnet ribbons tickling her chin were becoming more unbearable with the passing of each minute. She was as anxious now to be gone from the church as she had been earlier to trip across its threshhold. Her restlessness drew a sharp glance from Mrs Croft: the dead man had been a great friend, Lizzie knew, and the old lady was finding this day difficult.

'My father, Lucien Delacourt, was once a soldier—brave, honest and true—and these were the qualities he made his own throughout his life.'

Lizzie was startled. A new voice had succeeded the vicar's and it was electrifying. Tender but strong, as though honey had coated steel with a sweet warmth. It cut through Lizzie's irritation and compelled her bolt upright. Her eyes were drawn to the lectern and remained fixed there. A man she had never before seen had begun to read the eulogy. Her heart gave a strange little jump as she drank him in. He stood tall and straight, his dark clothing fitting him with a military precision, his face lean and tanned, as though he had spent most of his life out of doors. He was surely a soldier. She watched his hands as he read—strong and steady even at a moment of great emotion. Only his hair flew in the face of such determined restraint, abundant and gleaming, challenging the dreariness of the place and the day. Even the dim lighting could not suppress its bright glory, catching at highlights and dancing them in the air, until it seemed the man's head was circled by a veritable halo. Lizzie sat mesmerised as he spoke lovingly of the father he had known. The words themselves hardly registered, it was the music of his voice that caught at her, the power of his presence that kept her still and breathless.

The service was over and she forced herself to muster all the patience at her command while Mrs Croft slowly checked the contents of her reticule and began a search for a mislaid umbrella. *Hurry up, hurry up*, Lizzie pleaded inwardly, *he may be gone by the time we get to the door.* But he had not. A straggle of parishioners had lingered behind to offer their condolences and Sir Lucien Delacourt's son had a word for every one of them. While they waited in line, the clouds overhead began to mass into a thunderous blanket. It was doubtful they would make it out of the churchyard, she thought, yet alone reach Brede House before the coming cloudburst, but she was sure it would be worth the inevitable drenching.

At last the final parishioner had said his

final word and the young man was clasping her employer by the hand.

'Dear Mrs Croft, my grateful thanks for coming out on such a day.'

His voice was as beautiful as when he'd spoken from the church lectern, and it was not just his voice that was beautiful. He seemed even taller now, more upright, more hardened. Lizzie liked what she saw and, from the shelter of the laurel hedge, unashamedly looked her fill.

'How could I not come, Justin? Your father was a dear friend, a very dear friend. And to lose him so swiftly. I cannot believe he is no longer here with us.' Henrietta Croft dabbed her eyes with an already sodden handkerchief.

'Nor I.' He squeezed her hands warmly, but his lips compressed into a thin, uncompromising line. 'I had no idea how frail he had become.'

'He has not been well for some time,' Mrs Croft conceded, 'but the heart to fail! None of us expected that.'

'I should have been here, seen what was happening…' His eyes seemed to wander to a distant horizon and there was a bleakness in their depths. They were green—or were they grey? Lizzie wondered. They held a curious light, ever changing like the sea, and they spoke of restlessness, of constant motion. 'I should have realised how vulnerable he was.'

'You must not blame yourself, Justin—you have been fighting for King and country, and very bravely by all accounts. It is what your father would have wanted. And he has left you problems enough, I don't doubt. The estate must be in a sorry mess.'

'You excuse me too easily, but you are right. Chelwood has been badly neglected of late. I cannot make up for my prolonged absence, but I can at least set the estate on a smooth path before I leave.'

'You are planning to leave Rye?' Mrs Croft's voice rose in surprise.

'I must return to my regiment as soon as I am able.'

'But I thought—' her voice tailed off uncertainly '—I thought that now you have inherited the title and estate, you would be certain to sell out.'

'I shall never take that course, Mrs Croft. The army is my life. There can be no other for me.'

Lizzie's heart did another of those curious little bounces. She knew exactly what he meant, for did she not have the military in her very bones? He was a kindred spirit, she was sure, and she wanted to rush forwards and clasp those strong hands in hers. Taking a deep breath, she walked boldly from her shelter and into their conversation. Mrs Croft seemed surprised to see her, as though she had recently mislaid her companion as well as her umbrella, but was happy enough to perform introductions.

'Justin, this is my young friend, Miss Elizabeth Ingram. My cousin was kind enough to recommend her. Elizabeth has recently been a pupil teacher at Clementine's establishment.'

'Miss Ingram.'

Justin Delacourt bent his head in the smallest of bows and when he looked up, his eyes refused to meet hers. Or so it seemed, for Lizzie was certain that he had deliberately looked through her. She felt angry at him and angry at her foolishness. Why was she always attracted to unsatisfactory men? She should not have allowed herself to be beguiled: he was cold and indifferent and far too like another soldier of her acquaintance. He was also quite possibly short sighted, for she knew herself to be a pretty girl and was unused to such treatment. There could be nothing in her appearance surely to give him disgust.

The dove-grey gown had been carefully refurbished in deference to the occasion and a straw villager bonnet hid the dazzle of auburn curls. Did he perhaps not like women? Or was it simply snobbishness—she was a mere companion and therefore not worthy of notice?

'I found the eulogy you gave most moving.' She was determined he would take notice of her—he need not know it was his voice rather than his words that had moved her so powerfully.

'Thank you, Miss Ingram. You are very kind.' Another dismissive bow and he was turning back to his father's old friend.

'Such a splendid congregation, do you not think?' she prodded. 'They were most appreciative.'

'I am glad you feel so. It is difficult to distil into a few words all that one man has meant.'

'You must have succeeded. I did not know your father during his lifetime, yet I found myself touched by your words.'

She knew herself guilty of flummery but at least she had forced him to look at her. She saw his gaze travel over her figure and linger unwillingly on her face and though he might wish otherwise, he could not prevent his eyes betraying a flicker, a flash of interest. He gave a brief nod in acknowledgement and then abruptly looked away to address Mrs Croft once more.

But whatever he was about to say was lost. A well-dressed, middle-aged couple emerged just then from the shadows of the church and hurried towards them. There was a subdued murmuring of greetings mixed with farewells and in a moment Mrs Croft was leading the way from the churchyard with an unwilling Lizzie in her train. She would have liked the chance to make clear to Sir Justin Delacourt that she was not a woman to be ignored.

'How wonderful to see you back in Rye where you belong.'

Caroline Armitage held out impulsive hands to the young friend towering over her, but for a moment received no response. Justin was struggling to regain his composure. He had caught sight of a light-grey skirt half-hidden behind the greenery, but he'd had no idea of its owner. Then without warning she was upon them and he'd glimpsed a pair of the deepest-brown eyes and a profusion of errant curls the colour of fresh chestnuts tucked beneath her bonnet. He had been taken aback at how young and pretty she was, far too young and far too pretty to be anyone's companion, particularly a semi-invalid like Henrietta Croft. And far too interesting for his peace of mind. Experience had taught him that women were either manipulative or missish, and neither held any attraction, but he had sensed straight away that Miss Ingram was different. She was no simpering miss that was certain—she had a bold and lively spirit, but an honest one, he thought. She was also quite lovely. In truth, he had been unnerved by her and that made him feel ridiculous.

'Justin? How are you, my dear?'

He gave himself a mental shake and embraced Mrs Armitage with affection, extending a warm handshake to her husband.

'My very humble apologies for not having visited you both. It is what I most wanted to do but there has been so much to arrange at Chelwood and I have been home but a week.'

'We understand that well enough,' Caroline soothed. 'It has been the saddest homecoming for you.'

'Sad indeed, but I have the best of neighbours. I mean to pay Five Oaks a visit next week—once the formalities are over—and will hope to find you both at home.'

'You know that whenever you come, you

will be very welcome,' James Armitage said heartily. His eyes slid uneasily towards his wife and a warning hand was placed on her arm.

Justin saw it and wondered. The Armitages were lifelong friends and their son, Gil, his closest companion for as many years as he could remember. But a note of discomfort had crept into the conversation and that was odd. Perhaps they, too, thought he should have been at Chelwood caring for his father rather than fighting battles in Spain. In an effort to cover the awkward moment, he said, 'I collect that Gil is away on some adventure right now. As soon as he is back, he must ride over to Chelwood and tell me all. We will have much catching up to do—it must be over three years since I was last home.'

To his horror, tears began to fill Caroline's eyes and two large drops trickled down each of her cheeks.

'Mrs Armitage, what have I said?' Justin was genuinely alarmed. In all the years he had known her, he had never seen her cry.

'I'm sorry, it is not your fault,' she managed at last. Then the tears became too much and she retreated into the folds of a cambric handkerchief. Her husband signalled urgently to their waiting groom to escort her back to the carriage.

'I must apologise for my wife's tears.'

There was an uneasy pause until Justin asked, 'Can you tell me what ails Mrs Armitage?' He felt upset as well as mystified. Caroline had been more of a mother to him than his own and he loved both the Armitages.

'It was your mention of Gilbert, you see,' James said haltingly. 'The boy is missing.'

'Missing?' Justin's face was blank. 'But how, when?'

'He has been missing for three months and as to how, we have no notion. That is the problem. One day he was here and the next he had gone. He simply vanished from sight, taking nothing with him except…' James hesitated a moment '…except a little money and a family ring—but they would certainly not be sufficient to sustain him for long.'

'But surely someone must know where he is. His friends? Your family elsewhere in the country?'

'We've sent messages everywhere, but no one in the family has seen him. As for friends, Gilbert has few. It was always you, Justin— he needed no other—and since you have been away, I think at times he has felt very lonely.'

Another reproach to add to the already long list, Justin thought. 'I have been away too long and I am sorry for it—but is there no one in the neighbourhood that might have an inkling of his whereabouts?' It seemed impossible to believe that a healthy, young man could disappear so completely.

'The new excise officer was the only person he talked to. He spent a good deal of time with him walking the marshes and the cliffs, as he used to with you. But then the poor chap died. It was most tragic. It was Gil who found his body, you know, lying at the foot of the cliff. He'd fallen in the darkness, though there are rumours that it might not have been an accident. Whatever the truth of it, Gil was greatly upset and I have sometimes wondered if that might be the reason he disappeared. I have no real idea, though. I seemed to have lost touch with my son, long before he vanished.'

Justin's brow furrowed, trying to think himself into Gil's shoes, but he found that he was as much out of touch with his friend as James. 'Might he have gone to London?' he offered without much hope.

'We certainly considered the possibility and sent Robert—you remember Robert, I'm sure—he is as true a servant as you could hope for. We sent him up to London almost immediately to make discreet enquiries, but not a sound or sign did he gather. After two weeks we called him home. It was a hopeless task.'

The more Justin considered what James Armitage had told him, the more puzzled he grew. Gil was the best of fellows, but he had never been the most adventurous of spirits. As boys, it had always been Justin that had led the way: building dams, scrumping apples, climbing every one of the estate's five oak trees. It was always Justin who thought up the pranks which landed them in trouble. He hadn't seen his friend for three years but when they'd last met, he'd thought Gil more sober than ever—hardly a man liable to kick up his heels and vanish without a word.

'I imagine you have tried the local doctors,' he said tentatively, fearing that his friend had come to harm in some way, but unable to say so directly.

'I've checked with every doctor in Sussex,' Armitage said grimly. 'I've even visited the mortuary, but not a sign of him.'

There was a rustle of silk and a slight aura of perfume and Caroline had left the carriage and was almost upon them. 'You must help us, Justin.' Her eyes were large and frightened and the appeal went straight to his heart.

'Mrs Armitage, you know that I would do anything to help, but...'

'You must find him,' she said, her voice cracking. 'You must find Gilbert.'

Her husband wrapped a restraining arm around her. 'You cannot ask the impossible of our young friend.'

'If anyone can find our son, Justin can.' And she turned back to the carriage, her eyes already beginning to fill with fresh tears.

Justin shook his head. He felt enormously weary. His father's sudden death had shocked him far more than he'd thought possible. He had felt guilt, unbearable guilt, that he had shirked a sacred responsibility. And the guilt had only grown when he'd arrived home and found Chelwood in the most wretched disarray, a rascally bailiff having taken advantage of Sir Lucien and enriched himself at the expense of the estate. Weeks of work were before him if he were to put Chelwood to rights—even with a new and trustworthy man in charge. And if that was not bad enough, he had this minute learned that his dearest friend had gone missing without a trace, had vanished into the air like a magician's accomplice. What was going on? Whatever it was, Caroline Armitage expected him to discover it.

'Take no notice of my wife,' James was saying. 'She is naturally distraught. Of course, you cannot be expected to begin looking for Gilbert, with your own life in such turmoil. Please forget her words and forgive us for intruding so badly on a day when your own grief should be paramount.'

For an instant he had forgotten his father, forgotten Chelwood, forgotten even his beloved regiment. He had been remembering his dear friend and all they had meant to each other. In some strange way the image of the girl he had just met was entangled with the image of Gil. But why? It made no sense, but nothing about this day did. She was one complication he would be sure to avoid. There had never been space for women in his life and certainly not now; it was Gil he must think of.

'I'll try,' he said firmly. 'I doubt I will be successful, but I will do my damnedest to find your son.'

The rain had held off, the black rolling clouds travelling swiftly westwards, but in their place the October sky was left bleached, an eerie half-light pervading the world. The congregation that only minutes ago had poured from the ancient church and through the ivy-covered lych gate had seemingly been blown away on the wind. Not a soul was visible as they walked down the hill and towards the water, leaving behind the shelter of the Citadel, the small hilly enclave of houses and lanes that clustered around the church. She wondered if Justin Delacourt was still holding forth in the churchyard or whether he, too, had disappeared into the ether. He was a very attractive man, but he had angered her—he had been curt and uncivil. Yet despite that she could not stop herself from feeling intrigued.

'Who were those people, Mrs Croft?'

They were battling their way along the river bank against a furious wind. 'I mean the people who greeted Lord Delacourt so warmly—almost as a long-lost son.' And then when her companion did not answer, she said doubtfully, 'It *is* Lord Delacourt, isn't it?'

'Not quite.' Mrs Croft allowed herself a smile. 'You have elevated him. On his father's death, he became Sir Justin Delacourt, though I imagine he would prefer to be known as Major. And those people, as you call them, were the Armitages.'

'They seemed to know him very well,' Lizzie reiterated.

'They own Five Oaks. Their estate adjoins Chelwood Place and Justin Delacourt ran tame there for most of his childhood. The Armitages were very good friends of Sir Lucien and the two sons were the closest of companions, always playing together or learning with the same tutor.'

'He is fortunate to have such good friends with whom he can share his sadness.' Lizzie hoped her sympathy might encourage the older woman to talk, for she had found Mrs Croft to be annoyingly discreet, volunteering only the most superficial of news.

'They will have much to say to each other, yes—sadnesses aplenty to share, I make no doubt.'

The tone was vague and the comment cryptic, but when Lizzie dared to look a question, she was met by brisk dismissal. 'It can be of no interest to you, child.'

But it was of interest, or at least Justin Delacourt was. 'I gather Sir Justin is in the army.'

'Indeed, and seemingly wishful to remain

a serving officer, though I am not sure how practical that will prove.'

'How long has he been a soldier?'

'It must be some six years. He has done well, even though he went as an enlisted man. In the Light Dragoons, I believe. He wanted no favours, but his natural leadership has seen him rise very quickly through the ranks. That and this dreadful war England has been fighting these past ten years.'

Lizzie was silent, thinking of a father who had fought that war and was still fighting. She had not seen him for three years and the last occasion was one she chose not to remember. It was on her account that he had been given compassionate leave to travel to England. She blushed even now, remembering her disgrace.

'Soldiering must suit him,' she said, wrenching her mind away from the unhappy thoughts.

'Why would it not? Lucien was a splendid soldier himself until he was persuaded by that woman to sell out. Harangued into submission, more like.'

The old lady seemed to realise that for once she had said too much and finished brusquely, 'I have no doubt that his son will make certain to avoid the same fate.'

The wind by now was even fiercer, blowing directly from the sea and howling so loudly that it was impossible to speak more. Lizzie's bonnet was almost torn from her head and she quickly untied its ribbons and held it tightly to her chest. She had been entranced in her first few days in Rye to be living so close to water, but after several days of inclement weather, she had begun to wish that Mrs Croft's house was situated in the small town's medieval centre. The remnants of Rye's fortifications protected the Citadel's narrow, winding streets against all but the worst weather, but Brede House was open to a battering from every direction. To the south, the English Channel roared its might and to the north lay marshland and an even harsher landscape.

Today the path home seemed longer than usual and she had several times had to support her companion as they battled to stay upright. Below them the river stretched like an ocean of restless grey, every inch rucked by the fearsome gale into ridges of cold, foaming white. It was as though the sea had lost its way and come calling. Wave after wave of water hit the shingled mud with a fierce power, then retreated with a roar, sucking and dragging to itself everything in its path.

Above them gulls competed with the cacophony, dipping and calling in tempestuous flight, unsure it seemed whether to rejoice in the wild beauty encircling them or to take shelter from its dangers.

They had gone some half a mile along the coastal path when they heard a faint noise coming to them on the wind. Both ladies turned towards it, clutching their skirts and bonnets against the oncoming blast. A coach had stopped on the Rye road, running parallel to the path, and a figure was striding towards them.

'Mrs Croft, please forgive me.' Justin Delacourt arrived, only slightly out of breath from having battled the wind at a running pace.

She blinked at him, surprised by his sudden appearance when she had thought him on his way back to Chelwood.

'Please forgive me,' he repeated, 'You should not be out in such weather. I have been most remiss in allowing you to slip away in that fashion.' He kept his gaze fixed on the old lady's face and Lizzie prickled with annoyance. She appreciated his concern for her employer, but not that he was again choosing to ignore her.

He affected not to notice her baleful stare

and went on with his apologies. 'I fear that I was so taken up with talking to the Armitages, that I did not ask you to drive with me. I am a little tardy but please allow me to offer you a seat.'

'How kind of you,' Mrs Croft murmured. 'But there is really no need. We have only a short way to go.'

'You have at least another fifteen minutes to walk and, in this weather, that is far too long. Allow me to escort you to my carriage.'

'My companion...' Mrs Croft began. 'You are in your curricle, I believe.'

He shot Lizzie a swift glance. He had finally been forced to acknowledge her presence, she thought. She had been right about his snobbishness—in his eyes she was a servant and could happily be discounted. But it was Mrs Croft she must think of and she softly nudged the older lady towards the arm he was extending.

Seeing that lady's hesitation, he said in an even tone, 'I am sure Miss Ingram is hale enough to finish the walk on her own. If not, of course, my groom can dismount.'

'Surely not—a groom to relinquish his seat!' Lizzie was unable to bite back the words. 'That would never do!'

Henrietta Croft looked uncomfortably from one to the other, bewildered by the animosity slicing through the air.

'Naturally you are welcome to travel with us, Miss Ingram. Perkins will not mind walking the short way to Brede House.'

'And nor will I! As you say, I am hale enough.' She turned to her employer. 'Go in the carriage, Mrs Croft,' she said warmly. 'You are finding this weather very trying and should reach home as soon as possible.'

Justin gave the old lady an encouraging smile, but she was shaking her head. 'I think it best that I continue my walk with Elizabeth. She will take good care of me, you can be sure.'

But still he lingered and Mrs Croft was forced to renew her persuasions. 'You will have many calls on your time, Justin, and I'm sure you must wish to return to Chelwood as soon as you are able.'

He was dismissed and turned back to the road and the waiting Perkins, but as he walked away Lizzie's voice carried tauntingly on the wind. 'It must be so arduous, do you not think, Mrs Croft, being a soldier *and* a landowner?'

* * *

Within a short while they were turning into the drive of Brede House and its avenue of trees, where the wind blew much less strongly. The respite allowed them both to regain their breath and Lizzie to regain her temper. She began to feel ashamed of her rudeness and wished she could forget the wretched man, but annoyingly he was filling her mind to the exclusion of all else.

'Do you know which regiment of Dragoons the Major serves in, Mrs Croft?'

'You ask a vast amount of questions, young lady.' Henrietta had not appreciated the little drama they had just played out and wanted to speak no more of Sir Justin. 'What possible interest can Major Delacourt's regiment have for you?'

'My father is also a military man,' Lizzie responded, a hot flush staining her cheek. Any mention of Colonel Ingram always raised this peculiar mix of pride and resentment in her. 'He is even now in the Peninsula and has been for very many years.'

'I had no idea, Elizabeth.' Mrs Croft spoke more kindly as they reached the house and a maidservant struggled to open the door to them. A final gust of wind found its way between the trees and literally blew them into the entrance hall. 'You must take tea with me, my dear. It is the very thing to warm us and prevent our taking a chill.'

Henrietta divested herself of coat and hat, located the missing umbrella still in the hat stand, tutted a little and then led the way to her private parlour. Lizzie was soon perched on the edge of the satinwood sofa, but unable to relax. It was not her first invitation to the sanctum, but she always felt awkward. It wasn't just that the parlour lacked air and was stifling in its warmth or that the furnishings were depressing—Mrs Croft refurbished frequently, but always in brown. It was the fact that she was never quite sure as a companion where she belonged. Governesses suffered the same problem, she imagined—you were an educated gentlewoman forced to live within the restrictions of polite society, yet you were also at the beck and call of an employer. One day you could be greeted as a friend by those who came to the house, while on another you might be ignored. It made life difficult, for in truth you belonged nowhere.

'And where is your father at this moment, my dear?'

'To be honest, I have no idea. The last news

we received at the Seminary was months ago just after the battle of Vitoria. He sent a message to Bath to say he was still alive and well.'

A two-line message, she thought unhappily. That was all she warranted, it seemed. Now if she had been a boy... How many times had she dreamed of being able to follow the drum along with her father instead of this tedious life she was forced to lead.

'I am sure that very soon there will be more news,' her employer said comfortably. 'While you are with me, you can be certain that Clementine will send on any messages she receives at the school.'

'I'm sure she will,' Lizzie said dully. It was lucky, of course, that Clementine Bates had a weakness for military men, for Lizzie knew for a fact that Hector had not paid her school fees for many a long year and it was from charity that Clementine had allowed her to remain at school as a pupil teacher. His charm seemed to suffice for whatever was owing, but it left his daughter having to live her life at Clementine's behest. And right now her behest was for Lizzie to suffocate in a small coastal Sussex town with her cousin, a lady four times Lizzie's age.

'It must be very upsetting for you,' Henrietta continued, 'not seeing your father for such a long time. But there is always the possibility that he may be granted leave. Now that would enliven your days a little, would it not?' She sipped delicately at her tea and smiled at the young woman sitting across from her.

It was hardly likely, Lizzie thought, that her father would come to Rye. But something else *had* occurred to enliven her days. Sir Justin had arrived in her world and he offered an enticing challenge. He was aloof and ungracious, arrogant even, but she was sure that she could make him unbend. Men were not usually slow to fall for her attractions and she did not see why he should be any different. It was not the most worthy of ambitions, she confessed, but there was little else in Rye to excite her. Mrs Croft was a dear, kind lady but their life at Brede House was wholly uneventful. And after all, hadn't she been sensible for a very long time?

## Chapter Two

A hazy October sun greeted Lizzie when she pulled back the curtains the next morning. The storm had subsided and it was a day to snatch a walk, if Mrs Croft did not immediately require her services. As luck would have it, her employer had chosen to entertain an acquaintance from St Mary's congregation that morning and was looking forward to talking with her alone. A companion had always to know when her presence was not welcome, Lizzie thought, but this visit suited her well. She had expected life in Rye to be hedged around with every kind of petty rule and restriction and it was true that the work was tiring and the days monotonous. But when Mrs Croft did not require attendance, she seemed happy for Lizzie to spend her few precious hours of freedom walking the quiet lanes of the neighbourhood. The old lady might not have been so happy today, though, and it was best that she knew nothing of this particular ramble.

She had a very good idea in which direction she should wander and, after a hasty breakfast, set off towards the Guldeford Ferry. This small boat service was the quickest means of crossing the river to the marsh opposite and Lizzie had discovered that Chelwood Place was a mere three miles away, across the river and lying to the left of the marshland. A casual comment to Hester, Mrs Croft's maidservant, and she had the main direction in which to walk. Like so many estates locally, it was famous for the wool it produced and Hester warned her that if she found her way there, she might well have to walk through fields of sheep. Sheep did not bother Lizzie.

The sky was a misty autumn blue, the sun growing stronger by the minute, but she knew from painful experience that the weather could change at any time. Several foot crossings and the small ferry were all that separated Rye from the marsh and thick mists could descend at any time. Just a few days ago she had begun her walk in brilliant sunshine, only to be turned within minutes into a veritable sponge by rolling, wet clouds. This morning she would risk a light costume, she decided, but wear a protective cloak. She could always abandon the garment once she arrived and bundle it behind a bush. Intent on looking her best, she had selected from a meagre wardrobe her second-best gown, a dress of primrose-floret sarsnet. It was a trifle old-fashioned, bought for her by Colonel Ingram as a peace offering before he returned to the Peninsula, but she had tried to bring it up to date by trimming it with French flounces. With a bright yellow ribbon threaded through chestnut curls and a primrose-silk reticule, painstakingly made over the last few evenings, she had checked the mirror and thought herself presentable. She hoped she could persuade Major Delacourt into thinking so, too.

The ferry proved as dirty as it was ancient and she spread a handkerchief across one of its grimy seats before lowering herself carefully on to a broken plank. The ferryman gave her a disdainful glance, spat over the side and turned to the shepherd who had followed her on board. Their muttered conversation in an impenetrable dialect filled the short journey, but Lizzie was happy to be ignored—she was on another adventure.

Once on the other side of the river she found the path to Chelwood without difficulty. As the maid had described, it skirted the marshland at its edge and travelled in a semi-circle inland. Beneath this morning's high blue skies the marsh looked benign, but here and there the wooden structures marking a sluice gate raised their profile above the flat landscape, looking from a distance for all the world like a gallows. There was something primeval about this world, something deep and visceral, and brave though she was, she wasn't at all sure she would want to venture into its depths. She was glad that Chelwood lay at its very edge.

An hour's brisk walking had brought her to the gates of the mansion. They were immense, a rampart of black iron decorated with several rows of sharp-tipped spikes; they were also resoundingly locked. She saw to the side the lodge-keeper's house and wondered if she dared lift the knocker and ask to be admitted. But what reason could she give for her visit? To stroll casually up the carriageway

towards the house and 'accidentally' bump
into Sir Justin was one thing, but to demand
admittance on a formal visit when no invitation had been issued was quite another. Possibly there was a second way into the grounds,
an entrance less thoroughly guarded. Veering
left away from the lodge, she began to push
through the deep grass which grew around
the perimeter wall. She walked until her small
boots were sodden with dew, but without
finding any break in the masonry. The wall
was as old as the iron gates, old and crumbling, and here and there large stones had
come loose, sometimes falling to the ground
altogether. There were footholds for anyone
daring enough to climb and she stood for a
while, calculating whether she could manage the ascent without damaging either her
dress or her limbs. She would have to, she
decided. She hadn't donned her second-best
dress and come all this way merely to turn
around. But it was more than that. She didn't
know why, but it seemed important that she
see Justin Delacourt and see him today. She
would have to get over that wall. She chose a
section which was crumbling more quickly
than elsewhere, and, hoisting her petticoats up
around her knees, she reached up and began

hand over hand to climb. It was fortunate that
the lane abutting the wall was narrow and
largely unused for it would have been mortifying to be caught showing her stockings.
Once at the top of the wall she saw to her
dismay that a long drop lay before her, since
the inside of the wall had not succumbed to
the elements as badly and there was no easy
path to the ground. She took a deep breath,
closed her eyes and jumped, landing awkwardly on her ankle and bruising her shins.
But she was in.

A pain shot through her foot. She would
not stop to worry about it: she wanted to catch
Justin Delacourt before he left the house for
the day's business and she had already wasted
too much time. She had landed in a thicket
of trees that appeared to be part of a larger
spinney. The undergrowth was lush and uncut
and straggling branches obliterated her view.
Pushing past the trees, one after another, she
attempted to find a path, but there seemed
always to be another row of trees to negoti-
ate. Then the first drops of rain fell. She had
been so busy clambering over the wall she
had not noticed the blue sky disappear and a
menacing black take its place. The few drops
soon became a downpour and then a veritable

torrent. She pulled her cloak tightly to her, sheltering her hair beneath its hood, but in a short while she was wet to her very skin. The ground beneath her began to squelch ominously and she was dismayed to see the lower part of her dress as well as her boots become caked in mud. How could she accost Sir Justin looking such a fright? There was no hope for it—she would have to abandon her adventure and return to Brede House.

But she was lost. The spinney seemed to stretch for miles and she had no idea of the direction she should take. She could only hope that she would hit upon a road before she dissolved in the driving rain. She was bending down to loosen a twig that had become tangled in her skirts when she felt something hard and unyielding pressed into her back. A voice sounded through the downpour.

'Right, me lad, let's be 'avin' yer. Yer can disguise yerself all yer wish, but yer ain't gettin' away. Not from Mellors. Chelwood Place ain't open fer poachers—not now it ain't.'

She tried to turn round and reveal herself. There was a gun to her back, she was sure, but if the man who spoke knew her to be a woman, surely he would lower the weapon and allow her to go.

He was taking no chances. 'Keep yer back to me.' He prodded her angrily with the weapon. 'I knows yer tricks. Now walk!'

'But…' she started to protest.

'Keep quiet and walk. By the sounds of yer, yer but a striplin'. What's the world comin' to, eh?' And Mellors tutted softly to himself while keeping his weapon firmly levelled.

Lizzie had no option but to walk. She could sense the tension in the man and feel the hard pressure of the shotgun in her back. She did not think he would use it if she tried to escape, but she could not be sure and dared not take the chance. She was marched for minutes on end until they were out of the spinney and walking over smooth lawns towards the main driveway. This was the spot she had been seeking. A gig was drawn up outside the front entrance—precisely as she had imagined. The baronet would be leaving, she had decided, and as he came down the steps, she would trip up to the front door, telling some story of having become lost and wandered by accident on to his land, and looking a picture of primrose loveliness. He would wonder how he could ever have ignored such a delightful girl and, filled with contrition, immediately set about trying to please her. That was the fantasy. The reality was that her feet oozed mud, her hair dripped water and, far from tripping, she was being roughly frogmarched to an uncertain fate.

The man steered her towards the back of the sprawling mansion. She was being taken to the servants' quarters, she thought—at least she would be spared the humiliation of meeting Justin Delacourt face to face. Down a long passageway they trundled, a passageway filled with doors, but at its very end a large, airy kitchen. The room was bright and homely, smelling of baked bread and fresh coffee and Lizzie realised how hungry she was. Her tiny breakfast seemed an age away.

'Look 'ere, folks,' the man said gleefully, 'look what I've caught meself.'

The cook was just then taking newly baked cakes from the oven, but at the sound of Mellors's voice, she stopped and looked around. The scullery maid on her knees paused in her scrubbing and the footman held aloft the silver he was polishing.

'You best put that gun down,' Cook said crossly. 'Master won't like that thing in the house.'

Mellors did as he was told, but was unwilling to give up his glory quite so quickly. 'See 'ere,' he repeated and pushed Lizzie into the centre of the room. 'Take a look at me very first catch. There'll be plenty more of 'em before I'm through.'

The cook sniffed at this pronouncement and the footman allowed himself a small snigger. Wearily the scullery maid began again on her scrubbing.

Lizzie stood in their midst, dripping puddles on to the flagstones, her cloak still wrapped around her, the hood still covering her head. Anger at this stupid man coursed through her veins. It wasn't his fault that she was drenched, she conceded, but to be treated so disagreeably and then made a fairground exhibit was too much.

She pushed back the hood on her cape and shook her damp ringlets out. The cook, the maid, the footman, stopped again what they were doing and gawped, open-mouthed. Mellors, busy fetching a rope to bind his victim's hands, turned round, surprised by the sudden ghastly silence. Even in her present state, Lizzie looked lovely. What she didn't look was a poacher.

'What *have* you done, Mr Mellors?' Cook rubbed the flour from her hands with a satisfied smile on her face. It was clear that the new bailiff was not a popular man among his fellows.

Lizzie was swift to use the moment to her advantage. 'How dare you!' Her voice quivered with indignation. 'How dare you treat a lady in such a dastardly fashion!'

Mellors looked bewildered, but still managed to stutter a reproof. 'But yer wuz poachin', miss.' His obsession was all-consuming and he failed to see the absurdity of the situation.

'Poaching! Are you completely witless? Do poachers normally come calling in a muslin dress?'

There was more sniggering from the footman and the unhappy bailiff hung his head a little lower. 'No, miss, but...'

'And if I am a poacher,' Lizzie continued inexorably, 'where are my tools? Do you think I have hid them? Perhaps you would like to search me for the odd snare?'

The footman guffawed at this idea, but the look she shot him bought his immediate silence.

'And where, pray, are my illegitimate spoils? Why be a poacher and be empty-handed?'

'You could 'ave 'idden the stuff, miss,' he tried desperately.

'Hidden? Upon my person, perhaps? You are ridiculous.'

'Mebbe you warn't poachin', then, but you wuz still trespassin',' he continued doggedly.

'I am no trespasser, you scurvy man.' Lizzie drew herself erect, making up in dignity for what she lacked in height. 'I came to call upon Sir Justin Delacourt.'

Mellors shifted uncomfortably. His master's name gave him pause, but he would not yet own himself beaten. 'So what were yer doin' in the spinney, miss? It ain't usual for Sir Justin's visitors to come by that way.'

For an instant Lizzie was flustered and she saw a small, sly smile creep over Mellors's face. There was no alternative—she would have to behave shamelessly.

'I met Sir Justin for the first time yesterday,' she said in a low voice, 'but I was deeply moved by his sorrow. I had not the opportunity then of speaking to him of his dead father and I came here today only to pay my respects. I meant well, but look how I've been treated!' She began to sniffle slightly and managed to squeeze several realistic teardrops from her eyes.

'There, there, my pet,' the cook weighed in. 'Look what you've done, you clumsy oaf!' She turned to Lizzie. 'Come here, my dear. You need looking after, not lambasting. Poor lamb, you're wet through.'

Lizzie coughed artistically. 'I meant no harm, ma'am. You see, I was so touched by Sir Lucien's death and his son's grief that I merely wanted to say how sorry I was.' A few more tears trickled down her cheeks without robbing her of one mite of beauty.

Mellors and the footman looked on askance, but the scullery maid clasped her hands to her breast, drinking in the romantic possibilities. 'I am soaked to the skin,' Lizzie continued, her voice barely audible, her hands clasped together in anguish. 'I have been in these clothes so long that I shall likely die of pneumonia.'

Her sudden terrified wail startled her listeners into action. There was a general fussing and clucking as the cook and the scullery maid took her to their bosoms and Mr Mellors protested his innocence and the footman was sure that a fit young woman would not contract pneumonia from just one soaking.

'What the *deuce* is going on here?' Sir Justin strode into the kitchen and in an instant the uproar ceased and was followed by a strained silence.

'Perhaps one of you would care to explain this mayhem and tell me why I have been ringing for coffee for the last ten minutes without answer. Do I employ you to serve me or not?' His beautiful voice held a new severity.

All of a sudden he became aware of Lizzie, abandoned in the middle of the room, and still dripping ceaselessly on to the floor. An expression of blank amazement replaced the frown on his face.

'Miss Ingram?' he queried. 'Can it be you?'

'It can.' She gave a saucy smirk at the bailiff and, since there was nothing left to lose, announced boldly, 'I have come to call on you, Sir Justin.'

Justin remained motionless, stunned by the vision before him. Elizabeth Ingram was the last person he expected to find in his kitchen, and to find her dripping and mud stained was astonishing.

'How came you here, Miss Ingram?' He almost stuttered the words.

'At the point of a gun,' she said bitterly. 'You should not complain that your servants are tardy, Sir Justin. One of them at least is a little too eager.'

'What can you mean?'

'Your bailiff believes me to be a poacher!'

Justin looked even more stunned, his hand ruffling the fair halo of hair. 'Mellors?' he queried, hoping for enlightenment, and was immediately subjected to the bailiff's impassioned defence.

'The lady wuz in a cloak, Sir Justin,' Mellors protested. 'She 'ad her back ter me and, in the rain, I took her fer a boy.'

'Then I fear you may be in need of spectacles!'

The other servants cackled joyfully at this sally, but Mellors's face took on a truculent expression. 'It were an easy mistake to make, Sir Justin. We've 'ad a spate of poachin', you knows that. You told me yerself to be extra vigilant.'

'Vigilant, yes, foolish, no. You had better wait for me in the office—I may be some time... And take that gun with you.'

The man slumped to the door, still ruffled. 'She wuz trespassin' for sure,' he managed as a parting shot.

Justin Delacourt turned impatiently to face his audience who seemed caught in a trance and had barely moved since he had entered the room. 'You may forget the coffee—but make sure that tea is ready in the library in ten minutes.' His tone was even more severe and the servants, forgetting their earlier gaiety, speedily resumed their chores.

Striding across the room to the hanging line of brass bells, he sounded one vigorously. 'I have this minute rung for my housekeeper, Miss Ingram. Mrs Reynolds will be with you shortly to escort you upstairs, so that you may—um—tidy yourself.'

He accorded Lizzie a brief bow and, without another word, walked through the door.

He strode to the library and waited. What the devil was the girl doing wandering in his grounds? Was Mellors right when he said she was trespassing? She must have been, otherwise why had she not called at the lodge and asked the porter for admittance. And how had she got in? The lodge gates were the only entrance to the estate, a fact bemoaned by servants and masters alike for years, but nothing had ever been done to improve the situation. And nothing would be done now, for there was precious little money for refurbishment. But Miss Ingram. He had been stunned at the sight of her and not just because she had no place in his kitchen. Even in her sodden condition she had looked lovely, her soft brown eyes wide with indignation and her fiery curls already drying to a glossy mass. He hoped her dress was not completely ruined for he thought it likely that her wardrobe was not extensive. Until the gown could be laundered, Mrs Reynolds must find a replacement from one of the many wardrobes scattered across the house. It would probably not be to Miss Elizabeth's taste but then she should not have come calling in a downpour, or, more accurately, she should not have come trespassing. He would have some questions for that young woman.

It was at least half an hour before he could pose them and when she slipped quietly into the library, all desire to question her fled. Her skin, still luminous from the rain, was blooming with health and her dazzling hair had been marshalled into some kind of order. But it was the dress that mesmerised Justin. A deep blue of the finest silk, years out of date, but showing the girl's shapely figure to splendid effect. He almost gasped. His mother had worn that dress and she, too, had been beautiful and well formed. In body at least, he amended, for there was nothing beautiful about Lady Delacourt's nature. But what had possessed the housekeeper to alight on that particular gown? He could only imagine that it was one of the few dresses that fitted his unexpected guest.

A lace shawl was draped across her bosom—just as well, Justin thought, else the temptation to caress her two beautifully rounded breasts would be too strong. His thoughts juddered to an abrupt halt. He was shocked, shocked at himself that he could think thus of a girl he hardly knew. 'Come in, Miss Ingram.' He had to clear his throat which had become very tight. 'Come in,' he repeated and gestured to the table. 'Alfred has brought tea and there are fresh baked madeleines. I hope you will partake of some or Cook will be disappointed.'

She did partake and with gusto. Justin thought he had never seen a young lady so happy to eat and the sight was strangely pleasurable. She became aware that he was watching her. 'I had hardly any breakfast,' she explained naïvely, 'and walking in the rain has made me ravenous.'

It was not exactly the response a society

miss would have given, but then Miss Ingram was hardly a society miss. She was a hired companion who spoke confidently and looked good enough to eat herself. In short, she was a conundrum.

'Walking was not all you were doing, I imagine,' he said gently.

She flushed a little and looked defiant. 'No, it wasn't. I was being marched across your estate.'

'But why were you in the Chelwood grounds?'

'I became confused and lost my way. Then that clunch of a bailiff found me and took me for a poacher.'

'You must excuse Mellors. He is new and very eager to be seen doing a good job.'

'He hasn't exactly covered himself in glory this morning,' she noted, munching her way through her third madeleine.

'But you,' he said, determined to bring the conversation back to her. It was difficult when she was sitting so close and looking more lovely in his mother's gown than ever Lady Delacourt had. He tried again to focus his mind. 'The only way into Chelwood is through the lodge gates and you didn't come that way. How did you get into the estate and why?'

The question was bluntly put for he had given up any pretence of subtlety. He couldn't play word games, not while his body was reacting so treacherously.

'I climbed the wall.' Her defiance was even more marked. 'And as for why, because it blocked my way.'

'Do you normally scale walls if they're in your way?'

'I don't normally meet them. Most people don't feel the need to live behind locked gates.'

She had quite neatly turned the tables. 'My bailiff considers that locking the gates acts as a deterrent to law breakers. But then he is unused to adventurous young ladies.' *As I am*, he thought. The idea of any woman in his mother's tight little circle lifting one elegant foot to the wall was laughable.

'Adventurous? Do you think so?'

'Few ladies of my acquaintance would hurl themselves over ten-feet walls.'

'I didn't exactly hurl myself and your friends must be sad company.'

'Acquaintances,' he corrected. For some reason he did not want her to think he was part of the *ton* society he despised. 'But you are right, they lack courage! They would never make a soldier!'

'*I* would—and that is what I most wish for.' He was startled for he had meant the remark only as a pleasantry.

She saw him looking astonished and laughed. 'Don't worry! I know that a woman cannot join the army, but I would give anything to do so—to be in Spain at this moment, to feel the camaraderie, the excitement, the thrill of victory.'

'Victory is not assured,' he warned. 'We have lost almost as many battles as we have won and it is only recently that the tide has turned.'

'I know. At Badajoz and Vitoria.'

He was intrigued. 'You have followed the war closely?'

'My father is fighting in Spain,' she said simply.

'Your father?' Her name had had a familiar ring, he remembered, when Mrs Croft first introduced her, but he had taken little notice. He had been far too concerned with her prettiness to think of anything else and far too disturbed by his response to it.

'He is not by chance Colonel Ingram?'

'He is.'

She was transformed, her face alight, her smile glowing. It was clear that her father was a hero to her—and why should he not be? Justin knew him by repute as a very brave man. 'You have met him?' The words were almost breathless and the plate of madeleines pushed to one side.

'Once. I met him only once. It was after Vitoria. His regiment was taking over from mine and I was about to leave. I had just received news of my father's death and knew that I must return to England immediately.'

'And how was he?' She was all eagerness. 'After the battle, he wrote only two lines to say that he was alive.'

'He appeared well, but I was with him little more than an hour.'

'Then that is one more hour than I have known.'

He refilled her cup and wondered if he should say more, for her voice had become shadowed and her liveliness lost. At length he said, 'When did you last see him?'

'Some three years ago.' She jumped up from her chair and wandered to the window. 'You have a vast estate here.'

For some reason she no longer wished to

talk of her father and he wondered what had happened three years ago. He found himself wanting to ask, wanting to know more of her, but good sense reasserted itself. He must keep the conversation to polite trivialities. 'Yes, most of it is given over to sheep farming, though we have some pleasant acres of parkland and a thriving kitchen garden.'

'Everyone farms sheep here.'

'That's because it is profitable, especially now that taxes have been reduced and we can export to France without a huge levy. The smugglers have gone out of business,' he joked.

'There are smugglers here?' She had turned back from the window, her eyes wide and her voice humming with excitement. The girl's vitality was entrancing, he thought, but she had a raw energy that could easily lead her into trouble. Another reason, if he needed one, to keep his distance.

'The smugglers have long gone,' he said firmly. 'Once the taxes were rescinded, smuggling lost its profit and therefore its attraction.'

'But it cannot only be wool that was smuggled.'

'Spirits and tobacco, I imagine. Perhaps

even tea. But the last gang of smugglers were
hanged years ago and the preventives are now
everywhere along the coast.'

'The preventives?'

'Excise men. So you see, you are unlikely
to discover an adventure here.'

Her face had fallen and he had to stop himself smiling at her disappointment. 'You must
find life as a companion a trifle slow.'

'Mrs Croft is very kind,' she said quickly.

'But still a lady in her eighties. Why did
you take such a post?' The more he spoke to
her—indeed, the more he looked at her and
felt her charm, the more odd it seemed.

Her response was tart. 'Possibly because I
don't own an estate like Chelwood.'

He could have kicked himself. She had evidently to earn her own living—no doubt Ingram was in debt and unable to help. Most
soldiers he knew were, for much of the army
had not been paid for months.

'I'm sorry,' he began, wishing away his
crass comments.

'There is no need to apologise, Major Delacourt. I find military men in general are blinkered. They see only the narrow world that is
theirs and nothing of the world outside which

can be quite as difficult as any military campaign.'

'I'm sure it can be.' He could find nothing better to say, but to his own ears he sounded indifferent, even condescending.

When she spoke again, her tone was a little too bright. 'I must leave you in peace. The rain has stopped at last and I should return to Brede House before it begins again. If you would ring for your housekeeper, I would be much obliged. By now my dress should be dry.'

'Nonsense. I will make sure that your dress is returned clean as well as dry, but in the meantime I will drive you back to Rye. The gig is at the door and you can be home in minutes, rain or no rain.'

She looked as though she might refuse his offer but when she stood, it was evident that her ankle was paining her and she capitulated.

'Thank you. That is most kind of you.'

Neither of them spoke as they drove the five miles back to Brede House, but he was acutely aware of her warm body sitting snug beside him and of the slightest trace of jasmine filling the air. He tried hard not to think about her, to abstract his mind from her prox-

imity, but failed miserably. His sharpened
senses relished her very nearness and he could
only thank heaven that the journey was brief.
There was no space in his life for a woman,
for any woman. Women were the very devil—
he should know that better than anyone—and
could ruin the best of men's lives. From a
young age he had steered clear of entanglement despite others' best efforts and he was
not about to let a girl he had met by chance
destroy his peace of mind. She was a mere acquaintance, not even that, an acquaintance of
an acquaintance. But it seemed that she was
refusing to play the part assigned to her—she
had given him no clear answer as to why she
was wandering in the grounds of Chelwood
and he had the uncomfortable suspicion that
she had come looking for him. If so, alarm
bells should be ringing very loudly. Her physical attractions were manifold and they were
dangerous, he was quite aware of that. If that
was all…but he knew it was more than that—
there was an ardent soul behind those deep-
brown eyes and even in the small time he had
been with her, he'd found himself tumbling
towards its bright sun. That thought made
him crack the whip and the startled horse
immediately picked up its pace. He really

must curb such fanciful inclinations, he reproved himself silently. Elizabeth Ingram was no more than a shadowy presence in his life and must remain so. She was far too lively and far too attractive and he had sufficient problems already.

## *Chapter Three*

Lizzie bid a prim farewell to him at the entrance to Brede House. Crunching her way along the gravelled drive, she was careful to hold her head high and not look back at the carriage. He was just a little too alluring. What a pity that Piers Silchester did not exude the same attraction, for as Miss Bates was fond of pointing out, he was everything she should want: loyal, loving, stable. The trouble was that she didn't want it, or at least not enough. Instead she seemed continually drawn to men who offered fleeting excitement rather than a secure future. Soldiers lived in an exclusive world—she knew that from bitter experience—and it was a world in which women had no part. Justin Delacourt was most definitely a soldier, a gentlemanly one, but nevertheless a soldier. He lacked understanding of the cramped life she was forced to lead, knowing nothing of the narrow horizons which bound her. It would be years before he settled to any kind of humdrum life and in the meantime female company signified for him a little pleasantry, a little dalliance only.

Why was a woman's life so very difficult? A small sum of money was all it would take to give her independence, but even a little money was beyond her. Still a companion's life, for all its limitations, had to be better than marriage. Being married was too dull for words and being married to Piers Silchester, gentle soul though he was, the dullest of the dull. That was the choice that Clementine Bates had offered and she couldn't blame the woman—she knew herself to be a liability, a loose cannon prone to fire in any direction. It must have been a blessed day for Miss Bates when she learned from her blushing music teacher that he hoped one day to make Miss Ingram his wife.

Lizzie was old enough now, though, to know that she could not afford to lose her heart to an adventurer. One day she supposed she would have to marry, heart or no heart, and doubtless Piers would be the lucky husband. He was the most dependable man she knew and, most importantly, he was willing to adore her. He would make her his goddess. She tried to imagine Justin Delacourt worshipping at her altar and the thought made her chuckle.

She wondered if he even found her attractive. He had certainly stared long and hard when she'd entered the library wearing that dress, his ever-changing eyes shading from light to dark as his glance held. Goodness knew why, since the garment was the frumpiest thing imaginable. But he had stared nevertheless and not in a pleasant way. Mrs Reynolds had confided in the bedroom that the gown had belonged to the Major's mother, someone she called Lady Delacourt. Her tightened lips suggested to Lizzie that there was something odd about the woman. Was she dead? If so, why hadn't the housekeeper mentioned the fact, especially since Sir Lucien had only just died himself? And if she wasn't dead, then where was she? The dress was old fashioned, it was true, but she saw immediately that its material was richly luxurious and that it was beautifully made.

Lady Delacourt must at one time have enjoyed wealth, enjoyed being spoilt, enjoyed being adored. Perhaps *she* had been made a goddess. If so, it was unlikely to have been her son doing the adoring. After that first amazed stare, his face had registered a dour distaste.

She had reached the front entrance of Brede House and was about to raise the cast-iron anchor that served as a knocker when the door flew open and a figure dashed past her, nearly knocking her down. It was female, wild eyed and seemingly distraught. She had a brief glimpse of a face before the woman started down the drive at the most tremendous pace. Lizzie looked after her in astonishment. It was Mrs Armitage, she was sure, the woman she had seen in the churchyard. Why was she visiting Mrs Croft and why had the visit upset her so badly that she had tossed aside all vestige of propriety?

Lizzie walked into the hall and saw that the drawing-room door had been left ajar. Cautiously advancing into the room, she spied the remnants of tea scattered across the small occasional table that her employer used when visitors called—a plate of uneaten macaroons, a teacup tossed on its side. It seemed that this had been a social call, but what kind of social call ended with a flight such as Mrs Armitage's? Or for that matter left the hostess prostrate. Her employer was slumped into one of the armchairs, her hand to her forehead as though nursing a sick headache.

'Mrs Croft?' she said gently. 'Are you feeling unwell?'

At the sound of her voice, the old lady stirred and, seeing Lizzie's anxious face looking at her from the doorway, attempted to pull herself upright.

'No, my dear, I thank you, just a little tired.' Her voice was barely above a whisper. 'Socialising at my age can be a little trying, you know.'

Mrs Croft evidently did not wish to dwell on whatever had occurred and Lizzie wondered if she should leave the matter. It would probably be as well to escape now before her employer recognised the outdated dress she was wearing. But she could not leave her in such a mournful state.

'I saw Mrs Armitage,' she mentioned quietly. 'She passed me as I came through the door. She seemed very upset.'

The old lady did not look at her, but uttered

the deepest of sighs. 'I'm sorry you were witness to her distress. Caroline is grief-stricken and her behaviour at the moment is unpredictable.'

'But why? I mean why is she grief-stricken?' That sounded a little harsh, Lizzie thought, and tried to infuse more sympathy into her next words. 'I had not realised that Mrs Armitage was so attached to Sir Lucien.'

'Not Sir Lucien, my dear,' Mrs Croft said gently. 'It is her son she mourns. She has lost Gilbert.'

'Lost as in dead?' Lizzie queried, wide eyed.

'Lost as in lost. You might as well know, since it is now common knowledge. Gilbert Armitage disappeared some months ago and his parents have been unable to trace him. No one seems to know a thing about his disappearance.'

'How strange. And sad,' Lizzie added quickly. 'But why was she so distressed? She could have received nothing but comfort from you.'

'That is where you are wrong, I fear. I could not give her what she wanted. She has asked me to intercede with Justin Delacourt, to put all his other concerns to one side and search for her son. I told you, did I not, that Gilbert Armitage was the closest of friends with Justin?'

'You did. But why was she so upset with you?'

'Because I refused. I cannot bother Justin at a time like this. He has so very recently lost his father and been left an estate which is in near ruin. It will take him an age to put it right and I know that he is desperate to return to his regiment.'

'Could she not ask Sir Justin herself—if he is so very close to the family?'

'She has already asked him for help, but she wanted me to add my voice to her pleas. I could not in all honesty do that. Justin has more than enough to contend with. If he has promised to help in the search, he will do so—he is a man of his word—but it must be on his terms and at a time of his arranging.'

'And that is not what Mrs Armitage wants?'

'No, indeed. He must drop everything. I am afraid that she is slightly unbalanced at the moment. Her son was everything to her. He was a late child, you see, a delicate boy, or so Caroline always maintained. His disappearance has sent her teetering over the edge of an abyss and none of her friends' advice or her husband's care has been able to prevent it.'

'I am sorry that you have had such an uncomfortable afternoon, Mrs Croft.' Lizzie felt genuine concern for her employer, the old lady's pallor testifying to how badly shaken she had been. 'Can I bring you some water, perhaps, or fetch down the footstool for you to rest more comfortably?'

'No, but thank you for your kind thoughts, Elizabeth. I shall sit here a while and listen to the river. It is nearly high tide, you know, and already I can hear the waters lapping in the distance. It is a most soothing sound and will soon restore me.'

Lizzie took her cue and slipped out of the room and up the stairs. Once in her bedroom, she stood at the open window and listened to the same water tumbling across the small, stony beach which lay just beyond the garden. Taking up her sketch pad, she began to draw—not the river snaking below, nor the clouds above busily filling the sky. She drew a face, one she had studied well and but recently. When she had finished, she was pleased with her portrait—the strong, lean cheek bones, the eyes steady and appraising, the hair a wild halo—but she was not so pleased with herself. She should cast the Major from her mind. From the outset he had fascinated and his curt indifference when they'd first met had only sharpened her interest: he was an invitation, an enjoyable project to lighten the dull days ahead. But this morning it had taken only a very little time in his company to realise her mistake. He was far too attractive, certainly too attractive to treat lightly, and if she were sensible, she would keep her distance. She looked down at the paper on her knee. What on earth was she doing, drawing portraits of the man? She took the sheet of paper and tore it neatly in half, dropping it in the nearby waste bin. He was a footloose soldier and she must forget about him and instead school herself to appreciate the estimable Piers.

There was a soft knock on the door and Hester came in, carrying fresh bedding and towels.

'Is mistress feeling any better now, Miss Elizabeth?'

'She is resting. She wished to be left alone.'

'She shouldn't be put under that kind of strain, not at her age she shouldn't.'

'Mrs Armitage was very upset.'

'Mebbe. But that ain't no excuse for upsetting an old lady like she's done.'

Hester had been with Mrs Croft for years and had a fierce loyalty to her mistress. She knew everything that happened in the house, and no doubt in Rye itself, without ever being told. A thought wormed its way into Lizzie's mind and she could not stop herself from listening to it.

'Do you know anything about her son's disappearance, Hester?'

Why on earth was she gossiping with a maidservant? She knew why. It seemed that she was not yet willing to forget Justin Delacourt entirely and Hester might provide some small piece of ammunition in any future tussle with him. As so often, she was choosing not to be sensible.

The maid appeared unwilling to answer and looked fixedly down at her feet. 'You do know something, don't you, Hester?' Lizzie probed.

'Not rightly, miss. It's probably nothing and I shouldn't be saying it, but Mr Gil was fair taken with that gypsy woman and I've been wondering if she had anything to do with his going away.'

'A gypsy woman?' Lizzie tried hard not

to sound eager, but her nerves were tingling. Could there be a real adventure here?

'She weren't truly a gypsy. But she didn't seem to have a proper home. And she mixed with some queer company—still does for that matter.'

'So she is still in Rye? Who is she, Hester?'

'She goes by the name of Rosanna. A right heathen name, if you ask me.'

'Rosanna who? What is her last name?'

'There's no other name, leastways none that I know of.'

Lizzie thought hard. It seemed incongruous that someone of Gilbert Armitage's standing in the community should have made such a woman his sweetheart. But men under the influence of love could act completely out of character and contemplate the wildest of notions.

'And Gil Armitage was walking out with her?' she prompted. Was that the right term?

Hester snorted. 'He weren't doing that— walking out, I mean—not too boldly at least. He didn't dare be seen, but everyone knew that he was fair gone on her.'

'Why couldn't he be seen?' The question was ingenuous, but she was keen for the maid to keep talking.

'With a no-good woman like that and him a gentleman!'

'I understand.' Lizzie nodded her head sagely. 'I imagine then that his parents have no knowledge of Rosanna.'

'I wouldn't think so, miss. Reckon he would have kept mortal quiet about that particular friendship.'

'But when it became obvious that he was missing, surely someone must have mentioned the girl to them?'

Hester drew herself up to her full height. 'Folks round here don't gossip,' she said firmly. 'Leastways they don't gossip to the gentry. Mr and Mrs Armitage are well respected—nice people—and no one would want to hurt them by telling them such a thing. Not when their son wanted to keep it a secret.'

Lizzie shook her head, but kept her thoughts to herself. She had seen Caroline's face, wild with grief, and for an instant had shrunk beneath the intensity of its pain. What must it be like to lose your only child and not know what had happened to him? Surely it would be better to risk distressing the Armitages if it meant solving the mystery of their son's disappearance. But evidently Rye was a close-

knit community and secrets were secrets and
had to be kept. But not by her. A tantalising
thought arrived. She might be able to help
Mrs Armitage and surely the poor woman
deserved whatever aid she could offer. At the
same time she would annoy Justin Delacourt.
She had been left feeling flustered and gauche
by his closeness while he—he was just a little
too smooth, a little too in control. It would be
good to disturb that infuriating calm. Justin
was charged with the onerous duty of finding
his friend and he would need every small clue
he could lay his hands on. And she had one
now, and not a small clue at that. A very big
clue. She would dangle it before him, tease
him with it, and at the same time edge Caroline a little closer to finding her son.

The will was read and there had been few
surprises, since except for several small bequests to servants and close friends, everything had been left to Sir Lucien's son. The
lawyer from London had come and gone,
leaving Justin to distribute the gifts his father had bequeathed. A beautifully tooled
calf-bound volume detailing the delights of
Sussex and Kent was destined for Henrietta
Croft, in remembrance of the happy hours

she and Sir Lucien had spent poring over its expensive illustrations. His father had left a handwritten note with the book, asking Justin to deliver the gift personally. The dead man's request gave his son cause to sigh. It would mean a journey to Brede House and a possible encounter with the impossible young woman. He knew Mrs Croft left the house infrequently these days and how to get the book to her without meeting Miss Ingram presented a problem.

He had turned it over in his mind for several days without finding a solution, irritated with himself that he had so little control over his feelings that he shirked from visiting one of his father's oldest friends. It had been raining incessantly since the lawyer's departure and when on the third morning, he awoke to a cloudless blue sky, it seemed a sensible time to go in search of the old lady. She was sure to have kept within doors for the last few days, but hopefully would be unable to resist the promise of such glorious weather. There was a chance that he might overtake her on her way to the busy shopping streets of the Citadel and, if so, he could take her up in his carriage and present the precious gift to her there and then.

First, though, he must keep his word by visiting Five Oaks. Although it had been cold overnight, waves of sun-warmed air were already radiating off the land and chasing away all but the finest veils of mist. He steered the carriage through the Chelwood gates into the autumn lanes and was at once enveloped by a landscape of glorious colour: coppiced trees fountained upwards and linked arms to create a cavern of russet foliage, while here and there patches of sunlight pierced the canopy and mottled gold all they touched.

Despite the difficult morning ahead, he felt more optimistic than he had for weeks, ever since that first dreadful intimation that his father was dead. It must be the blissful weather, he thought, for little else had changed. The estate was still in desperate need of renovation, his friend was still missing and his regiment still awaited his return. Yet some kind of magic was being woven for his heart felt unaccountably light as he sped his horses on their way.

At Five Oaks he was greeted with great affection, waved into the sunny drawing room and plied with refreshments. Relieved that no mention was made of the task Caroline

Armitage had laid on him, he talked animat-
edly of the various schemes that he and Mellors were devising to set Chelwood to rights.
After half an hour he rose to take his leave
and remembered Sir Lucien's bequests only
when he had reached the front door.

'I had almost forgot!' He delved into the
old carpet bag he had unearthed from the
hall chest at Chelwood. 'The will has now
been proved and I have several gifts to distribute. My father wanted you to have his collection of old maps. I have them here', and he
brought forth several rolls of stained cream
parchment.

'How very kind of Lucien,' James responded warmly. 'He knew my interest in the
history of the area. But would you not wish
them to remain at Chelwood? I remember
them decorating the walls of his study there.
It would seem a better resting place for them.'

'His study is now mine, Mr Armitage, and
is covered in schedules for the advancement
of the estate. There is even the odd illustration of a rare pig! My father knew how much
you would value these—far more than I—
and I hope you will accept them as a small
remembrance of him.'

James clasped the younger man's hands in

his. 'I would be honoured to have them, Justin. They will be accorded pride of place in my own study.'

Justin hesitated. He had yet one more gift for Five Oaks, but he did not know how to introduce it. Caroline saw his hesitation. 'What is it, Justin? You have something more?'

'Mrs Armitage, please forgive me. I am clumsy. I should never perhaps have brought it with me, but I am legally bound to carry out the provisions of the will.'

The Armitages were looking at him, puzzled expressions on both their faces. He drew from the bag a small carved wooden object. 'It is a native Indian curio that my father purchased when he was serving in America—'

'And it is for Gilbert,' she finished for him.

'Yes,' he admitted, not knowing how to proceed.

'How very kind of your father to remember Gil's collection. Of course you should have bought it.' Her voice had only the slightest tremor. 'But will you do one thing for me before you go and take it to Gilbert's room.' Her voice was cracking now. 'You know where it is, you know where he kept his collection.'

Justin sprang forwards, relieved to be doing

something. 'I promise to find the perfect place for it.'

He was past the waiting couple and up the stairs before Caroline's tears began to flow. He felt angry with himself that so far he had done nothing to help the Armitages. He had been too busy with estate matters and, he told himself crossly, too busy with the girl. True she had taken up only an hour of his time at Chelwood, but simply thinking about her had wasted precious hours, too. He had not day-dreamed like this since he was a boy and he needed to snap out of it.

Gil's room was just as its owner had left it, just as Justin had seen it the last time he had visited: bedclothes uncreased, cushions plumped, fresh paper on the desk and a newly sharpened quill and pot of ink in the writing tray. The mirror reflected the same pictures, the mantelshelf held the same ornaments. He remembered being here three years ago, laughing and joking with his friend, twitting him over his ever-growing collection of native artefacts. You need to travel, Gil, he'd said, and not just in your mind.

He strode over to the large, wooden display cabinet that filled one corner of the room and opened its two glass doors. The shelves were already full and it took time to find a space into which he could fit his father's small offering. He reached up to the top shelf which seemed a little less crowded and shuffled several objects closer together. There appeared to be some resistance towards the back of the shelf and with some difficulty he reached over and pulled forth a sheaf of papers that had been taped to its underside.

Immediately he saw they were part of a private correspondence. He should not look at them. They were Gil's. He went to tape them back and by accident caught sight of the subscription which headed the first page.

'My darling.' My darling? Surely not. Surely not Gil. He was no ladies' man himself, but Gil was even less of one. He could not recall a single instance when his friend had shown the slightest partiality for any woman. They must have been written for someone else. He took the papers over to the desk and flicked through them. They continued in like vein. 'My darling', 'My sweetheart', 'Dear Heart', followed by protestations of love and longing that the writer would soon be with his beloved for ever. His eyes scrolled to the bottom of each page. There was no doubt. He had recognised his friend's hand, but a vague hope that Gil might have penned the letters for someone else died when he saw the unmistakable signature. But who had his friend be writing to? There was no clue. And he had not sent the letters, so what did that mean? He had written them, one after another judging by the dates, day after day, but he had never sent them. It was another puzzle. It was almost as though Gil had been leading a double life that nobody, least of all his parents, was aware of. What had James said—that he no longer knew his son?

Justin sighed. The letters did not advance his quest one iota—indeed, they complicated it and they would not help Caroline in her misery. The only thing to do was to tape them back where they had come from and forget he had ever read words meant for another. Who that other was, he had no idea and probably never would have. He was certain, though, that the unknown had nothing to do with his friend's disappearance. Gil had been gone for three months and if he had eloped with a sweetheart, he would by now have confessed his wrongdoing and been reunited with his family, perhaps a little in disgrace, but nevertheless welcomed home with love. No, there was no sweetheart, Justin decided. It was simply wishful thinking on his friend's part. If there were a real woman, she was a distant figure only and Gil had been worshipping from afar, lacking the temerity to approach her. Instead he wrote letter after letter, finding a release for his emotions, but saying nothing to anyone. How lonely he must have been, Justin thought, to have fallen in love with a dream and to have confided his deepest feelings to a few sheets of paper.

He was tempted to drive directly home after his unwelcome discovery, but knew it for a cowardly choice and instead pushed on towards Brede House. Not that he had any intention of calling there, but he still hoped that he might catch Henrietta Croft walking towards the town. As he neared the long, winding drive to the riverside house, keeping a careful look-out, he saw the skirts of a much younger woman disappearing in the direction of Rye. It was Lizzie Ingram, straw bonnet masking those glorious chestnut curls, and a basket swinging from her hand. Henrietta must have sent her to do the marketing, a little late in the day, but most fortunate for him. He could visit now without fear of meeting the girl.

Immediately he entered the small parlour looking out towards the river, he could see that Mrs Croft was not in the best of spirits. But her forlorn expression gave way to a welcoming smile as soon as she saw him and, getting to her feet with some difficulty, she came forward to clasp his hand.

'How lovely to see you, Justin. And how kind of you to spare a few minutes of what must be precious time.'

He felt a twinge of guilt, but said as convincingly as he could, 'It is always a pleasure to see you, Mrs Croft, and today especially—I have come on a very particular mission.'

She looked enquiringly and, in response, he withdrew the leather-bound book from its protective covering.

'I have come to bring you something I think you will treasure. Sir Lucien thought so at least. Here.' And he handed her the soft calfskin volume.

'So many happy hours,' she murmured, 'so many hours gone, friends gone.'

Justin did not know what to say. His hostess was evidently feeling downpin and he had not the words to comfort her. He need not have worried. As he struggled to find a cheering sentiment, the door opened abruptly and Lizzie stood on the threshold.

She smiled saucily at him. 'Major Delacourt! I was wondering who could have come calling and in such a very smart curricle! Is it new? And how heavenly to drive out from Chelwood on such a morning!'

He had stiffened at the sight of her, but managed a small bow. 'Good morning, Miss Ingram.' His face was bereft of expression. 'The day is indeed beautiful and you are dressed for walking, I see. Were you perhaps thinking of taking the air? If so, I can recommend the coastal path—it is at its best when the sun is shining and there is little wind.'

Her smile did not falter. 'What a delightful suggestion! But unfortunately I must engage myself elsewhere this morning. It is my ribbons, you see.' And she pulled from her basket a shining length of jonquil satin. 'I thought this morning to go to Mercer's to match this very lovely yellow, but I had gone no more than a hundred yards when I realised that I had left my purse behind.'

So that was the reason for her return. Or at least the reason she claimed. But had she perhaps caught sight of his carriage and made the decision to return to Brede House? To return and torment him. He would put nothing past her—her trespass at Chelwood had been shameless. Well, he could be shameless, too, and make it difficult for her to stay.

'I believe the haberdasher closes at noon so, if you are wishful of purchasing more ribbon, you would be wise to set forth immediately.'

She was still smiling, an uncomfortably satisfied smile, he decided. 'That is most thoughtful of you, but I am in no hurry. I find Rye lives at a slow pace and it is necessary to match one's own rhythm to it. Whether I get the ribbon today or tomorrow or the next week hardly matters.'

It was a brazen contradiction, for a minute ago she had insisted that she had not the time to go walking. He felt a growing exasperation, but he could press her no further without appearing blatantly discourteous. His hostess was already looking at him askance. Miss Ingram had decided that she was at Brede House to stay that morning and he must make the best of it.

'I seem to have interrupted your conversation,' she was saying. 'Please accept my apologies.' Her lips curved provocatively, lips that were full and warm and red, he noticed.

His thoughts stumbled and he felt himself

growing hot—how could he allow his mind such licence? Trying to regain his equilibrium, he said in as toneless a voice as he could manage, 'There is no need for apologies. I came only to give my father's present to Mrs Croft.'

'And a beautiful present it is, too,' Henrietta intervened, obviously relieved to get the conversation back on to firmer ground. 'But will you not stay for some refreshment, Justin?'

'Thank you, but, no. I must return to Chelwood. There is much to do, as you will appreciate. I will call again very soon and perhaps then we can talk at greater length.' But only when I can be absolutely sure that Miss Ingram is nowhere in the vicinity, he told himself.

'Before you go, Justin...' The old lady caught at his arm. 'I think I should warn you—' She broke off, unable to find the right words, and then with difficulty, murmured, 'It is Caroline, Mrs Armitage.'

'What of her?'

'She is in great distress.'

'I understand that, Mrs Croft, and I am aware of her suffering.' He gently disentangled her arm from his and began walking towards the door. But she was on her feet and following him, her voice unusually urgent.

'I am sure that you are. How could you not be? I understand that she has asked you to aid her in the search for Gilbert. But she has been here, too, to ask something similar of myself.'

Justin stopped in surprise. 'That you should aid her? Surely not!'

'That I should add my voice to hers in persuading you to commence your search immediately. I refused, I fear. I know how much work is before you. I know, too, that the Armitages have tried almost everything to find their son and not succeeded. How she imagines that you can perform miracles, I do not know.'

The Armitages had said nothing to him this morning of the visit. Perhaps James was ignorant of his wife's call and Caroline ashamed now of the disturbance she had caused.

He pressed the old lady's hand in reassurance. 'Mrs Armitage is overwrought—understandably so—and we must not be too alarmed if she behaves unusually. But I confess that her reliance on me is worrying though Gil was, is, my friend, and I have promised to do all I can.' He smiled wryly.

'My promise was well meant, though I am at a loss where to start.'

'That is hardly surprising. If all the enquiries the Armitages have sent out over these past months have come to nought, how can you, newly arrived and in the most difficult of circumstances, be expected to fare better?' Henrietta looked searchingly up at her visitor. 'It would not be wrong to forgo your promise, Justin, for it was unfair to have extracted it from you. Your focus must be on Chelwood and Caroline knows that. She will come to her senses soon and when she does, she will see what an impossible task she has given you.'

'I can only hope so.' He reached the door as Mrs Croft rang the bell for Hester. 'But I do not want you to be worried by this business. If Mrs Armitage should call again, you must refer her to me.'

'I doubt that she is likely to do so.'

As soon as Hester had escorted their visitor to the front door, Lizzie bounced from her seat. She had been listening intently, but made no reference to the conversation. Instead she gestured to the sun beaming its way through the parlour window.

'As the weather remains so kind, I think that perhaps I will walk to Rye, after all, Mrs

Croft, if you will be comfortable for an hour. The haberdasher will not be closed for long. My second-best reticule is badly in need of retrimming and I can buy you the new cap you were mentioning.'

Her employer nodded assent and settled herself wearily back into the armchair. In seconds Lizzie was slipping out of the front door just as Sir Justin jumped into the curricle's driving seat. He saw her out of the corner of his eye and had no alternative but to offer to drive her into Rye. It was not at all what he wanted, but for the second time that morning, fortune appeared to favour him.

'I prefer to walk, Sir Justin. It keeps me fit and healthy, or hale, as you would say.' That was true enough, he thought—her slim figure filled the simple sprig muslin in all the right places. He wished he could stop noticing, but it seemed an impossibility.

'There is something I might be able to do for *you*, though,' she said pertly, 'something you might be interested in knowing.'

Her words took him aback and he paused for an instant before reluctantly deciding to clamber from his seat to stand beside her. The reins, though, remained firmly within his grasp for, whatever it was she had to impart, he had no intention of lingering.

'And what exactly might I be interested in, Miss Ingram?'

'You have been charged with the burden of finding your lost friend. I may just have the information that you need to begin your search.'

He very much doubted that. The Armitages had searched high and low. The whole of Rye knew that Gil was missing and were on the alert, while Lizzie Ingram had been here but a few weeks. What could she know? Nothing, he thought. It was a ploy to draw him in, or simply to irritate him. He imagined that she was used to male admiration and his refusal to pay her the necessary compliments no doubt rankled.

'If you can help in any way, I will be most grateful.' He kept his voice impassive, but there was that smile again, provocative, tilting at him, teasing him with its promise.

'Do you know of a woman called Rosanna?'

What was this nonsense? 'No, I cannot say I do. Should I?'

'Not necessarily, but your friend did.'

'Gil?' He was shocked out of his formality. The thought of the letters loomed large.

'Yes, Gilbert Armitage. Apparently he had a close relationship with a woman called Rosanna. If *I* were looking for him, I would want to speak to her.'

'That is impossible,' he stammered his incomprehension. 'And who is this Rosanna?' He had put the letters down to fantasy, nothing more. Now this girl was naming a flesh-and-blood woman. Was she teasing or could she really be serious?

'I believe she is a woman of some mystery. She is not exactly a gypsy, but neither does she live a settled life. I am told, too, that she keeps dubious company.'

'In that case, Gilbert Armitage would have had no commerce with her.' His tone was uncompromising and he made to remount the carriage. His suspicions had disappeared— Gil would never have taken up with such a woman.

'You should not dismiss her so lightly. I make no doubt that Rosanna is a fascinator of men and even your friend might have been vulnerable to her attractions.'

'I know my friend and, if you will forgive me, the idea that he would become embroiled with such a woman is a hum.'

She took a deep breath, drawing herself up

to stand ramrod straight, her eyes flashing a clear challenge. '*I* will forgive you, Sir Justin. But will the Armitages?'

## *Chapter Four*

He watched her, basket in hand, as she began
to walk along the winding drive towards the
Rye road. He wanted to run after her, ask her
for more details, ask her to offer some kind
of evidence, but it was clear that he would
get nothing more. She must know that she
had dealt him a knock and he was sure she
was enjoying it. She had said just enough to
torment, but not enough for him to discount
the news completely. The notion of Gil in an
intimate relationship with any woman was
astonishing enough, but with a woman such
as Lizzie Ingram had described it had to be
impossible.

Yet there were those letters. They might
never have been sent, but they could, after all,

have been written to a real woman. Reading them, he had been so astonished that he had imagined a fantasy sweetheart, but was that because he still saw Gil as the boy he had been and not the man he had become in his absence? Or was it, perish the thought, because it was easier to assume that there was nothing to explain his friend's absence and therefore nothing to investigate. If he had once been tempted to think so, that no longer held. There were not only the letters to Rosanna, if such they were, but the fact that the woman kept dubious company. If Lizzie were right, that could be greatly significant. Of course, she had quite deliberately thrown that piece of gossip into the conversation in an effort to intrigue or, more probably, annoy him. But that didn't mean it was untrue. There was no hope for it, he thought heavily, he would have to explore further. For the next day or so Mellors would have to carry on alone with the work at Chelwood, at least until he had disproved the suspicions the girl had planted. He had made the Armitages a promise and he would fulfil it.

For a good half a mile Lizzie danced along the river path, elated by the fact that she had confounded the infuriating Major. His expression when she'd mentioned his friend's involvement with the mysterious Rosanna had been satisfyingly dumbfounded. He deserved to be put out of countenance, she thought. It was evident that he had set out to visit Brede House when he knew she would not be there. The minute she'd remembered leaving her purse on the bedroom chest, she had turned back towards the house and seen his carriage at the entrance to the drive. It appeared to be lingering there, unwilling to commit itself to any particular direction, but then the horse had plunged forwards as though relieved of a burden. She'd realised in that instant that she was the burden. Justin Delacourt did not want to see her and had taken advantage of her absence—it had been quite deliberate.

She had thought him snobbish, too high in the instep to acknowledge a humble companion, but after the visit to Chelwood Hall, she'd had to revise that view. He might have shown himself oblivious to the constraints that hedged her life, but he had treated his uninvited guest with courtesy and without a hint of condescension. So why was he so desperate to escape her presence that he chose to visit Mrs Croft in secret? Was it that he felt uncomfortable in the company of young females? She thought it unlikely. He was a soldier and must have had plenty of dealings with women over the years. Was it a particular woman then, Lizzie Ingram, that he found unnerving? She hoped very much that it was so. It would only be fair since each time they'd met, she had felt similarly unnerved. In church she had been captivated by his wonderful voice, driving with him from Chelwood she had not been able to stop her skin from prickling in a most peculiar fashion, and just now standing so close to him in the porch, the warmth of his body, the hardness of his form, had alerted each and every small fibre within her. It was only the fact that she possessed crucial information that had kept her mind steady, but it had been difficult to maintain a calm exterior while her body was responding so disturbingly. She had been almost glad to see him regain the driving seat and set his horse in motion.

But not glad that he'd rejected so completely what she had told him. He had not believed her or, more likely, had not wanted to believe. He had refused to accept that his friend was capable of falling in love with a low-born and possibly impure woman. Why was he so stubborn? He might know his friend, but she knew women better and if this Rosanna had set her sights on Gilbert Armitage, Lizzie had no doubt that she had succeeded. And surely it was right that Caroline be told of anything that might lead her to her son. As she walked, her earlier elation slowly drifted away and was replaced by a strong sense of irritation. Why were men, why were soldiers, so blinkered? She had thought the information gold dust and yet he had dismissed it without pause. It would serve him right if she herself followed up the clue she had unearthed.

Her mind began to buzz uncomfortably and she told herself to forget whatever mad thoughts she was having. Below her the river flowed smoothly today with hardly a ripple breaking its surface and she focused herself on embracing the calm. But it was to no avail—her thoughts had broken loose and she could not curb them. She had imagined this a staid town, yet in the last few days adventure had beckoned from every quarter: the talk of smugglers, the disappearance of a local gentleman, a secret love affair with a mysterious woman. It had beckoned faintly, it was true, but why could she not turn this into a real adventure? She set to wondering what Rosanna looked like, who Rosanna really was. Justin Delacourt had no intention of finding out but why shouldn't she?

When she reached the haberdasher's, she found the shop still open but crowded. Until Mr Mercer was free to serve, she riffled through the buttons and ribbons that he always laid out for display in long wooden trays. An elderly customer in an unfashionable poke bonnet was at the counter, making an anxious choice of a length of silk organza for her granddaughter's first party dress and all the time maintaining a mumbled commentary on the high cost of the material.

'Prices have risen, Mrs Cartwright,' the shopkeeper was saying, a trifle tight lipped. 'I make little enough profit as it is.'

'I am sure that is so, Mr Mercer,' the woman agreed, her tone placating, 'but I cannot forget the time—you, too, I'm sure—when we were able to buy the most exquisite silks from France for next to nothing.'

He looked warningly at her and she caught his glance. 'Don't mind me, I am an old woman. I realise those days are gone and are best forgotten. We must be glad that the law is no longer broken with impunity.' She did not look particularly glad.

A younger woman, weighed down by the heavy pannier she carried, cut across the conversation. 'We *should* be glad that Rye is no longer a den of thieves,' she said emphatically, 'and that people can walk through the town freely without fear.'

There was a murmur of assent among the several women standing behind her. 'You have only to think of what the Mermaid used to be, to know that's so!' A red-faced woman, looking every inch a farmer's wife, perspired quietly at the back of the waiting line. Her words loosed a torrent of condemnation from the other women.

'They say the Mermaid has a hidden cellár and secret passageways to other inns—no wonder it's been a villains' haunt for so long!'

'And still is, I reckon. Have you seen those men, lording it up, sitting in the window, as bold as brass as though they own the town.'

'It's not just the men!'

'No indeed. Have you seen that woman…?'

'She should not be mentioned in decent society.' The elderly customer patted the brown paper package Mr Mercer had handed her, as though seeking reassurance. 'We must protect our young folks.'

Lizzie's hand had stopped on the brocade she was fingering. She had been engrossed by the conversation as it see-sawed between members of the group. The person they had just spoken of, could that be Rosanna? It had to be: a woman who consorted with a gang of desperate men and who outraged society. She had been right, she thought—there was an adventure here and she could not resist its siren call.

Abandoning any desire to buy yellow ribbons, Lizzie slipped out of the shop. She closed the door quietly behind her as the haberdasher continued to complain of high prices and the women to lament the moral threat to their town. She had seen the signpost for Mermaid Street when attending services at St Mary's. Mrs Croft always refused to take that way to the river and had warned her of setting foot in the street. But now Lizzie's curiosity burned too brightly and she hurried up West Street towards the church, then swerved left, winding her way around the churchyard to arrive at the top of the infamous road. Its cobbled length fell steeply towards the river and the cluster of small boats bobbing on the incoming tide. A third of the way down on the right-hand side, an old black-and-white Tudor building raised its head. The Mermaid Inn! A few carts rumbled their way over the cobbles making for the quayside, but there were no other pedestrians. It was as though the population had chosen this street out of all of those in Rye to put into quarantine. She kept to the left-hand pavement, her face shadowed by the brim of her bonnet, but her eyes surreptitiously keeping watch on the other side of the street. Soon she had drawn nearly opposite the tavern and slowed her pace to a crawl.

She saw them immediately. A sizeable group of men, roughly clad in stained leather jerkins, were sitting at a downstairs open window, pint pots in their hands, heads wreathed in noxious clouds of smoke. They lazed at their ease, an untidy circle around a table scattered with empty tankards and the remnants of food. And amid this detritus—was that a pistol, she could see? She tried to look more closely. It *was* a pistol, in fact, several pistols, and they all looked to be cocked and ready for use. Her knowledge of firearms was limited, but a cocked gun meant it was loaded and she was in the direct line of fire! She knew that she should scurry down the hill as fast her

legs would go, but instead she could not stop
looking. They were the ugliest collection of
men, she thought, bearded and unkempt and,
most likely, unwashed. One man in particular
she noticed—he did not at first fall vividly on
the eye, nor was he in any way flamboyant.
But there was a stillness about him, a malevo-
lent stillness. His hair was tow coloured, his
eyes lightless, but his brows thick and black.
He had the look of an other worldly creature,
an avenging demon. It was a hauntingly evil
face.

At that minute, a voluptuous figure swam
into view and Lizzie was so stunned by the
woman's appearance that her feet seemed to
grow roots and anchor her to the ground. The
woman *was* vivid, she *was* flamboyant. Her
hair was black and her eyes even blacker. She
was beautiful, Lizzie thought, beautiful in a
bold, brazen fashion. Miss Bates would have
called her a hussy—or worse. She was wearing a red dress, the material so thin that you
could almost see her naked skin beneath it,
and so tight that it left nothing to the imagination. As Lizzie watched mesmerised, the
woman placed the tray of tankards she was
carrying on the table and began to sway in and
out of the chairs, stroking the men's beards

and leaving light kisses on their foreheads.
Her kiss for the tow-headed man seemed to
linger. This had to be Rosanna. Lizzie gulped.
She should have nothing more to do with
this—*walk on, walk to Brede House*, she told
herself, *and forget you ever witnessed this
little tableau*. But her spirit of devilment, her
thirst for the uncommon, was too strong. If
she could only get Rosanna alone, she might
discover exactly what had happened to Gil
Armitage, for one thing was very clear: this
woman was the enchantress that Lizzie had
predicted, and she most certainly could have
enchanted Justin Delacourt's friend into submission, or worse.

It was several days before Lizzie was able
to put into practice the plan she had formu-
lated. Mrs Croft had been badly upset by
Caroline Armitage's visit, more than the
household had realised at the time, and she
needed constant attention—first from her
doctor and then from both Hester and Lizzie.
But as the old lady gradually recovered her
spirits, her interest in the world returned and
with it the desire for new books. A branch
of the circulating library had been set up the
previous year in small premises next to the

George Hotel on Lion Street and Lizzie was despatched on a mission to find reading material for the recovering invalid. It proved a difficult task since Mrs Croft was a voracious reader and over the months the circulating library had been thoroughly plundered. But eventually after an hour of searching, Lizzie had secured two volumes she thought might satisfy her employer.

She was glad to leave the stuffy air of the library behind and feel again the sea breeze blowing off the river, but more than disappointed to realise how fast the light was fading. She had hoped to use this time to further the plan she'd conceived. But she should have remembered that it was October and each day brought an earlier dusk. She would have to make haste back to Brede House before darkness fell. The image of Rosanna teased at her still and she dared once more to walk down Mermaid Street on her way to the river path. This time the inn's window was closed against the cold air and there was no sign of any of the men she had seen before. A strange mix of regret and relief swept over her. She tripped lightly down the street, gathering speed as she went. She could almost feel the sky darken above. A flash of red in the distance caught her attention and held it. It was a dress and it was disappearing into the warren of narrow paths which branched from the bottom of Mermaid Street into what she had learned was the poorest part of the town. A red dress! Who else wore such a garment? The figure ahead was Rosanna's, she was almost sure. But she had not the time to go after her for she must return as quickly as possible to Brede House. That was the sensible thing to do. But she had never been sensible, she reflected ruefully, and set out to follow the woman's swaying figure.

Reaching the end of Mermaid Street, she saw the slightest glimpse of red vanishing around the next corner and hurried in pursuit. Past the Ship Inn, avoiding several of its already drunken clients, and still shadowing the figure ahead, she turned left again. The thoroughfare here was even narrower, and every kind of dirt and rubbish had been strewn across the bare earth that constituted a path. Carefully Lizzie picked her way along the filthy lane, sending up thanks that she had worn her stoutest boots. A cacophony of noise emanating from the mean cottages that lined either side of the narrow byway accompanied her every step—doors were banged almost

off their hinges, cooking pans crashed into
crude sinks, angry curses flew through the
air. A few faint spots of candlelight shone out
of the dusk in one or two of the cottages, but
the sky above was thick with cloud and offered no trace of moon or stars to leaven the
inky night that was falling so swiftly. Out of
the corner of her eye, she spied the silhouette
of a ragged black crow perched on a half-
ruined wall. The bird emerged, spectre like,
out of the shreds of mist now stealing ashore
from the river, an omen of desolation, she
thought. But she could not turn back now. She
was close to her quarry, so close—she had to
keep going. If she could see in which of these
houses Rosanna lodged, she would brave the
inhabitants and ask to speak with the woman.
Surely her courage would be rewarded.

She reached the end of the street and scur-
ried to a halt. A crossroads confronted her and
she had no idea which path to take. The red
dress that had been like a beacon shining her
onwards had seemingly disappeared into thin
air. She could have cried with vexation. She
would have to choose one of these pathways,
but which? As she hesitated, a figure stepped
out from behind her, a figure that had been
waiting silently in the shadows. She felt an

iron grip close around her arm and her heart somersaulted in fear.

'You should go no further, Miss Ingram.'

Her mind blurred at the sound of the familiar voice. 'What…!' She tried to twist around, but remained locked in Justin Delacourt's hard grasp.

'You are hurting me.' She was breathing fast, more from the shock of his sudden appearance than from any pain he was inflicting.

'Forgive me, but I had to stop you from venturing any further into this den of villainy. We must retrace our steps immediately.'

'I will leave as soon as my business is finished and not before.' Indignation had replaced the initial shock and her limbs no longer trembled. She was so close to her goal and no one was going to stop her, certainly not the man who had shown contempt for the information she had brought him.

But Justin Delacourt had other ideas. 'You will leave now,' he said simply, his tone implacable. 'You will place your arm on mine and we will walk to the end of the street as calmly as though we were out for an evening stroll.'

'But…'

'No buts. We are being watched and, if I am not mistaken, we could be attacked at any moment. That is a fine ruby ring you are wearing and I had not the forethought to remove this handsome timepiece from my jacket.'

'I cannot leave yet. I have a most important task still to accomplish.' Her protest was half-hearted for his hand was still firm on her arm and she knew that he could make her do exactly what he wanted.

'Enough,' he commanded. 'Whatever your mission, you must abandon it. Now take my arm. We will walk slowly and all will be well.'

She had no alternative but to do as he wished. She felt the sinews of his arm against hers and his hand guiding her firmly towards the broader streets that ran upwards to the Citadel and eastwards towards the bustling port. She had been so focused on her quest that meeting him in that unlikely place had come as a shock, and it had been an even greater shock to realise the danger she was in. The minute she had spied that red dress, her quest had become all-consuming and she had blithely ignored the very real possibility that she might be attacked.

They retraced their steps until once more

they stood at the bottom of Mermaid Street, the coastal path lying ahead of them. She felt braver now, brave enough to disentangle her arm and to throw out a challenge.

'I thank you for your escort, Sir Justin, though I am unsure what right you have to determine where I walk.' She knew he had acted with good sense, but she had no intention of acknowledging it.

'I have no right, Miss Ingram, simply a wish to save you from unpleasantness. You should not be walking in that area and particularly not at nightfall'

They stood facing each other. The river below them snaked its way blackly to the sea. Here and there when the clouds above parted, licks of silver danced across its surface, but on the far bank the marshy plain lay flat and dark, crouching like some latent beast ready to strike. She shuddered involuntarily.

'Allow me to escort you home.'

'Thank you, but there is no need. The path is straight and I know it well.'

'I hate to contradict a lady twice in one evening, but I consider there is every need. Please take my arm again and I will see you safely to Brede House.'

Something in his voice made her do as he

asked. Something in her wished to do it, to feel the warmth of his thigh as she walked close beside him, to feel his comforting nearness.

'Why were you there?' he asked conversationally and out of the blue.

'I lost my way.'

'Really? You have a habit of losing your way, it seems.'

She was grateful that the dusk hid her spreading flush. 'Why were *you* there?' she countered.

'I will come clean,' he said engagingly. 'I was looking for the woman you called Rosanna.'

'So you did believe me!'

'It wasn't a case of believing or not believing. You gave me information and I felt duty bound to follow it up.'

'And what did you find?'

'A great deal—and yet, at the same time, nothing.'

Her mouth hardened into a severe line. 'You are setting out deliberately to puzzle me, I collect,' she said coldly.

'Forgive me, Miss Ingram, that is not at all my wish. I discovered that Rosanna is an intimate of several unsavoury gentlemen who are suspected of having formed a new smuggling gang. Also that an excise man—presumably on their trail—fell to his death just before Gilbert Armitage disappeared and that it was recorded as an accident by the magistrate. It is how all these things fit together that mystifies me and makes me feel I have got nowhere. It would seem, though, that Rosanna is the key.'

'I told you so,' she said triumphantly. 'And if you had not stopped me, I would have discovered just what she knows of your friend's whereabouts.'

'Again, I must disagree. The woman you were pursuing had disappeared. She had melted away and could have been in any one of those buildings. If it is any consolation, I lost sight of her at the same time as you. There are bolt holes aplenty in that wretched quarter and you would never have found her—and might well have had your throat cut in trying.'

'Are you not being a little melodramatic?' She tried to shrug off his warning, but her voice was shaky.

They had reached the beginning of the drive to Brede House and he came to a halt and stood facing her. In the clouded light his expression was solemn but concerned. 'I am the last person in the world to cry wolf,

Lizzie, and when I tell you that you were in great danger, you must believe me.'

She was charmed by the way in which her pet name had unconsciously slipped from him. *That is how he thinks of me*, she thought, *as Lizzie—not Miss Ingram*.

He captured her hands in a hard grasp. 'You must never go to that part of the town again!'

His touch was making her feel light-headed, or was it simply fatigue? She struggled to maintain her composure for she had an argument to make. 'Then how are we to discover the truth? I am certain that Rosanna lodges in one of those houses. We must find her and question her.'

'*We* are not going to find her. You will leave this investigation to me, do you understand?'

She pulled her hands from his. 'You are so used to giving orders that you think to command women as though they were part of the military.'

'I doubt that I could command you.' His smile was laconic. 'And did you not express a wish to be a soldier? That involves taking orders, you know.'

She tossed her head angrily and began to walk towards the house when he grabbed hold of her arm to detain her. 'Tell me, whatever possessed you to go searching for the woman?'

'You made me very angry when you refused to believe me,' she returned candidly. 'I decided to show you how wrong you were.'

'If I admit to my fault, will you promise to let the matter lie?'

She looked at him thoughtfully. 'It wasn't just that I wanted to prove you wrong. It was an adventure as well.'

He raised his eyebrows at her confession. 'And that is important?'

'It promised to enliven my life.'

'It would certainly do that. But I cannot imagine that adventure can be so important to you that you would deliberately walk into danger.'

'You cannot imagine because your life is one long adventure. Mine has been spent in a seminary. Think of it—the whole of my life in a girls' school, and in Bath of all places.'

'It sounds a trifle dull.' There was sympathy, but it was edged with caution.

'It was abysmally dull.'

'And you were at the school because your father was serving abroad?' She nodded. 'But did you have no female relations to care for you? What of your mother?'

'You need not worry,' she said seeing the concern in his face. 'My mother died when I was a baby and I know nothing of her.' She fingered the band on her finger. 'I have only this ring as remembrance. An elderly aunt looked after me until I was seven and then she died, too. Perhaps I have that effect on people.' Despite the joke, she could not prevent a note of wistfulness.

'And then…' he prompted.

'And then my father placed me at the Bates Seminary for Young Girls and there I've stayed ever since—well, with a few exceptions,' she said unguardedly.

'And what exceptions would they be?'

'I did try to escape.'

'Tell me.' He leaned back against the iron gatepost, clearly entranced.

'When I was nine I packed my most treasured possessions in a large handkerchief and started to walk to Bristol. I must have seen an illustration of Dick Whittington. Bristol is not that far from Bath, you know—though perhaps a little too far when you are nine,' she added pensively.

He burst out laughing. 'I would imagine so. What happened?'

'I got as far as Twiverton. It's a small village where everyone seems to spend their time watching everyone else. Anyway the local beadle caught me and would not let me go until he had made enquiries. Of course, he found out where I came from and I was duly returned to Miss Bates.'

'How did she respond to your bid for freedom?'

'She was kind, I think. At least not too cross—not as cross as she was when I tried to join the travelling circus.' She saw the astonishment on his face. 'I didn't actually want to join them, but they were on their way to Southampton and it seemed a good opportunity.'

'Does Miss Bates by any chance sport white hair?'

'She does—but I'm sure she had it before I ever came on the scene.'

'I don't share your confidence. But why this desire to get to the coast?'

'I wanted to reach Spain,' she said simply. 'Well, the first time I wanted to get to Canada—my father was still there after he fought in the American War. Later it was the

Peninsula. Canada or Spain, I had little idea where either country was—I just wanted to find my father.'

'And the circus was your last bid to travel abroad?'

'Oh, no.' She was abruptly downcast. 'But it is all history.' She had no intention of disclosing that particular episode, it was too shameful.

The breeze had picked up as they talked and she shivered a little from her inadequate clothing.

'Here', and he removed his jacket. 'How ungallant of me to keep you talking while you are slowly freezing to death.'

'Now that *is* melodramatic,' she said shyly, 'but thank you.'

He sheltered her with his jacket, pulling her very slightly towards him as he did so. She felt her face brushing his broad chest and the sound of his heart beating through her. His hands lingered on her shoulders, then stretched themselves towards temptation. She felt the lightest touch—fingers stroking her neck and slowly tangling themselves in the strands of hair that had come loose from beneath her bonnet. For a moment the clouds parted and a fingernail of moon floated across the dark arc of the sky, illuminating his golden halo of hair. Everything about him was beautiful, she thought. Everything. His lips were so close she could see their outline. His mouth hovered and she could almost feel its warmth on hers. She waited, her breath stilled, her body softening towards him.

'Come,' he said brusquely. 'We must get you indoors before you become any colder.'

She felt a confusion of emotions: anger, humiliation and deep, sinking disappointment. To cover her turmoil, she turned without another word and walked down the drive towards Brede House. He strolled silently beside her, neither of them speaking until they reached the front entrance.

'You must leave finding Rosanna to me,' he reiterated. 'I want you to promise.'

It was as though their earlier conversation had never been interrupted, as though the moment of intimacy between them had never happened. She was forced to nod her agreement for there was nothing else she could say or do. Misinterpreting her dismay, he tried to reassure her.

'I will undertake to talk to the woman as soon as I can. You can be sure that I will find out whatever she knows.'

She tried to collect herself, tried to pretend that his touch had been as unimportant to her as it evidently was to him.

'That is all very well, but what if she will not talk to you?' It was a last attempt to save her adventure.

'She will,' he said, grimly.

And Lizzie had to believe him.

## Chapter Five

Justin woke the next morning feeling strangely unsure. Every day of his life and virtually every minute of every day since he joined the army six years ago, he had been quite certain of who he was, where he was going and what he was doing. But today he felt unsure. Finding the woman Rosanna might not be as easy as he hoped, but that was not what was concerning him. He guessed that a few greased palms would help to track her down and similar largesse might get her talking. He did not share Lizzie's conviction that Rosanna would lead him to his missing friend, but if the woman could add anything to the sketchy picture he had so far managed to construct, it would be worth the effort. If he could pass on to the Armitages the slightest piece of new information, he would feel better.

And it would show Lizzie Ingram that he had fulfilled his promise to her. She was the reason, of course, that he was feeling insecure. How foolish—a girl he barely knew, a girl he'd met only days ago, and a wayward one at that. She had thought nothing of wandering at dusk into the worst parts of the town and all in the name of some unspecified adventure. Her childhood exploits had made him smile, but last night she could have been seriously harmed and that was not so amusing. It was not amusing either that he had come near to kissing her. No wonder he had woken this morning feeling decidedly uncomfortable. What had possessed him to get so close? He was honest enough to admit that she had got under his skin from the moment he'd seen her, but that if anything should have made him more circumspect. Instead, having rescued her from the danger of Rye's back streets, he had pushed them both towards an even greater danger. Even as he'd felt the touch of her breath on his cheeks, he'd sensed her body soften towards him and seen her full lips raised to his. The image returned with devastating clarity—it was enough to send a man crazy.

Is this what had happened to his dear father? Had he experienced such overwhelming desire that he'd thrown his whole life into chaos—his career, his family, his estate—in order to satisfy it? And what had been the result: nothing but disillusion and bitterness. He had grown up with his father's pain and sworn when he was little more than a child that he would never, ever follow in Sir Lucien's footsteps. So what on earth was he doing last night? He was no better than a moth singed by the flame, he chided himself, unable to resist the auburn curls, the dark-brown eyes, the saucy smile—above all, the smile. It was a novel experience and he did not like it. It made him restless and impatient with his life when his whole concentration should be on getting Chelwood on a secure footing before he returned to his beloved regiment.

This morning he abandoned any idea of sitting down to breakfast and went instead to the estate office. Mellors was already there and greeted him with a gloomy face.

'Beggin' your lordship's pardon, but I've been goin' through the account books fer the last few years and the estate's losin' money by the month. We don't charge proper rents, Sir Justin, that's the nub of it. There's some tenants paying what their grandfathers did. We must raise our rents, there's no 'elp for it.'

Justin turned away from the stack of ledgers hugging the table. 'I have no wish to bleed my tenants dry, Mellors.'

'Nothin' like that, sir. Just a modest increase, I'm thinkin'. It'd be more than justified. There's farmers over Hawkshead livin' high on the hog while we can't afford to mend the stable roof.'

'So what do you suggest?' Justin's voice expressed all the weariness he felt. Remorse was still biting deep—Sir Lucien had died alone while his only son was a thousand miles away, happily ignorant of Chelwood's problems. If only he had not stayed away so long, if only he had known how burdensome the estate had become to an increasingly frail man.

'We need an inventory, sir. That'll be the ticket—an inventory detailing the rents for every tenant, the size of their farm and the general state of repair.'

'There is no inventory!' Justin was shocked to think that he had not even considered the possibility.

'There were one, years ago...' Mellors scratched his head '...leastways I believe so. But 'appen it's been lost and not replaced. Sir Lucien was seemingly not one to worry over-much about paperwork.'

'No, indeed. And no doubt that accounts for many of our troubles. You're right—we need to know what rents the whole estate is earning. There may even be tenants who are behind with payment, but I have no idea.'

'So I can begin work on a new schedule?' Mellors looked more hopeful than he had for days.

'Yes, make a start now. But I don't want to worry people.' Justin's brow creased into tiny furrows. 'My father may not have been good with paper, but he was respected and well liked. I don't want that to change.'

'Reckon we should call a meeting, sir.' Mellors warmed to his theme. 'Explain our difficulties and tell them 'ow the estate can't afford to rent out farms at sums that 'ave been around for a 'undred years or more. Prepare them for the changes, as it were.'

'I suppose we will have to. But I've had no time so far to meet my tenants and I would rather that is not my first encounter with them. Perhaps we could offer them a more sociable occasion beforehand—a chance for me to get to know at least some of the larger land holders. I remember that years ago my father used to throw open the doors of Chelwood in the autumn for a celebration of the harvest and of the year that was just finishing.'

His face shadowed for a moment. Those evenings had ceased when his mother had abandoned Chelwood for good and Sir Lucien, left alone in the great house but for his young son, could not face the curiosity of local people.

'It'll be expensive,' the bailiff warned.

'You sometimes have to spend money, Mellors, to accumulate it. And it need not be wildly expensive. We are in mourning for Sir Lucien and that will preclude any extravagant entertainment—a simple buffet, perhaps, a little champagne even, some pleasant music. We could invite some of the townspeople, too—those well-wishers that I have not yet had time to visit.'

Mellors's gloom was back but his lugubrious expression only made Justin more determined. 'Yes,' he said with conviction, 'a meeting of town and country will be an excellent way to celebrate my father's life and mark a new beginning. Before you start on the inventory, draw up a list of those we should invite. Make sure that you include the Armitages—and Mrs Croft.'

And, of course, her companion. Was that why the idea had such appeal—that he could once again bring Lizzie Ingram to Chelwood? Surely not. There was a perfectly legitimate reason for the evening's entertainment, a very good reason, he assured himself. And naturally he could not leave Henrietta Croft from the guest list. Where Mrs Croft came, so did Miss Ingram. It was really quite simple. Having settled the matter to his satisfaction, he turned to the sheaf of papers his architect had left him for the renovation of the west wing. One day he might even have the money to carry out the ambitious plans.

Try as he might, he could not concentrate on the tasks that clamoured for his attention. The Chelwood celebration was to be held on the Friday evening and he was eagerly looking forward to it, more eagerly than he could ever remember when his father had presided over similar gatherings. He constantly checked on the arrangements: had Mellors booked the string quartet travelling all the way from Canterbury, had Cook ordered additional titbits from the most prestigious caterer in Tunbridge Wells, would his butler bring up as much champagne from the cellar as the sideboard would hold? His staff tried to smile through the barrage of commands, but with increasing difficulty, and it was only a sudden remembrance on his part that saved him from their rebellion. He must go to Rye for he had a woman to find! And he needed to find her before Friday evening.

As he'd suspected, it took only a short time and several sovereigns before he was confronting Rosanna. But as soon as he saw her, he knew that he had been wrong: he would not need to pay this woman or metaphorically twist her arm to get her to talk. Rosanna would always be happy to speak to a gentleman, more than happy to speak to a good-looking gentleman, who bore a military title and dressed in expensive superfine. She was beautiful, he thought, if you liked that kind of ripeness and he could well understand why her sultry attractions might allow her to manipulate others—men would be malleable clay between her slender hands.

She tried flirting with him, subtly at first and then, when he proved unresponsive, more overtly. He had no intention of succumbing to her charms. He had sought her out only because he had questions he needed answering, but in the event he was to be disappointed. Yes, she had known Gilbert Armitage, but only as an acquaintance. He had been friendly with the excise man, she knew, the man who had so tragically fallen to his death. It was all very sad. The last time she'd seen Mr Armitage had been a chance meeting with him in the market place, but the encounter was unremarkable and she remembered nothing much of it. Of course, like everyone else in the town, she had been shocked to hear of his friend's disappearance, but had no idea what might have become of him. Patiently Justin put the same questions to her several times, but her response was always the same, her eyes unwavering, looking frankly into his. He would get no further, he could see, and could do nothing more but bid her a courteous farewell and walk away. He doubted that she knew anything, but beneath her seductive exterior he sensed a sharp mind at work, and if she did possess information she was not about to disgorge it. Lizzie would not be pleased to find the trail had gone cold again, but there was little more he could do.

\* \* \*

Mellors had been commanded to deliver invitations for the Friday entertainment to the outlying farmers on the estate, while Justin had undertaken to call on the various townspeople who were to be invited. Brede House was next on his list and he found Mrs Croft sitting quietly in her armchair, her book cast aside.

'How good to see you, Justin, and how very kind of you to invite me to Chelwood. A celebration of Lucien's life and the life of the estate—that is most fitting.'

'So you will come?' He wished he did not feel so anxious to hear her reply.

'I would love to, my dear, but these last few weeks I have been feeling my age—I am getting old, there's no denying it—and an evening party is too difficult for me.'

He could not quite conceal his disappointment and she said quickly, 'I'm sure that Elizabeth would be happy to be my representative. This place is tedious for her, you know, and she is such a lively young woman. But perhaps I have spoken out of turn and you were not intending to invite her?'

'I could not invite you without your companion,' Justin said gallantly, 'but will Miss Ingram be happy to leave you and come alone?'

'I am well enough on my own—in fact, I enjoy the solitude. Another sign of old age, I fear. But Elizabeth can take my maid for company, if you are happy to send your carriage to convey them both to Chelwood.'

'Naturally I will be delighted to send Perkins.'

'Good,' she said, surprisingly brisk. 'Of course, you will have to ask Elizabeth yourself. I believe you will find her walking in the cove. She has been working very hard this morning, taking down and rearranging an entire wall of books for me, but she is an indefatigable walker.'

His smile was wry. 'So I have noticed, Mrs Croft.'

He walked through the long, narrow garden that separated Brede House from the river. The leaves were already russet, many lying on the ground in tall heaps, gathered there by the wind which funnelled its way upstream from the Channel. Picking his way through the path's coating of crackling fronds, he passed the stone folly built years ago to overlook the river by some sailor nostalgic for the sea and reached the wicket gate which led directly to the water.

Out of the gate and down the worn, wooden steps to the small cove lying sheltered beneath the cliff. Many years ago he remembered playing here with Gil. The cliff was riddled with caves and there had been a game of dare they'd played with each other all through one long summer—who could travel furthest through the caves and towards the sea before the tide turned. Some of the caves had been so low and narrow that they'd had to wriggle their way through, while others were wide open caverns, stunning in their immensity. Sometimes they had clambered their way until they'd almost reached the sea, when the sound of it in their ears became a warning to turn back. One day, they'd been so intent on exploring cave after cave that they had not heard the sound of waves drawing nearer until their boots were suddenly leaking water. They had run and wriggled their way back through the chain of caves with terror in their hearts and arrived at the cove with the river already lapping at their feet. They had never played that game again, he reflected.

\* \* \*

She was standing by the river's edge, the water lapping at the shingle beach around her feet. The rocky outcrops on either side glinted in the late-autumn sun and she had raised her hand to shade her eyes as she looked across the quick-flowing river to the marsh beyond, almost black in this newly intense light. Beneath her shawl, she was wearing a simple muslin dress that hugged itself tight to her trim figure and her hair this morning hung free, caressing the nape of her neck. His heart did a small flip. He wanted to reach out and touch that hair, to feel his hands again tangle the softness of those auburn curls. He cleared his throat and she looked around, surprised by the intrusion.

'Forgive me, Miss Ingram, I had not meant to startle you.'

'You may startle me at will.' She smiled at him, a warm, welcoming smile, and he felt again that small insistent lurch. 'You have news for me, Sir Justin?'

'Some news,' he said cautiously. 'But first, tell me how you have been since your adventure. I feared that you might catch cold from our evening walk.'

'I am not such a weak creature,' she laughed.

'I am glad you have taken no hurt for I am hoping that you will be willing to brave the night air once more. I am throwing a small celebration at Chelwood this Friday and wished for both yours and Mrs Croft's attendance. She tells me that she no longer feels able to manage an evening entertainment, but perhaps I may persuade you to come alone.'

She looked surprised. 'You wish me to come to your party?'

'It is not precisely a party—a small gathering only, to celebrate the end of the harvest and the year that has passed. Some of my tenants are invited and a few townspeople and local gentry. My father hosted the same event for many years and I have decided to reinstate the tradition.'

'That seems a most thoughtful way to honour him.' It warmed him that she had immediately recognised the deeper meaning of his gesture.

'He was a good man and much admired.' For a moment he stared fixedly at the fast-flowing river. 'He deserved a longer life.'

'You loved your father greatly, I think.'

'How could I not? He was my rock, the dearest person to me in the whole world.'

'People don't always love their parents.'

She appeared to hesitate. 'I imagine that you did not care much for your mother.'

He was taken aback by her perception and a tinge of colour stole into his tanned cheeks. 'You are frank, Miss Ingram. Is my distaste so very evident?'

'I wore her dress at Chelwood,' she reminded him, 'and your face told its own story.'

'It's true that my mother spread little joy. She was not a happy woman.'

She gave him a quick glance before venturing, 'She is dead?'

'As good as—dead to Chelwood, at least. She left the house fourteen years ago and never returned.' Except once, he reflected, but he would not think of that.

'Where did she go?'

'Everywhere and nowhere. Mostly London, living with whoever was her latest—friend.'

Her eyebrows shot up at this matter-of-fact statement. 'You will hear the stories soon enough,' he continued. 'I'm surprised that you haven't already. It speaks volumes for Mrs Croft's discretion!'

'All Mrs Croft ever told me was that your father was forced to give up soldiering. I think she forgot for the moment who she was talking to. I believe her words were that "*he was harangued into submission by that woman*".'

His lips twisted. 'Mrs Croft spoke truly. My mother always got her way.'

The tide was coming in now and pushing the river water further up the deep channel it had furrowed inland over the centuries. Lizzie's slippers were in grave danger of drowning and she moved quickly back from the water's edge to perch herself on one of the many rocks that enclosed the small bay. Smoothing its warm, flat surface, she gestured to him to take a seat beside her. The sun had settled low in the sky and glinted richly chestnut through her tangled ringlets. In the breeze a few stray tendrils of hair had blown across her cheek and he itched to smooth them back into place. Somehow he forced himself to keep his hands locked against the rock's hard surface.

'You have not called on your mother since your father's death, then?'

'Why would I wish to? I have made it my business to avoid her and the rackety set she runs with.' That was hardly to be wondered at, he thought, not after the most humiliating experience of his life. 'In truth, I rarely think of her—and at the risk of sounding callous, my life over the past few years has been so crowded that it has been easy to forget she was ever my mother.'

Lizzie nibbled at her lip. 'You have been in Spain for years and involved in the bloodiest of conflicts, but now that you are in England…'

'I doubt that I will find it any more difficult. The people here know the worst there is to know of my family and will not speak of her. And my mother is the one person who will not be attending the celebration and causing discomfort!'

Lizzie drew a slow circle on the rock with her finger. 'You might not find the party as comfortable as you expect.'

He looked slightly bemused and she murmured, 'You have invited me to Chelwood.'

For a moment he was caught unawares. Of course, he would not find it comfortable to have her beneath his roof again. On the contrary, he would find it deliciously uncomfortable. And though he should be fighting such feelings with every ounce of his willpower, he could not stop himself relishing the emotion. She was looking at him quizzically, waiting for him to speak. Please God, he had not betrayed his thoughts.

'I will stand out like a sore thumb among the wealthy farmers and the local gentry,' she explained. 'I am a servant, Sir Justin.'

So that is what she had meant! 'You are a companion and that is very different,' he countered.

But she was insistent. 'For many that is synonomous with a servant.'

'Perhaps,' he had to concede, 'but for a very few only. Many more will welcome your being there. The Armitages, for instance. I am on my way to Five Oaks with their invitation.'

'You have news for them?' Her eyes sparkled almost amber. Her eagerness to carry on the adventure was a delight and he hated that he must disappoint her.

'News that is, in fact, no news. I hope, though, that they will welcome the little I have discovered.'

'You have found Rosanna!' Her cheeks were flaming with pleasure and he longed to fan them with his breath, to cover her soft skin in butterfly kisses until his mouth reached the entrancing hollow at the base of her neck.

'You have found Rosanna?' she repeated a little unsurely.

With a huge effort he pulled his thoughts

back to the business in hand. 'I have found her and spoken to her, but…' his strong fingers reached out and covered her small hand '…but I fear that I have discovered little. Rosanna knows nothing of Gilbert's disappearance. She admits to knowing him, but very slightly. He was a pleasant gentleman, she said, and they would exchange a few words when they encountered one another. The last time she saw him was on market day when she bumped into him by chance. She spoke to him for a few minutes only and never saw him again.'

Lizzie broke through his hand's clasp and jumped abruptly to her feet. She stood facing him and her expression was scornful. 'And you believed her?'

'I must believe her.' He rose to stand tall beside her. 'I can see no reason for her to lie. And she confirmed something that James Armitage had already hinted——that Gil had made a friend of the excise man who died and that the man's death upset him greatly. She wondered if Gil might have fallen prey to the blue devils because of that and his disappearance was the result.'

'So though she knew your friend only slightly, she could discern when he was greatly upset and liable to depression!'

He felt irritated at her evident distrust. 'I imagine the man's death was a topic of general conversation in the town—until the magistrate ruled that it had been an accident. She would have no doubt exchanged words about it with Gil and he was never a person who could hide his feelings.'

She turned away from him, her shoulders hunched angrily.

'Why can you not accept what she says? I asked her the same questions two or three times and always received the same answer.'

She was facing him again, looking straight into his eyes, her expression unwavering. 'She is lying. I cannot believe you were taken in by her.'

'Why are you so certain that she is lying? I am a good judge of character, Miss Ingram, and I can assure you that I was not taken in by her.'

'We are not talking character here. We are talking of a beautiful woman, who no doubt fluttered her eyelashes, smiled sweetly and spoke softly.'

He flushed angrily. 'That does not necessarily suggest that she is a liar.'

'It does suggest, though, that you have been duped.'

'I resent that accusation.' He did not take kindly to having his word challenged and felt an overwhelming impulse to shake her. He had no interest in Rosanna, seductive as she was. He had no interest in any woman. No, that was no longer true. He *should* have no interest in any woman, he corrected himself. He could not be certain that Rosanna had told him the truth, but without an alternative, he must believe she had spoken in good faith.

'Resent it you may, but it rings true. She has wound you round her small finger, as she does all the men of the town. She has told you a pack of lies. Of course, she knows more than she is saying and you were too besotted to make her tell you. She has deceived you.'

'You are entitled to your opinion.' His voice was sharp with suppressed anger. 'I have done what I promised and can do no more.'

'You disappoint me, Major. I had thought you more resourceful.'

He would have liked to grab her there and then and shown her just how resourceful he could be, but he had himself under control now and his tone was deliberately measured. 'I am sorry that you are disappointed, but I trust that you will still feel able to come to

Chelwood on Friday. I will send my carriage for you.'

'Please do not concern yourself,' she said icily. 'If I wish, I am quite able to get to Chelwood by myself.'

His response matched hers in rancour. 'Of course you are. How stupid of me! I had forgotten your last visit.'

And with that he turned on his heel and, without another word, strode towards the wooden steps.

# *Chapter Six*

Lizzie stared sightlessly at the water eddying in small circles so close to her feet. She was angry and she was disappointed. Justin Delacourt had allowed himself to be duped! She was furious that he had not seen through such obvious duplicity, but disillusioned, too. Within minutes of meeting Rosanna, he had obviously succumbed to the woman's flattery; at the first flutter of her eyelashes, he had capitulated. He was no more subtle than that, no more reliable than any soldier, no more dependable than the father who had abandoned her. Had she really allowed herself to think that just possibly she had found a man who measured up to her dreams: a man of action, brave and daring, yet one who was also steadfast and trustworthy? If so, she was more foolish than she would have believed possible.

She turned to make her way back to Brede House, feeling out of sympathy with the whole world. She needed to walk off her animosity for she was too restless to take up a book or settle to her drawing, but she could not leave the house.

Mrs Croft was in her room taking a late-afternoon nap and would need her services when she awoke, but Lizzie had to relieve her stifled feelings or she would burst. She would attack the parlour! Hester had cleaned it that very morning, but she gave that not a thought. Grabbing a dustcloth and feather duster, she began ruthlessly to scour and polish the furniture. With every vigorous lunge, she imagined her fists to be pounding a row of military chests, with every swish of the feather duster, she was decapitating a line of soldiers. The more she cleaned, the more furious her movements, so that she became a whirl of activity, filling the small room. Several ornaments wobbled beneath her hand and nearly fell from the mantelshelf, a vase narrowly avoided being swept from an occasional table, but when she snatched up the tea tray left there from Mrs Croft's nuncheon, she did so with such violent motion that the china slid dangerously to one side and her employer's favourite teapot left the tray and toppled towards unyielding floorboards where it broke into small pieces. She was brought to a sudden halt and was standing aghast at the carnage when Mrs Croft came slowly into the room.

The old lady blinked, surprised into stating the obvious. 'You have had an accident, my dear.'

'I'm so sorry, Mrs Croft. I thought to get the parlour sparkling for you and look what I have done.'

'Accidents will always happen, my dear. I am sure you were trying to help.' Lizzie had the grace to feel ashamed. 'Get Hester to clear the pieces before we sit down, will you?'

'There's no need to bother Hester. I can clear it quite easily myself', and she began to shovel the sad fragments into the dustpan. 'I know that you loved this teapot, Mrs Croft. I promise to replace it as soon as I can if you tell me where it came from.' She could only hope that it was not an heirloom or so expensive that it was beyond her purse.

'You must not worry yourself, Elizabeth. The pot is of no value—I believe I bought it last year from a stall in the market. It has been a good pourer, but I'm sure I must have a dozen other teapots in the cupboard.'

'Maybe, but this one was your favourite and you must allow me to buy you another,' Lizzie said firmly. 'Tomorrow is market day and, if you will excuse me for just one hour, I shall get there bright and early and return with an exact replica!'

She was in the town before ten o'clock the next morning, still feeling shamefaced at yesterday's outburst. What was it about Justin Delacourt that made her so angry? It was perhaps better not to question herself too deeply, for she had an uneasy suspicion that she would not like the answer. She must simply put him out of her mind. He was not the man on whom to pin her dreams—there never would be a dream man and Miss Bates was right when she'd advised Lizzie to be sensible in contemplating the future and to settle for a secure life. Her heart must be given to a man she could depend on, or, if not her heart, at least her loyalty.

The market was already in full swing as she turned the corner of West Street and found herself outside the white frontage of the George, the oldest coaching inn in Rye. Farmers had gathered there to do business and a chatter of conversation filtered through the open windows and into the street. Lizzie walked past, her eyes fixed on the line of stalls stretching into the distance, trying to locate where she might begin to look for china. A loud cry of 'Milk!' rang in her ear and, alarmed, she almost cannoned into a milkmaid, painfully burdened by a wooden yoke and brimming pails, but intent on selling her wares. She walked on, passing stall after stall, amazed at the bounty on display. There were dozens of wooden trestles groaning with every conceivable fruit and vegetable and several stalls outside the baker's with pile after unsteady pile of flat breads for sale. Everywhere mounds of clothes—men's, women's and children's, of every hue and style—were tumbled together and spread on linen sheets to protect them from the dirt and damp of the cobbles. The smell of roasting meat floated in the air and mixed with that of sweetmeats, making her feel slightly nauseous. Several people were already eating, seated on upturned barrels or using them as makeshift tables.

The market snaked right into Lion Street

and she followed the line of stalls until at last she came to those displaying china at the quieter end of the thoroughfare. Here a street artist had set himself up, perched precariously on a folding stool, but vociferous in his invitation to the passing crowd to have their likeness drawn. She wandered slowly from stall to stall, picking up a cup here, a saucer and plate there, looking for the elusive pot. There were numerous teapots, but none that seemed a match for the one she had so carelessly destroyed. She turned and walked back down the road again, once more past the artist and once more refusing his offer. She could draw her own likeness if she had a mind. But in pausing to walk around the seated figure, she discovered a stall she had not seen before, half-hidden by the man's bulk. She saw the pot immediately and pounced. Surely it was an exact match. She was about to ask its price from the stallholder when a small ripple ran through the crowd. Almost a *frisson* of nervousness, she thought, seeming to affect all those around her. The buzz of chatter dwindled to nothing and the stallholder's attention was lost; he was no longer looking at her, but up the street in the direction she had come. She followed his glance and caught her breath.

It was Rosanna, her voluptuous curves gowned this morning in bright emerald silk and her ample bosom sporting a neckline so low that she was almost unclothed. It was downright indecent, Lizzie thought. No wonder the crowd had held their breath. But accompanying Rosanna was a man, one of the group Lizzie had spied days ago at the window of the Mermaid Inn. It was the tow-headed man, the man with a face that spoke wickedness! Rosanna was clinging to him, gazing dotingly into his eyes, occasionally pressing her lips to his as arm in arm they strolled leisurely along the pavement towards the High Street, looking neither to left nor to right. People instantly made way for the couple, averting their eyes. They had passed Lizzie now and were disappearing around the corner; an almost audible sigh flowed through the crowd, a gasp as everyone once more began to breathe easily.

Lizzie turned to the stallholder. 'Who was that?'

'Them's folk yer don't want to know, miss.'

'Everyone else seems to know them.'

'That woman ain't fit for decent society.' The man spat disparagingly on to the cobbles.

'And the man?' Lizzie persevered.

The stallholder lowered his voice. 'He's a bad lot, a very bad lot. Name of Thomas Chapman. That's all yer need to know.'

It meant nothing to her. 'Is the name of Chapman important then?'

'You'm a furriner, I take it. You keep clear of all the Chapmans, believe you me. Them's a bad lot,' he repeated.

'But how?'

'You'm a persistent one, ain't you, missy? That man's grandfather was George Chapman, *the* George Chapman, but no doubt yer never heard o' him?'

'No,' she said, bewildered.

His voice dropped again, almost to a whisper. 'Gibbeted he were, on Hurst Green.'

She stared. 'Shocked yer, haven't I? But he were part of the worst gang ever. Notorious they were. The Hawkhurst Gang—a bloodthirsty lot, cruel and violent. They terrorised this part o' the world fer years and George, well, he murdered a revenue officer who were doing his duty. Then he paid the price.' His tone expressed satisfaction.

'So George Chapman was a smuggler?'

'Told yer, didn't I? One o' the Hawkhurst gang.'

'And this man?'

The stall holder spat again. 'Like father, like son. Or in this case, like grandfather.'

'Thomas Chapman is a smuggler?'

The man hastily shushed her and looked warily around. 'Never say that. Remember, them's that asks no questions ain't told no lie—watch the wall, my darling, while the Gentlemen go by!'

'But I understood there was no longer smuggling in this area.' She remembered what Justin had told her. 'There are preventives along the coast, is that not right?'

The man snorted. 'What use are a few of them against that band of cut throats? There are two revenue cutters…' he held up his fingers, counting them out, one, two '…two between here and Poole! *The Stag* were here last week and we won't see the ship again for nigh on a month. Plenty of time for the mice to play, wouldn't you say?'

'But there are revenue men on shore. Excise men? I heard there was one based in Rye until a short time ago.'

A frightened look crossed his face and he hastily took the teapot from her hand, wrapping it in string and brown paper. She wanted to ask him more, ask what he knew of the dead excise man, but his face told her that he would say nothing. He might even refuse to serve her if she persisted in her questions and send her away empty-handed. She passed over the coins and turned for home.

Her mind was teeming. From the first time she had set eyes on Thomas Chapman, she had known that he was bad through and through. She had not known why, but every nerve in her body had told her that it was so. And now it appeared that Rosanna was an intimate of his, in fact, far more than an intimate. She was not simply the woman who happily replenished the men's tankards at the Mermaid Inn, but Thomas Chapman's lover. She must know what had happened to the excise man, Lizzie thought, and more to the point, she *must* know what had happened to Gilbert Armitage. But what was Justin's friend doing with a woman who was so evidently another man's lover? Had he not known of the relationship? He could not have done and Rosanna had played him for a fool. It was the only explanation. Gil Armitage was a wealthy young man and ripe for the plucking. She had no doubt played him cleverly, encouraged him in his infatuation to shower gifts on her and expensive gifts at that. She would get precious few from Thomas, Lizzie was sure. But what a tangle! Rosanna was in thrall to the evil Thomas while Gilbert was in thrall to her.

She walked swiftly back to Brede House, feeling vindicated. She had been right and Justin Delacourt had been wrong. It hardly mattered, though. His friend had fallen into the clutches of a desperate gang of men, it seemed, and wherever he was, he needed to be rescued. The only person who could do that was Justin. But he knew nothing about Rosanna's insidious connection and would have to be told. The future happiness of the Armitage family depended on her sounding the alarm, she realised. But how was she to alert Justin? He was unlikely to visit Brede House in the near future. She could write him a letter telling him of her discovery, but would he even read it? They were hardly on speaking terms, after all. And if he did read the letter, would he believe her? Past experience was not encouraging. But she had to speak to him, make him see that he must act immediately if Gilbert were to be saved. Despite her prom-

ise to keep away, she must go to Chelwood—
there was no other option.

'I hope you will feel able to go to Sir Justin's entertainment, my dear. Hester can accompany you.'

Mrs Croft fixed Lizzie with an anxious gaze as the young girl poked the fire into a comforting warmth. She was settled for the evening in her favourite chair, but something was marring her contentment. She had been speaking of Chelwood, as she often did, though always in relation to Sir Lucien, her mind taking pleasure in wandering the byways of the past. It saddened Lizzie to see the way that the world narrowed so drastically with age, and the ability to look forwards was overtaken by the enjoyment of looking back.

'I would like to go, Mrs Croft,' she said, excusing herself the small, white lie.

Her employer's face cleared. 'That is good news, Elizabeth. I feel that one of us should be there, but I very much feared that you had decided not to attend.'

'My gown has been concerning me.' Another white lie. 'It is sure to be a grand affair, despite Sir Justin's mourning, and it has worried me that I might appear poorly dressed in a gathering of Rye's finest.'

The old lady leant forwards, her face warm and her eyes alert. 'If that is the problem, I may be able to help you.'

Lizzie looked puzzled. Was Mrs Croft about to double her wages? She did not think so. And surely she could not be suggesting that she donated one of her own gowns. Lizzie was a fine needlewoman, but the stiff taffetas and voluminous skirts of the old lady's generation would defeat even her dexterity.

'My granddaughter—' Mrs Croft broke off, finding it difficult to continue. Lizzie looked astonished. She had not known there was a granddaughter or even that Mrs Croft had once been married. She'd hardly considered the matter, but if she had, she might have concluded that the Mrs was simply a courtesy title, so very spinsterish was Henrietta.

'I had a granddaughter,' the old lady tried again. She paused for a moment and with an effort gathered herself together. 'She was most fashionable in her time, you know. My dear Susanna.' Her eyes filled with unshed tears and she hurried to finish what she wished to say. 'Of course, the dresses Susanna left are no longer fashionable, but their materials are not so very different from those young women wear today and they have maintained their depth of colour and their texture. I know you to be most adept with a needle, so if you would care to take a look…'

Lizzie was touched. Mrs Croft had lost a loved grandchild, but bore her sorrow in silence. She would like to have asked what unkind fate had destroyed the old lady's happiness, would have liked indeed to express her sympathy, but she knew instinctively that it would not be welcome. Instead she said in her most practical tone, 'That is most kind of you, Mrs Croft. I would love to look.'

'Then you must go to the room at the very end of the corridor in which you have your own bedroom. There you will find a large wardrobe. It is unlocked. You may take what you wish.'

Lizzie thanked her profusely and made haste upstairs. If she was to remake a dress for tomorrow evening she would have to work swiftly. The oak wardrobe was exactly where Mrs Croft had directed. A strong smell of rose petals flooded the room as she opened the door. A row of gowns, all carefully protected by linen covers, lined up to face her and one by one she took them down and ran a practised eye over them. As the old lady had promised, they were beautifully cut, but now unfashionable. The materials, though, were lustrous in feel and hue. She guessed that Susanna must have possessed much the same colouring as herself for virtually every gown was a perfect complement for her hair and complexion. At the bottom of the wardrobe, she found a large bag spilling over with lace trimmings and spools of ribbon. The wardrobe was a treasure trove indeed.

After a good thirty minutes of unpacking and repacking, Lizzie had chosen her gown. It was of shimmering eau-de-nil silk with a matching lace trim at the hem. She found a spool of deeper green ribbon which she could fashion into love knots as trimming for the waist and sleeves. Fortunately Susanna appeared to have been a good deal taller, which would allow Lizzie to lift the waist and cut the skirt to a much narrower shape. The puff sleeves and bodice required no alteration. The gown must have been chosen at a time when the stiff skirts and petticoats of an earlier age were beginning to be replaced by the freedom of current fashions. Once the skirt was cut to size, there would be sufficient material left to fashion a matching reticule. Excitedly Lizzie bore her trophies to the parlour, wishing to thank her benefactress, but Mrs Croft was already slumbering by the fire and she did not feel it right to disturb her, for the sight of the dress could only reignite painful memories.

Instead she retired to the kitchen where there was a large scrubbed wooden table, perfect for the intricate cutting she must do. She found Hester drowsing by the open stove and a wave of impatience took hold. What was she doing in this house of sleeping women? Once she had settled this business with Justin Delacourt, she must take hold of her life and drift no longer. She cleared the table with an impetuous sweep, rousing Hester as she did. The maid blinked herself to full wakefulness. Intrigued by Lizzie's plans for the dress, she found a sudden new energy and plunged into the preparations with unusual vigour, unpicking seams, fashioning love knots and finally pinning the gown to exactly the right shape.

'The dress will look some lovely, miss,' Hester opined, 'once you've done all the fancy stitching.'

'I hope so or I will have wasted some very expensive material! Mrs Croft's granddaughter must have had excellent taste even though her dresses are now a little dated.'

'She did that, miss. A lovely lady was Miss Susanna.'

'She never married, then?'

'Bless you, no. She were too sickly ever to marry. Her mother died giving birth and it was two to one that the baby would follow. But the little mite survived—just. And it were thanks to her grandmother's care.'

'What happened to her father?' It was the inevitable question for Lizzie.

'He disappeared, thinking both his wife and child had perished. Mrs Croft sent looking for him, but he never came back.'

'So the baby lived here?'

'All her life. She was the mistress's angel. So close they were.'

'But she was always sickly, you say. Poor Mrs Croft, to lose her so young.'

'She were sickly, it's true, but if it hadn't been for that man...'

'What man?'

'We don't talk about it, miss, not in this house.'

'You have talked about it, just this minute.' Lizzie's tone was tart for she had pricked her finger from inattention. 'Who was he?'

'Nobody knew. He were a stranger but here in the garden. Scared the daylights out of Miss Susanna when she went to call the cat. She doted on that cat.'

'But how could that have led to her death? Did he attack her?'

'Not exactly. But her heart was weak and seemingly when he jumped out at her in the dark, it faltered and then stopped.'

'How very dreadful. And she did not live to identify him?'

'All Miss Susanna could whisper was "A man". I heard her myself for I had run out into the garden when I heard her scream. "A man," she said. "A man" and "behind me".'

'And was there was no investigation?'

'There were nothing to investigate, miss. Just a few words from a dying girl who everyone knew to be sick.'

Lizzie thought this the saddest story she had ever heard and her respect for Mrs Croft rose. To lose your daughter in childbirth was dreadful, but then to lose the child you had raised and loved in her stead was truly terrible. She would make sure that this dress was something that Miss Susanna could be proud of. She sewed on furiously and by midnight was ready to try on the rough toile she had made. Both women held their breath while Hester slipped the gown over her shoulders and stood back. It was a perfect fit.

Lizzie had worked late into the night and for most of the next day, but by seven o'clock that evening she was dressed in a fashionable new gown and ready to leave. Since she had refused the ride in Justin's carriage, they would need at least an hour to walk to Chelwood Hall. Hester had tried to persuade her to recant her decision, but she had been resolute in refusing. She was no longer angry, but she was still disillusioned. He had been led by the nose—and by such a woman! She was going to Chelwood only because she had compelling news and she was doing it, she reasoned, more for the Armitages' sake than for his. Nevertheless she could not help but feel a tremor of excitement. This was the first party she had attended in Rye, indeed the first party she had attended alone and without the eagle eye of Miss Bates overseeing her every move. The first time, too, that she had dressed just as she wished.

While she waited for Hester to collect her cloak from the scullery, she studied her image in the mirror, anxious that no crease marred her gown, no smudge sat on her nose. Miss Bates would doubtless have found fault with her appearance this evening, but she was delighted with it, knowing that she would be the equal of any woman there. The maid had helped tame her luxuriant curls into the popular Roman style and glistening ringlets now cascaded from a carefully arranged topknot. A string of pearls wound its way in and out of the ringlets and she had artfully feathered a few stray tendrils of hair to frame the perfect oval of her face. The slightest blush of rouge to her cheeks—Miss Bates would certainly not have approved that—and a smear of rose salve to her lips completed her *toilette*.

'You look lovely, miss. A real picture!' Hester was as delighted as she with the result of their hard work.

She was not as pleased though with the tramp along country roads that awaited them, for at this hour of the day there was no possibility of taking the ferry which would have shortened the journey considerably. From the outset Lizzie set a spanking pace with the maid dawdling a little in the rear. She had ignored Hester's advice that she wear boots until they reached the Hall for she could not bear anyone to see her so attired for a party. In-

stead she had donned the flimsiest of evening
slippers and after half a mile, the slippers—
so beautiful, so creamy—began to pinch.
Gradually they grew more and more painful and by the time they had covered another
mile, Lizzie could barely walk.

'There now, miss, didn't I tell you. We'll
never get to Chelwood at this rate.'

'We will.' Lizzie's tone admitted no argument. 'And why are *you* complaining—you
have boots to walk in!'

'And whose fault is that?' Hester muttered.
'If we ever get there, it will be a miracle and
we'll be so dirty, we won't be worth setting
eyes on.'

Their progress was becoming slower by
the minute. The lane they were walking was
heavily used by farmers' vehicles and they
were forced to zigzag from hedge to hedge in
an effort to avoid the worst potholes and here
and there patches of deep mud. When a cart
coming from the opposite direction rounded
the bend a little too quickly, they found themselves stranded in the middle of the track with
a horse thundering down on them.

The driver managed to bring the beast to a
sudden halt, missing them by a whisker.

'It's Mr Jefferson, that it is,' Hester exclaimed, her bonnet knocked askew.

'Well, what have we here?' The farmer's face broke into a wide smile. 'Two damsels in distress!'

Lizzie scowled at him and started to walk on, but was stopped by Hester clamping a fierce hand on her arm. 'We are in a little trouble, Mr Jefferson. The carriage we ordered never came and, as you see, we've been left to walk in our party clothes.'

Lizzie gaped at the maid's dishonesty, but before she could contradict her, Mr Jefferson had jumped down from his box and was moving bales of hay around in the back of the open wagon. 'We can't have that, can we, me dears?'

In a few minutes he had arranged the cart to his satisfaction and held out his hand to Lizzie. 'There now, ladies, your carriage awaits. Seats fit for a queen, I swear. And where might you be wanting to go?'

'Chelwood Hall, please,' Hester said quickly before Lizzie had time to protest.

The farmer propelled Lizzie upwards into the wagon and on to the nearest hay bale where she sat fuming at her own stupidity. Why on earth had she insisted on wearing these slippers, for now she must suffer the indignity of travelling in a hay cart. Hester had no such qualms. Smiling contentedly, she took a seat beside Lizzie as the cart lurched forward and once more began its swaying progress.

In less than half an hour they were clip-clopping up the drive to the entrance of Chelwood Hall. As they drew near, Lizzie could see the house ablaze with light and hear the sounds of distant music, its faint ripples escaping into the night.

She felt herself freeze. If she could hear music singing through the air…the huge oak door stood wide open! She cursed her luck for she had wanted to bid the cart farewell before anyone could see her. But, no, the front entrance was ajar and who was standing there but Justin Delacourt himself. Of course he would have to be, she thought bitterly. He had positioned himself so that he might greet his guests one by one, but he could not have bargained on such an arrival. He had seen the whole sorry spectacle and it was mortifying. She tried not to look at his splendid figure walking towards her and failed. He was dressed in the deep-blue jacket of the Dragoons, gold buttons gleaming and a white-silk sash crossing his powerful chest. Tight grey pantaloons clung to a pair of muscular legs and on his feet the lightest of evening slippers. For a moment the image of another uniformed soldier floated across her vision and she felt a great lump rising in her throat. But not for long. She looked again at the fine, sensitive face and her father was forgotten. A golden halo of hair and a pair of smiling eyes was quickening her heart and sending her stomach twisting and turning in the most alarming fashion.

He came level with the cart and she felt sure that he was struggling to keep his face straight, but barely a quiver ruffled his polished tone. 'Welcome to Chelwood, Miss Ingram.'

He helped her down from the vehicle, carefully brushing the stray straws from her cloak. 'I am delighted that you have been able to attend our small affair. You must come in and meet my other guests.' He turned back to the maid. 'Hester, you will find a ready welcome in the kitchen, I believe.'

Hester bobbed a curtsy and Lizzie, unable to say a word, found herself steered expertly towards the open door.

## Chapter Seven

'You must have had an uncomfortable ride, Miss Ingram. I wish you had sent me a message—my carriage was entirely at your disposal.'

'Thank you, you are most kind, but really how I travel is of no account.'

She was an extraordinary girl, he thought. Most women would have been close to hysterics if they had been discovered in such a predicament, but she was brushing the matter aside as though arriving on a hay cart was a daily occurrence.

He tried once more to break the ice between them. 'The evening air has a chill about it these days. I hope that you have not caught cold.'

'On the contrary, I find it most invigorating.'

Her tone remained curt and he knew himself unforgiven. 'Here, let me take your cloak. One of the footmen can banish any lingering straw.'

She glared at him. It must appear that he was enjoying her difficulty, he thought, but she allowed him to slip the cloak from her shoulders and hand it to a waiting servant. He saw her snatch a quick glance at the long, ornate mirror that hung to the right of the door and smile slightly at her own reflection. She seemed relieved that her beautiful silk gown had come to no harm and that she still presented a creditable appearance.

To Justin she was more than creditable. He stood behind her, the two of them gazing at her image in the mirror. She looked lovely, utterly lovely. The eau-de-nil silk of her dress shone lustrously and skimmed her body in the most enticing fashion, setting off to perfection the soft cream of her skin. Beneath the branches of candles that lit the flagged hallway, auburn ringlets flashed sparks of fire, sufficient to warm a man's body through and through, he thought. He was staring at her, staring too hard and too long. He must stop right there. Surely a military man could discipline himself sufficiently to get through this evening with feelings as hazardous as these under strict control. He straightened his shoulders and offered her his arm into the drawing room, where champagne was working its magic and the scatter of voices had become an ever-increasing buzz.

She made no move, but remained standing at arm's length, a defiant expression on her face. 'I will play at being your guest, Sir Justin—' her voice was coldly clipped '—but I have come tonight for one reason alone and that is to pass to you crucial information. As soon as we have talked, I would like to return to Brede House.'

He felt scorched. For a moment he had been caught in a dream: an enchanting woman emerging from out of the night, young, lissom and lovely, and here this evening only for him. But in a few words the dream had folded— she had come not as his muse, but to resurrect a tiresome quarrel. He felt himself begin to bristle as he remembered what had passed between them in the cove. She had been wrong to accuse him of weakness when they had last met and she was wrong now. He had not been weak, simply pragmatic. He had Rosanna's measure, he was sure, and no amount of flattery or fluttery had influenced him. Gil had been mooning over a woman, it was clear, and if by any chance that woman had been Rosanna—and he still found the idea ridiculous—adoration from afar was all there would have been. Gil was too timid to embark on a full-blown love affair and Rosanna would never have got close enough to know anything useful about his disappearance. He knew his friend and Lizzie Ingram did not.

Lizzie's brow puckered. She had thrown down a challenge and was waiting for his response. 'Naturally, Miss Ingram, you may leave whenever you choose. You have only to tell me and I will have my carriage take you back to Brede House. I hope, though, that you will be happy to meet some of our neighbours and perhaps enjoy a little music. The Cheriton Quartet is reputed to be excellent.'

'I am sure they are, but I have not come to listen to music. I am here for quite other reasons.'

He groaned inwardly. The evening was heading for trouble. It was like swimming towards submerged icebergs with the tip of their next quarrel hovering just above the water line. He did not want to fight again with this lovely girl, but it seemed inevitable, for what could she possibly know? Some unimportant snippet of gossip she had gathered from her last visit to the town? Really, all he wanted was to take her in his arms and kiss away this whole worrisome business. His reaction shocked him, but then, ever since their first meeting, he had been shocked by the feelings she provoked.

'I understand that you have information for me,' he said in a level voice, 'but for the moment, I must remain at my post to welcome any late-arriving guests. As soon as I am able, I will seek you out and we will talk.'

He was not going to escape, so better to advance immediately into enemy territory. Once all the guests had arrived, the quartet could be formally introduced and with everyone engrossed in the musical recital, it should be easy to extract Lizzie from their midst. She deserved a hearing after braving the hay cart—the least he could do was listen.

She thanked him crisply and allowed herself to be escorted into the adjoining room. It had been simply decorated for the occasion with posies of wild flowers lining the buffet table and branches of greenery hung from the panelled walls. Nothing too festive or fancy, he had told his people, and they had managed a backdrop which fittingly celebrated his father's life and work in the community he had loved.

'Allow me to introduce you to some of our neighbours.'

They hovered on the threshold of the drawing room and nearly every pair of eyes were on Lizzie, many of them warmly admiring. He felt a stupid pride that he had the most beautiful woman in the room on his arm and, for the moment, forgot that they were hardly on speaking terms. One or two of the younger men hastily broke off conversations and began to advance towards them, but before they could reach their goal James Armitage was there, bowing low to Lizzie and tapping Justin's arm in a friendly fashion.

'You must introduce me, Justin. This is a lady I have not yet fully encountered in Rye, but I feel I most definitely should!'

'Miss Ingram, this is Mr James Armitage, our very good friend and neighbour at Five Oaks. Mr Armitage, Miss Elizabeth Ingram—she is staying with Mrs Croft at Brede House.'

'So you are quite used to being beaten and battered by the elements, Miss Ingram! What

a house that is. I wonder that Henrietta can
bear to live there still what with—'

Justin cut in. 'I must return to my post, but
will you escort Miss Ingram to the buffet? I
imagine she has not yet eaten.'

'It will be my pleasure.' James Armitage
bowed elegantly in Lizzie's direction. 'Caroline is already enjoying your hospitality,
Justin.' He gestured towards the long dining
table which had been set up against one of the
panelled walls and was crammed with dishes
of every variety of savoury and sweetmeat.
'Come with me, Miss Ingram, and meet my
wife.'

He had not introduced her as Mrs Croft's
companion, Lizzie noted. Was that because
Justin Delacourt was ashamed of inviting a
servant to his party or because he wished to
show delicacy towards her feelings? She had
tried very hard to remain cold and reserved,
but it had been difficult to stop herself from
falling back under his spell. She had felt his
hard gaze on her and knew herself admired.
She had wanted him to admire her, wanted
him to desire her as she desired him and had
done from the very first moment they'd met.
Even now, with irritation so strong within her,

she was unable to protect herself from these most inconvenient feelings. Just the warmth of his body as he had walked beside her to the drawing room had made her heart beat erratically. And it was the strangest thing, but she felt secure. She felt herself relaxing into safety when she was with him, as though he offered a haven, a pair of arms in which she could rest. It made no sense—in fact, it was plainly stupid. He was far from safe: excitement did not go with security. Piers was security and she could not remember enjoying one exciting moment with him. And unlike Piers, Justin Delacourt could not be relied upon. Had he not let her down in succumbing to Rosanna's charms? And once he had put Chelwood Hall to rights he would leave the district, he would return to Spain and to the war. It was inevitable. He might look at her admiringly, but she was simply a pretty object to him, an item to appreciate before moving on.

James was guiding her towards the buffet table and towards his wife. She wondered if Caroline Armitage would remember seeing her from the time she had rushed wildly from Brede House. She hoped not. James was a charming man and no doubt his wife was equally charming, but she could have wished to be talking to someone else. In the light of what she now knew, it would be difficult, painful even, not to blurt out the most dreadful suspicions that had begun to fester.

Caroline came towards her, a gentle smile on her lips. Lizzie saw with relief that the woman had not recognised her, but it was a relief that was shortlived, for she found herself forced to make polite conversation with a woman whose heart she knew was breaking beneath the social mask she wore. Yes, Lizzie was enjoying living in Rye. She found the countryside pleasant and the sea air invigorating. Mrs Croft was a dear lady and a kind employer. She would love to visit Five Oaks and there was no need to send their carriage for her. She was a keen walker and who knew, she might meet Mr Jefferson and his cart— though she kept the latter thought to herself.

'Can I get you some food, Miss Ingram? A glass of champagne?' James was at her side.

'Champagne would be very pleasant, but I am not hungry, thank you.'

She could not eat, not while she had this information gnawing away at her, not while she was in the company of the Armitages. It was fortunate that just then Caroline's attention was claimed by acquaintances who had recently arrived and, for the moment, Lizzie felt she could relax.

While James busied himself fetching the champagne, she looked around. A mixed gathering of people were clustered beneath the drawing room's three fabulous chandeliers, enormous crystal constructions, which tonight blazed with the light of a thousand candles. She had not seen this room on her previous visit and the space was stunning. A bank of arched windows to the rear of the house looked out upon acres of rolling lawn, while another bank of windows in the opposite wall gave on to the gravelled carriageway which wound a sinuous path through flowering shrubs and ancient trees. Between the two sets of windows, there were beautifully carved, oak-panelled walls, smothered in intricate pattern—fruits and flowers and what looked to her like *fleur-de-lys*. Had not Mrs Croft told her that Delacourt was a French name? Such a very old family must have come from Normandy and was still living in the place they had first landed. The carving became even more elaborate in each corner of the room: snakes, she was sure, coiling themselves around wooden pineapples and through wooden palm leaves. She wondered if any

Delacourt ancestor had travelled beyond Europe. She had hardly spoken to Justin of his family and suddenly she wanted to know everything about them. That was stupid of her, too, for once she had spoken her piece, she would walk out of Chelwood's front door and never come back.

James Armitage was steering his way around the knots of chattering people, holding aloft several glasses of champagne. Lizzie was dismayed to see that he was not alone, but accompanied by a fresh-faced young man, eagerness writ large on his face. And just behind him, more young men appeared, as though the fetching of the champagne had signalled a barrier being lifted. It was the last thing she wanted: she had no wish to attract attention, no wish to be forced into rebuffing advances. Tonight was too important. Thankfully she heard the first strains of the violins and cello being tuned—the music would save her.

'We should take our seats, Miss Ingram. The recital is about to begin.'

Caroline had returned and was shepherding her towards three rows of chairs which had been laid out in the shape of a semi-circle. In front of the chairs, a playing space had been created and a temporary dais erected. The quartet had already settled themselves and their music. Glass in hand, Lizzie slid quietly into a seat on the edge of the furthest row. The news she was carrying had begun to feel like a burning brand and she was desperate to unburden herself, but she had no idea how long she would have to wait. After welcoming everyone to Chelwood and introducing each member of the quartet by name, Justin had disappeared! She could do nothing but settle herself to listen, though her mind was everywhere but in the room.

Five minutes into the 'Air' from *Suite in D*, she felt a strong hand on her arm. Slipping noiselessly from her seat, she followed his figure into the hall. He walked to the far end of the flagged passageway and stopped outside a room she remembered well.

'We should not be disturbed here.'

The library looked much the same as it had done on the day she had trespassed at Chelwood. Why had she been tempted to do such a foolish thing? Because her vanity was so overweening that she could not bear to think a man she admired did not similarly admire her? She felt ashamed at her shallowness, but she had been amply punished since, for with every one of their encounters, she had become more and more spellbound.

A fire had been lit in the immense stone grate and its heat was ferocious. She was temporarily stunned by it and stepped as far away from the hearth as she could.

'We could walk on the terrace if you would prefer,' he offered. 'I have a shawl here, should you need it.'

She was touched that he had thought to keep her warm and responded with more grace than she had so far managed that evening. 'I would like that very much. The air is quite still and the moon bright enough to light our footsteps.'

The sultry heat of the library was left behind as they passed through the long doors which led on to the terrace. She had not noticed them on her first visit, but that was hardly surprising. It had been a vexatious morning.

'The shawl is your mother's?' she ventured, as he placed the gorgeous length of Norwich silk around her shoulders.

'It is. It would appear she has her uses at last—her dress, her shawl.'

'She certainly had a taste for the luxurious. Her clothes are still elegant despite the passing years.'

'They are clothes befitting a beauty—a diamond of the first water, or so I'm told.'

'Lady Delacourt must have had many suitors.' She should not be prolonging the conversation, she scolded herself. She should say her piece and leave.

'Dozens, though she treated them with indifference.' Justin seemed as unwilling as she to confront the troublesome business between them. 'My father was one of her most ardent admirers and felt himself lucky that he was the man ultimately to win her. As it turned out, he was anything but lucky.'

'But surely she must at some time have been in love with Sir Lucien?'

A sardonic smile lit his face, encouraging her to make her case. 'If she were the beauty you say, she could have married the most prestigious of titles and become the mistress of a vast estate—she could even have become a duchess! Plenty of beautiful women have over the years. Instead she chose to come to Rye. There must have been a very good reason.'

'There was, but it was not love. She was certainly a beauty, but she didn't "take"—

I think that's the phrase—so that when Sir Lucien met her she was already in her second Season and without an offer to her name.'

Lizzie puckered her forehead. 'Not a single offer—how strange! I understood that acclaimed beauties in *ton* society always make splendid marriages. Are you sure you have it right?'

'Quite sure. I had it from my old nurse—she did not share Mrs Croft's discretion, alas, but she did know everything there was to know about the inhabitants of Chelwood Hall. She put my mother's failure down to her waspish nature. Even the most adoring of men will baulk at living with a termagant.'

'But not your father?'

He could not stop the sigh that had been building. 'It was my father's misfortune to fall deeply in love with her. Lavinia's younger sister was due to be presented the following Season and I imagine that she was desperate—bitter that her beauty had not won her the matrimonial prize she thought she deserved—so that when my father made his offer, she accepted. The Delacourt name was, after all, an ancient one—they came from France with William the Conqueror.'

'I am impressed! But surely the family

must have liked the match, or they would have intervened.'

'The "family" was, is, very small—just my father and grandfather at the time. My father was a grown man, he had been a soldier for years and my grandfather a semi-invalid. He was hardly going to question his son's choice.'

'And how did he like his new daughter-in-law?'

'He didn't. They were forced to live together at Chelwood while my father served abroad and that proved intolerable. My father never blamed my mother, but it became clear to me as I grew up that she had pressured him greatly until he promised to sell out and return to Chelwood. The army was his life, but he gave it up for her. For nothing, as it turned out.'

'It does not seem a happy household.' Her tone was thoughtful and he wondered at her interest in a history that was best forgotten. 'I imagine, though, that Lady Delacourt was glad when your father returned to live at Chelwood.'

'Intermittently glad, perhaps.' He was trying to be honest. 'My grandfather died a few years into the marriage and my father inherited the title. That kept her content for a while and naturally he lavished money on her. She spent whatever she liked and the estate suffered for it—even then, it was a struggle to keep things going. But life no doubt became tedious for her. Rye is a small place and the spread of gentry in this part of Sussex very thin. She craved company and when she had done her duty by finally producing an heir, she chose the fun and gaiety of the capital.'

'And your father—did he go with her?'

'That was not a choice. He would never have been happy in town, but he agreed to her staying with friends. The visits to London grew longer and more frequent and the times she returned to Chelwood fewer and fewer. Then they stopped altogether—that's when the lovers began.'

He saw the soft brown of her eyes darken with shock. He should not be telling this tale of unhappiness to such a young woman and one he barely knew.

'Shall we walk?' He offered her his arm once more and side by side they strolled along the terrace, its flags washed by moonlight and with the faintest scent of a few late-blooming roses. Above, the night sky was a sheet of polished glass, its ebony sheen broken only by a sprinkling of wayward stars.

'You cannot wish to hear more of this, Miss Ingram. Tell me instead how I can serve you.'

But for the moment Lizzie seemed to have forgotten her mission. 'As a boy, did you know of your mother's—activities?'

If she wanted the truth, she would have it. 'I could not escape knowing,' he said simply. 'She was the talk of the county—my father, too. One lover followed another until he could stand the humiliation no longer. They were divorced on my twelfth birthday.' Imagine how that felt, he almost said, but bit the words back. 'It was a shameful business. My father took the blame and allowed her to divorce him. Of course he did. She made a fool of him to the very end.'

'And now?'

'Now she lives in London—though given her scorched reputation, somewhat reluctantly, I imagine. But Europe is off limits and has been since the war began. I believe she has actually married her latest lover. No doubt she was getting a little old for dalliance and eager to strike while her cicisbeo's feelings ran high. He is obscenely wealthy, I'm told, so what more could she want? She has money, position and half-a-dozen estates. She need never be bored again.'

He closed his lips. He must say no more of the woman who had wreaked such unhappiness and wished he had not allowed himself to say as much. Lizzie Ingram had pierced his armour and he did not understand why he had let her do so.

He stopped and turned to her, his face pale and his hair almost silver in the spectral light. 'So, Miss Ingram. The information you have for me?'

'I understand that you are sceptical of anything I might tell you,' she began stiffly, 'and I would not again have exposed myself to your disbelief if I did not think that what I have to say is important, indeed critical to finding your friend.'

His expression mixed impatience with the slightest spark of interest. 'I hope that I am fair minded enough to listen impartially to whatever you have to say. If you have indeed discovered something that will lead me to Gil, I will be most grateful.'

'It is not gratitude that is required, but action,' she returned swiftly and then regretted the stinging nature of her response. 'What I am trying to say,' she appeased, 'is that the situation is urgent. Rosanna—'

She was sure that she heard him tut. 'What?'

'Nothing,' he said hastily. 'Please continue.'

'Rosanna has a lover. No, not Gilbert Armitage, though I believe he thought himself favoured. She has a lover called Thomas Chapman.'

She saw that the name had some meaning for him. 'Thomas Chapman is the grandson of a man who was hung for killing an excise man.'

'Yes, it's an old story.'

'It is not only a story. It is a fact. People here know the Chapmans' history and by all accounts his grandson is as violent and cruel as his ancestor.'

'Forgive me, but I cannot see a connection to Gil.'

'You will,' she said with certainty. 'Thomas Chapman heads a gang of smugglers. I know you believe that smuggling is extinct along this coast, but you are wrong. Ask any of the local people and they will tell you differently. I've seen the gang myself, sitting in the Mermaid Inn, their loaded guns on the table for all to see. I also saw Rosanna with them, but at the time I thought only that she was a barmaid, nothing more.'

'And now you think she is more intimately connected with Chapman?'

'She is his lover—there is no doubt of it. I saw them yesterday at the market, walking boldly together, arm in arm, openly kissing each other.' She flushed a little at the frankness with which she was forced to speak, but he appeared to notice nothing untoward.

'Your friend—'

She broke off what she was saying as he began to pace along the terrace. After a few yards, though, he turned back, his voice spilling with frustration. 'What has any of this to do with Gil?'

'Don't you see?' she said impatiently. 'Your friend hoped he was Rosanna's sweetheart. No doubt he bought her gifts, showered her with money. He hoped he was the loved one, but her heart belonged to Chapman and still does—and *his* heart is as black as coal. Together they used Gil's devotion against him.'

Her words had an effect. Justin was looking distracted, his hand cleaving a path through well-ordered locks and rumpling its bright strands into dishevelment. 'I found letters,' he began. 'Letters that Gilbert had written.' She stared at him for this was the first she had heard of them.

'Who were the letters meant for?'

'I have no notion, only that they were written to a woman he loved—page after page filled with his innermost feelings. I read only a little. I could not…but I got the general idea. Whoever he was writing to, she meant a great deal to him. But he did not send the letters.'

She pounced. 'Which means that he was unsure they would be welcome. He had doubts about Rosanna, he suspected she loved elsewhere!'

Justin leaned on the walled balustrade and looked out on to the peaceful garden, the bushes of the parterre transformed in the moonlight into a small army of magical soldiers. 'That is pure speculation. We cannot even be sure that Chapman and Rosanna are lovers.'

'Of course we can,' she said scornfully. 'As sure as anyone can be. Even a soldier should be able to recognise desire when it is walking down the road.'

It was his turn to flush. 'I see you have made a study of them.'

'I did not. I was too nervous yesterday to look at them closely. But so was every other person on the street. People were terrified. Chapman is evil, Justin.' In her excitement,

she had called him by his first name and
reached out for his arm to clasp it tightly. 'I
have no idea how far your friend was involved
with the gang, whether he was simply pursuing a hopeless love for Rosanna or whether he
allowed himself to be pulled into their wrongdoing. But whatever his involvement, I am
convinced that's where you will find the answer to his disappearance.'

He shook his head, trying for clarity. 'I
cannot believe that Gil would ever do such a
stupid thing as to involve himself with a crew
of miscreants.'

She stamped her foot. 'Whether he helped
them or not, it hardly matters. He is in
danger—surely you can see that. He may
have got close enough to discover something
they wished to keep hidden. He was a friend
of the excise man who died, remember, and
not one person in Rye believes that death was
accidental. If your friend knew something the
smugglers wanted to conceal, then they would
need him to disappear. They may have kidnapped him, may even have carried him over
the water.'

When he said nothing, she grabbed his arm
quite roughly. 'We need to rescue him!'

'Who is this "we"? You do not even know him.'

'It feels as though I do. And I am desperately sorry for his parents. I want to help.'

'You may have done so, though I find it almost impossible to reconcile the man I knew with what you say.' He was looking thoughtful again. 'You might as well know that the Armitages mentioned to me that money has gone missing from the family accounts. They are also missing a ring, one that belonged to Gil's grandmother.'

She looked triumphant, but he was not quite ready to concede. 'That does not mean anything on its own, of course. The ring could have been lost anywhere. Gil might not have withdrawn the money.'

'But he did, I'm sure, and spent it on Rosanna. Go to her again,' she urged. 'Use your charm to make her talk.'

'I have charm? That is surprising news, but none the less very welcome.'

She walked a little away from him, priming herself to make an apology. 'I'm sorry that we quarrelled. I'm sorry that I doubted you.'

'And I am sorry I disappointed you, Lizzie. It grieves me to acknowledge that I might have been wrong, but I will make amends, I promise!'

She liked the sound of her name on his lips and smiled up at him. 'I will go with you, if you like. We will confront Rosanna together.'

'You are worried that she will once more cast her spell over me?'

'I would not blame any man for being entranced by her. She is very beautiful,' Lizzie conceded.

'Some may find her so, but my taste is more refined.'

He was looking down at her, his fascinating changeful eyes unusually intent. His hand reached out and with his finger he traced a line down her cheek.

'You are far more beautiful and infinitely more enchanting.'

She flushed a deeper pink. 'That is poetic talk for a soldier,' she teased.

'When I am with you, I tend to forget I am a soldier.' He tipped her chin upwards and gazed into her glowing face. 'You are very lovely and—and I cannot stop myself from kissing you.'

He bent his head and his mouth found hers. At first it was a soft brushing of lips. Then his mouth grew harder and she sensed his body flex. A hand was in her hair, tangling her curls through his fingers, while with the other he pulled her towards him. She went willingly, her lips still fastened to his as though never to be parted. He kissed her over and over again, longer and more deeply with every kiss, until sheer breathlessness forced them apart. They stood for a moment looking at each other, dazed, shy, then his lips were back on her mouth and his tongue delicately probing. They leant against the stone walls of the house, still warm from the afternoon sun, and his body was pressing into hers and hers softening in response. Slowly he lowered his head to her bosom and touched his mouth to the soft skin between her breasts. She felt herself tauten and raised her arms in a gesture of surrender, her hands reaching up to stroke his cheek, to ruffle his wonderful golden hair. Her dress was crushed, but she cared nothing for that. She wanted no dress, she wanted to be naked and to feel him naked against her. It was the most wonderful feeling. Her skin was hot, flushed and prickling with anticipation. Her legs dissolved into water and her stomach was somersaulting wildly. Nothing had prepared her for this torrent of emotion, this overwhelming wave of passion that was opening her defences.

Without warning the library window was flooded with light. A branch of candles was being held aloft and they heard the sound of footsteps coming towards the open door. They stood still and silent in the outside darkness, catching their breath, trying to slow the beat of their hearts.

'It is Alfred,' Justin whispered in her ear. Then, at the sight of her bewildered face, 'The footman. His evening duty is to close the curtains and lock the doors.'

'Then we should…' she began, finding it difficult to speak.

'We should.'

'And we should not have…'

'No,' he agreed, 'we should not have.'

But she knew that neither of them was sorry, only sorry that they had not finished what they had begun.

'How good an actress are you?' he asked.

'I don't know, but shall we put it to the test?' And with her hand on his arm, they walked back into the library, faces schooled into blandness. Alfred looked up at their entrance, surprised to see them.

'I am sorry, Sir Justin, I had not realised you were on the terrace.'

'We have been taking the air,' Justin said casually. 'Miss Ingram found the heat of the library a little oppressive.'

They walked in dignified silence past an impassive Alfred, but once in the hall could not stop giggles from bubbling to the surface, as though they were naughty schoolchildren who had been lucky to escape punishment.

Once at the front entrance, though, Lizzie grew serious again. 'Promise me that you will see Rosanna as soon as you can.'

He took her hands in his and gave them a squeeze. 'You can depend on me, Lizzie. I will not let you down—and this time I'll not be deceived either. On the contrary, I have every intention of being the deceiver if I must.'

She frowned. 'I'm not sure I like the sound of that. What is it you intend to do?'

'That I can't tell you. Consider it a military secret! But don't worry yourself. I am an excellent strategist and will do only what I have to, and then only if I am certain it will work.'

'Are you sure you need no aid?' She pressed his hands more firmly. 'I might be very helpful to you.'

He laughed and his eyes, now misty grey in the candlelight, were happier than she had ever seen them. 'You *are* helpful to me, more helpful than you can ever imagine. But this might be dangerous work and I would prefer you to be a million miles away.'

'But...'

'Sometimes, Lizzie, it is the duty of soldiers simply to stand and wait.'

And with that, she had to be content.

## *Chapter Eight*

~~~

Before she tumbled into bed that night, Lizzie took her sketch pad and pencils to the window seat and drew. It was another portrait of Justin, as handsome as ever, but now the eyes were lit with tenderness, the expression was warm and loving. After she had finished she sat looking at the face, touching it softly from time to time, even kissing the full lips she had sketched. She was euphoric, filled with a nameless delight. It wasn't just that Justin had believed her story. Nor that he had trusted her sufficiently to promise he would finish the job she had started. It was much, much more. That evening on the terrace she had lain in his embrace and felt his lips on hers, felt the heat of his mouth warming her skin, caressing a path to her very breasts. She had melted against him, trembled with every touch and taste of him—and had known herself desired. For he, too, had been overwhelmed in that magical, moonlit world, drowning in a passion he could not suppress.

Eventually she climbed between the sheets, certain that she was too happy ever to close her eyes. True to her prophecy, she slept only lightly, waking just after dawn when the first streaks of grey light crept through her curtains. It was barely six o'clock, yet she could sleep no more and she felt inexplicably downpin. She tried to make sense of her megrims and at length decided that it could not have been happiness that kept her from deep sleep, but the first stirrings of unease now tempering her joy. She slid from the bed and padded towards the washbasin, the euphoria of last night's lovemaking dwindling as she walked. Why such a reversal? She had succumbed too eagerly to his caresses, that was the problem. She had been without shame, allowing herself to be kissed in a way that no modest woman should. Her face burned at the thought of the licence she had allowed him. For all his quiet courtesy, Justin Delacourt was a soldier and she should never forget that. Soldiers were wanderers, opportunistic by nature, and even the most discerning of their company would take what was on offer. And she had offered herself—openly. She had always suspected that if he kissed her, she would not be able to resist. And she had been right. Had she not slid into his arms, matched him kiss for kiss, wrapped herself around his body and felt her breasts harden to his lips? She had wanted him in a way she had never before known. And it was not simple desire that plagued her, but a desperate aching for him, for his voice, his smile, his laughter. She hardly dared put a name to it, but it felt very like love.

But it must not be; she could not allow herself to love him. Her emotions might skitter this way and that, but her mind was clear: in a precarious world, she must seek a man who was secure and dependable, a man who would cleave to her and her alone, a stolid helpmeet for the years to come. Yet her mind and her heart were fearsomely at odds. Vaguely she had imagined a day in the years to come when she would resign herself to a convenient marriage, but after last night, how could she ever wed in that way? The image of Piers Silchester had been slowly fading and was now vanquished entirely. If Alfred had not chosen to light the lamps at that very moment…

Disgrace would have followed swiftly, that was certain. She would have been without a home, without a job—without any home, in fact, for Miss Bates would never allow her to return to the Seminary under such circumstances, not after the mistakes she had already made. To allow Justin Delacourt a permanent place in her heart would be the worst of all mistakes. He was an honourable man, she knew, but he would expect her to recognise boundaries and if she chose to flout them, then on her own head be it. He would walk the dangerous path with her, she was sure, and revel in their mutual pleasure, but his life would continue as it always had, his future unhampered by a woman, for his allegiance was first and foremost to the army and to his regiment. So how was she to save herself from certain disgrace, from certain pain? She had only one weapon—to keep her distance or, at the very least, to ensure that she never again met him alone. She could no longer trust herself with him, not even for a minute.

Careful not to wake the household, she washed and dressed and crept downstairs.

She would walk, she decided, walk and hope to shake off the thoughts that plagued her. She tripped down the gravel drive, fearing the crunch of her footsteps might wake her employer, for Mrs Croft's bedroom was at the front of the house and she was a light sleeper. But the road was reached without mishap and she followed it for some way towards Rye. When after some half a mile, it began to wind its way inland towards the town, she branched off to the left, taking the much narrower coastal path which snaked along the clifftop. Far below her the river lay shrunk to a thin, silver thread.

She walked with purpose, pushing her disquiet to the back of her mind. Justin had been adamant that she should not involve herself further in the mystery and she would do as he asked, but she was curious about the excise man who had met his death in this apparently peaceful landscape. The magistrate believed it an accident, the rest of the town did not. Who was right? she wondered.

When she came upon the spot it was clear that there had been a disturbance, even though many months had elapsed. Bushes had been uprooted and lay sad and withered to one side, a rough patch of earth showed scuffing and stones were piled into an untidy heap as though feet had gouged them from the ground. It might still have been an accident, she thought. The man might have lost his footing—it had been raining that day, someone had said, and the ground underfoot would have been slippery. He could have lost his footing and grabbed at any bush he could get his hand to, trying to get a purchase. If he had, it had been to no avail. He had toppled over the cliff, leaving a trail of destruction behind him.

Cautiously she peered over the edge. It seemed a very long way down to the shingle beach. No wonder the man had broken his neck. But then she looked again—there seemed to be a ledge about ten feet below her. Very carefully, she leaned out further and, yes, there was a ledge which ran immediately below and continued around the next spur of the cliff. The man would have slipped over the edge rather than fallen, she thought, since his grabbing of the bushes would have slowed him. He would have tumbled to the ledge and no further. A broken bone or two perhaps, but from there he could easily have been rescued by a rope. But he hadn't been; he had crashed to the bottom. Yet surely to avoid the ledge, a body would have to be travelling at speed—it would have to be thrown outwards! Her heart began to pound and blood to thrum noisily in her ears. The excise man's death could not have been an accident!

Even as she stood quaking from her discovery, a murmur of voices drifted towards her on the air. The noise was coming from below and, taking a deep breath, she plucked up courage to peer over the cliff edge once more. Two men had appeared on the ledge, talking together several feet beneath her. She could catch no words but the conversation was short and sharp. One of them was a rough-looking individual, hair greasily matted, and dressed in patched breeches and a stained leather jerkin. And the other...the other was surely Justin Delacourt. She ducked down behind a small bush, hoping that she was completely hidden, her mind a frenzy of speculation. What on earth was Justin doing on the coastal path at this hour and in such dubious company? It could not be simple exercise that brought him here—he could have walked undisturbed for miles at Chelwood— so why come, and why speak so intently to the unknown man? She was sure their meeting was no casual encounter.

As she watched, the rough man turned to walk away while Justin began to follow the ledge back, climbing gradually upwards until he regained the greensward and was standing only a few feet from her. She held her breath, waiting for discovery. But in a moment he had struck out along the path towards the Rye road, evidently on his way back to Chelwood. No horse, she thought, no carriage and not a servant in sight. He had come to the meeting completely alone. She wondered if he realised the kind of men he was dealing with, the kind of men who could hurl another human being over the cliff to certain death. He would have to be a fool not to realise, and Justin Delacourt was no fool. So what was behind this encounter?

A dreadful thought lodged in her mind. Was it possible that he had become entangled in the same mesh as Gil, that he was not as impervious to Rosanna as he claimed? It was a crazy idea, yet…he was a soldier and nothing about him was certain, no matter how upright and honourable he appeared. For what did she really know of him beyond his title and his house? Only what her heart told her and her heart had proved spectacularly unreliable in the past. Hadn't it sent her on a fruitless search for her father and put her in danger along the way?

She hurried back to Brede House, trying hard to forget what she had witnessed. Whatever the truth of the meeting, it had nothing to do with her. She must leave Justin to solve the riddle of his friend's disappearance and dismiss him from her mind altogether. In the grey light of an October morning, last night's tryst had begun to seem the most foolish impulse to which she had ever succumbed. It was painful to acknowledge, but their lovemaking was something best forgotten, and he must feel the same. Doubtless he had forgotten already.

In that she was wrong. In the days that followed the party, Justin had ample time to relive the events of that evening. And he did constantly. While he walked his estate with the bailiff, discussing the pastures they might fence, the crops they would sow, the improvements they could afford, he thought of little else. He had lost control of himself that night and he dared not contemplate the likely consequences. He had almost seduced Lizzie

Ingram! If Alfred had not appeared from no-where, he would have made love to her right there and then. Exquisite love, he thought, but utterly wrong. He had been insane to allow things to get so out of hand between them and now he was faced with extricating him-self and her from the abyss into which they had fallen. Since that night, he had managed to avoid a meeting, but that would not an-swer for ever, and then what? She was young and heedless, impulsively throwing herself into life and love. But he was not and he be-rated himself for his folly. Despite her entic-ing loveliness, he should have been strong enough to remain aloof. Instead he had been unable to resist and the control of a lifetime had foundered. That must never happen again—there was no future in such a liai-son, no future for either of them. In a short while, he would be leaving Rye, leaving En-gland, and he did not know when or even if he would return. But that was not the crux of the problem, was it? Even if he emerged from this endless conflict unscathed, he was inca-pable of loving a woman in the way Lizzie should be loved. Any feeling he could offer would be a misshapen, half-formed thing—

you could hardly call it love—and she deserved a great deal better.

It was only the arrival of a letter mid-week that for a few hours cast Lizzie from his mind. He read the missive, read it again in mounting anger and then stuffed the sheet of cream vellum behind the stack of books which littered his study floor. He would not think of it or its contents. He would walk out to his furthermost field and check the progress of the men who had been hired that week to hedge and ditch. In that way he could keep his mind a deliberate blank.

He had passed the bailiff's office and was following the path which wound along the boundary of the estate, when he almost cannoned into Lizzie travelling in the opposite direction. They both stopped in their tracks, for she was as taken aback as he. His eyebrows rose in silent query and just as mutely she held out the basket she carried, as an explanation.

'It's a pie,' she said, when he had taken hold of the handle. 'Mrs Croft was insistent I bring it. It contains pheasant—your cook apparently has a great liking for Hester's pheasant pie.'

The words were delivered dully as though she were finding it troublesome to speak and he thought he knew why. She was regretting their indiscretion as much as he and he must make this encounter as brief as possible for both their sakes.

His greeting was courteous, but formal. 'It is very good of you to walk so far, Miss Ingram. The pie is a most kind thought of Mrs Croft.'

'It was Mrs Croft's express wish that I make the delivery.' She was making it clear, he thought, that she was not here willingly.

He tried to keep his eyes averted, but could not fail to see that in her green-velvet spencer she looked as lovely as ever. She had tied an emerald-green ribbon through her chestnut curls and he could not take his eyes from their bright sheen.

Fighting to bring his wandering mind back into order, he asked, 'Would you wish me to take it to the kitchen or perhaps you would prefer to present it yourself to Cook?'

'It would help me if you could deliver the gift yourself. I have much to do at Brede House. Mrs Croft has been unwell and needs my constant attention.'

Before he could ask after the health of his father's old friend, Lizzie had turned and begun to retrace her steps. He watched her retreating figure in silence, but then, quite suddenly, she stopped and twisted around to face him.

'Who was that man you were talking to by the river?'

For the moment, he was bewildered, then enlightenment dawned. 'What man was that?'

If he had thought to distract her, she was not to be put off. 'It was a few days ago, in the early morning. You were on a cliff ledge and talking together.'

'Yes, I remember,' he was forced to admit, 'but where were you? I did not see you.'

'I was walking,' she said vaguely. 'Who was he?'

He would need to be evasive, Justin decided. 'No one you would know, Miss Ingram, but someone perhaps who can help me. If you remember, I made a promise that I would get to the bottom of the mystery.'

His voice had grown strained at the mention of the pledge made to her that night, but she was not to be deflected.

'You will not tell me, then, who he is or why you were meeting him,' she said flatly.

'It is far better that you know nothing, Lizzie.' He could not maintain the formality, for she would always be Lizzie to him.

She was staring into the distance with her lips pursed and he could see that she wanted to kick against his refusal to say more. She felt cheated, he supposed, that in some way she'd had her adventure taken from her.

'It really is better this way.' Despite his vow to stay aloof, he could not stop himself smiling and she could not help but return the smile, her crossness disappearing beneath the warmth of his expression.

'I did wonder...' she said uncertainly.

'You must not worry. The man you saw is a means to an end, that is all. Things will turn out well, you will see.'

She gave a small nod and was making ready to walk on when he blurted out, 'Will you allow me to escort you to Brede House?'

What was wrong with him? The words had come instinctively, but what was he doing? He should let her go quietly and be grateful their conversation had been unexceptional, but here he was inviting himself to walk with her.

'You have to deliver the basket,' she pointed out.

'Yes.' He flushed. 'Of course, I had forgot.'

'You could leave it by the hedge. No harm will come to it until you return.'

\* \* \*

What was wrong with her? What was she doing accepting his escort? He had not properly explained his meeting with the villainous man, yet she was immediately willing to trust his assurance. It was her heart doing the talking—yet again—and it was telling her that he was too beautiful a man ever to do wrong. Or for that matter to care seriously for her. Hadn't she decided that she must never be alone with him? Yet here she was walking by his side. It was because she had met him so unexpectedly, she tried to reassure herself. He had startled her, appearing out of nowhere, filling the image she'd held in her mind since they last met. And filling it wonderfully.

They started along the path together, walking in silence, painfully aware of each other. He did not attempt to take her arm, but she could feel his warmth, his step matching hers, his body so close. He wore what she imagined were working clothes, though he looked smart enough for a parade. His face above the crisp white shirt was tanned and lean, his hair a bright sun in the overcast day. She wanted to reach out and touch: hold his hand, clasp his arm, ruffle his hair, smooth his cheek, feel his lips. This was madness, she told herself. One step along that road and she knew she would succumb to him completely and what would be the result? She would be a lost woman, that was what. She must stop thinking, stop imagining what might be, and start talking. Anything to break the tense silence that had grown alongside their bodies' longing.

'How is your work at Chelwood progressing?' she asked, her voice uncomfortably thin.

'Well, I thank you.' His own was studiously neutral. 'The horrible Mellors is proving worthy of his salary and taking much off my shoulders.'

'Is he still waging his crusade against poachers?' she could not resist asking.

Justin smiled slightly. 'Since that misfortune, he has acted more prudently and in time I am sure he will make a bailiff of which Chelwood is proud.'

She cast a sideways glance and was quick enough to see his smile fade and a frown take its place.

'You still seem worried.' It was a mistake, she knew, but she had ventured into the personal.

'Not about Chelwood—there is a great deal of hard work ahead, but Mellors and I are both clear what we must do to bring the estate back into profit.' There was a pause before he added abruptly, 'I have had a letter from my mother.'

She glanced across at him again and saw him shrug his shoulders, as though by doing so he could shrug away the parent he so disliked.

'You have unwelcome news?' She ought not to concern herself, but it seemed impossible to stand aside.

'Her husband—the duke I told you of, the one who drips money—has left her. He appears to have found solace in Italy. I cannot say that I am surprised. It was only ever going to be a matter of time before the marriage failed.'

'I am sorry to hear such news.'

'So am I,' he said grimly. 'Particularly as her letter hints that she may wish to return to Chelwood.'

Lizzie let out a little gasp. No wonder he was so perturbed. He must have hoped his mother's marriage had relieved him of all responsibility for her. But from what Justin had said, Lady Delacourt and Chelwood would seem a poor match. 'I imagine that your mother would prefer to stay in her London home.'

'You would think so, but there is a possibility that the less-than-honourable duke will sell it beneath her feet and so render her homeless. There is also the little matter of embarrassment. Having boasted to her cronies of the opulent life she was leading, it will come hard to confess that she has been abandoned, an ageing woman, and without a penny to her name.'

When he spoke so bitterly he seemed another person, Lizzie thought. It was clear that whatever he had suffered at his parent's hands, he had neither forgotten nor forgiven. They walked on and the sound of their footsteps echoed in the silent air. Eventually she plucked up courage to ask, 'Will you allow Lady Delacourt to return to Chelwood?'

'I have little choice in the matter. Whatever else she may be, she is my mother and if she has nowhere else to go... She will have grown frailer with the years and age must command some respect, I have always believed. But it sticks in my craw to have her here.'

'Perhaps it will not prove as difficult as you fear.'

'You are ever the optimist, Lizzie. I wish you were right.'

'Surely the power she once wielded is gone.

Your father is dead and can no longer be hurt by her.'

'No, thank God. She can hurt neither of us any more. I suppose I must write to her and tell her that if she is in distress, she may come, but she is to come alone. No entourage.' The two words chopped menacingly at the cold air.

'What kind of entourage does she have?' Lizzie asked wonderingly. It was a glimpse into another world.

'The horde of banshees she runs with. They will not be welcome at Chelwood—ever.'

'Are they so bad?'

'They are. You have no conception.'

'But once you return to your regiment, your mother would be quite alone at Chelwood. She will be in need of a friend, I think.'

'If she comes here, she comes alone or not at all,' he said inexorably. And then, when his intransigence drew a questioning look from her, he burst out, 'I am a grown man and there is not a harpy alive who can discomfort me. But I have not forgotten what it was like to be eighteen and at the mercy of such a one.'

'Then let us hope, for both your sakes, the duke is generous,' was all she could say.

They were nearing their destination and

covered the short distance that remained in silence. His words had brought home in stark fashion how strongly the past was still with him, how fiercely he would fight anything that threatened to make him vulnerable. She had suspected that he would never give himself wholeheartedly to love and here was the proof: his fear of humiliation was too great. No wonder his transient life as a soldier suited him so well.

The gates of Brede House were visible and its avenue of trees beckoning. At this hour the sky above them seemed enormous, its huge expanse flushed by warm light, apricot mixed with a cold, bright blue. In the distance she glimpsed the river lying calm, not a breath of wind touching its surface as it meandered its way to the sea, unravelling like a broad twist of beaten metal. The main gates remained locked for no carriages had come or gone from Brede House that day, but a small wicket stood to one side and it was this that Justin opened. The space was narrow and she could not help brushing against him as she passed. A spark, electric in its intensity, surged through her. Then the familiar weakness, her limbs losing their strength and her stomach dissolving into water.

The gate remained open behind them for he had not turned to close it. She felt his hand sweep her ringlets to one side and his lips on the nape of her neck scattering soft, small kisses. Now his mouth was nibbling at her ear, pulling and tugging gently at her lobe, until she could not stop herself uttering a small cry of pleasure. His arms enfolded her, wrapping themselves around her waist and pulling her urgently into him. She felt the hardness of his body through the muslin of her dress, felt the longing it contained. His hands moved upwards to cradle her breasts, caressing them slowly, rhythmically. His fingers brushed against her nipples, circled and returned, his touch intensifying all the time. Somewhere deep inside she was pierced by an indescribable ache. When it seemed that she could bear no more, he spun her around and his mouth clamped fast to hers.

'Lizzie,' he groaned.

Her lips parted in readiness. She wanted him, she wanted him. But she must not allow herself the surrender she longed for.

Wrenching herself away, she said in a voice she hardly recognised, 'We are in clear sight of the upstairs windows', and she gestured towards the house. 'Hester or Mrs Croft might look out at any moment.'

His arms dropped to his side and his shoulders slumped. 'Forgive me, Lizzie. I had no right... It is just that...' His voice tailed away.

They stood gazing at each other, rumpled, breathless, unable to avert their eyes, still balancing on the tightrope of desire.

Then he drew himself upright and said decisively, 'You are right, of course. It was the most foolhardy thing to have done. For my part, dishonourable, too. You must know that I delight in your company, but I have allowed my feelings too much licence. I hope you will forgive me.'

She could not find her voice; all she could do was to bow her head in acknowledgement. At the top of the driveway, they murmured a brief farewell before he turned to go. She heard the crunch of his footsteps on gravel, a creak of the wicket and then silence.

She hurried to her room, hoping she could snatch a few minutes before Mrs Croft rang the bell. Since her illness, the old lady could be tetchy and at this moment Lizzie felt unequal to dealing with her demands. She was still trembling with the shock of desire—the force of her passion *had* been shocking. After their lovemaking on the terrace at Chelwood, she should have been prepared, but if anything her need for him today had been even greater. Did that mean that every time they met, desire would get stronger? If so, the ending was inevitable. She knew that she could not fight such overpowering feelings for much longer and it scared her greatly.

And what of Justin? He was as weak as she, it seemed. He could not keep his hands from her body or his lips from her mouth. But just now he had said something that caught at her very soul. He had confessed that he delighted in her company, had suggested that his feelings for her ran deeper than simple physical desire. Was it possible that even a soldier could fall in love, genuinely in love? She could hardly believe so, but at the thought her anxious expression fled and in its stead a bright glow suffused her face. Then her mind raced on and her pleasure came to a sickening halt. If he *were* falling in love, and she could not really believe that it was so, his love would not endure. It could not endure.

Justin had upbraided himself for his lack of honour, but what would he say if he knew

the things she had done? She had behaved so
very badly. True, she had been a mere girl at
the time—but that made it worse. At an age
when she should have known only innocence
she had schemed in the most shocking way,
manipulated a man for her own ends, and only
by accident had ended the loser in that encounter. She could never tell Justin her story.
It must remain a secret for ever. If he knew
the depths to which she had sunk, his love for
her, his desire even, would wither instantly.
He would not wish to know her.

Lizzie had forgotten that Mrs Croft had
nominated this day for the autumn cleaning
of the conservatory that clung to the south
side of the house, but as soon as Hester re-
ported her returned, the work began. Plants
were brought indoors, wicker tables and
chairs covered and exiled to the folly, the
light voile curtains taken down and washed
and in their place heavier brocade curtains
were hung. The day was filled with activity
and by tea time both Hester and Lizzie were
extremely tired, since the old lady's instruc-
tions were as numerous as they were conflict-
ing. With some effort Lizzie had managed to
keep her mind on the tasks in hand and only

occasionally allow her thoughts to stray into dangerous territory. So it was with considerable surprise that she found one of the footmen from Chelwood Hall at the door around seven o'clock that evening. Her heart jumped as she saw his outline in the doorway, behind him the sun already setting and turning the sky to a pink marshmallow. It was a splendid evening, an evening for lovers, Lizzie thought, and she dreamed forlornly of spending it with Justin. But it was his footman who was standing before her, a posy of autumn flowers in one hand and a stiff white envelope in the other.

Hester was fidgeting behind her, shifting from foot to foot, impatient to know what or who had called. Lizzie made haste to thank the man and shut the door. Without a word, she took the posy upstairs, leaving Hester in the hall, her eyes wide with astonishment.

The envelope contained only one sheet of paper and the message inside was brief.

*Will you come to Chelwood tomorrow? I want to show you all the improvements I am making. No need to trespass this time!* It was signed simply J.

These past few days she had imagined Justin to be every kind of man: a thrilling lover who conquered her with his passion, a dashing soldier taking pleasure where he found it and, just hours ago, a blighted man too hurt ever to care deeply for any woman. And now? Now it seemed that he did care, cared enough to want her close. The thought made tears prick at her eyes. What she would give to visit Chelwood as his special guest, to eat at his table, to walk and talk with him, to share his innermost thoughts. But she could do none of these things. If he knew her secret… if she told him the whole story, he might not blame her for what had happened, but he would not condone her conduct. He was a man of principle and her story would turn a sincere lover into a disapproving acquaintance. She could not bear to see the distaste on his face, the same distaste that he reserved for his mother and her friends. No, she could not suffer that. She would keep his posy as a memory of what might have been, but though it broke her heart, she would not reply to the invitation.

For most of that day Justin had been in a state of chronic indecision, his thoughts wavering this way and that. Outside Brede House, he had once again found himself at the mercy of feelings so powerful that he had no idea how to command them. From the moment of their first meeting, this lovely, lively girl had intrigued him. He had known her immediately for a free spirit. He recognised now that she had been far more than that. She had been his own spirit, his own soul, though he had tried to shrug off such feelings as fanciful nonsense. Instead he had told himself that she was simply a young woman living in the neighbourhood, a girl who would become a stranger once he'd returned to the fighting and to Spain. And that was all to the good. Despite her manifold charms, Elizabeth Ingram was a woman like any other, and that in itself was a strong reason to pass her by with no more than a casual greeting. Yet he had found himself hoping to meet her whenever business took him to Rye, found himself enjoying their conversation and now, latterly, enjoying a great deal more. It was as though the emotions he had so carefully stored away had broken through an invisible barrier and were now impossible to recapture.

Only a few days ago on this very terrace, they had teetered on the edge of mutual seduction. He had known her to be as willing as he and after that disturbing encounter, he had told himself that it must never happen again. He must avoid her and concentrate entirely on Chelwood. In under a month, he would return to his regiment and he could not afford to be wasting his energy. In that way he had dismissed or tried to dismiss the devastating passion she aroused in him.

It had taken only a few minutes today, he reflected wryly, for such indifference to ring utterly false. Once more he had been unable to resist her and the realisation had come to him that he did not want to. He wanted to give himself to her body and soul. Extraordinary feelings had washed over him, ones he could never have imagined, and the years of bitterness had simply fallen away. Lizzie was *not* like any of the women he had known. She was fresh and young and innocent. She was passionate and loving and he wanted her. For the first time he questioned whether he had been misguided in devoting himself to a life of privation and hardship; whether the camaraderie of the regiment could ever be sufficient to make up for the love he had hitherto dismissed.

It was as though the premise on which he had built his adult life was under threat and he did not know how to respond. All that was

clear to him was that he needed to see her
again, needed her here at Chelwood. Their
parting had been abrupt, both of them over-
come by the sheer strength of their feelings.
Spiralling emotion had overturned long-held
beliefs for both of them, but they would find
a way through, he was certain, a way perhaps to happiness. The decision was made.
He rang the bell and summoned his gardener
to the library. Latimer was to pick the choic-
est blooms from the estate's one succession
house and he would sit at his desk and pen the
invitation. But that proved more difficult than
he could have imagined and after four spoiled
attempts, he was forced to settle for the brief-
est note he had ever written. He hoped that
Lizzie would understand its message.

When Alfred returned from Brede House
without a response, he felt a thud of disappointment and imagined that for some reason she had been prevented from answering
that evening and would send a note on the
morrow. But she did not. Nor did she on the
next day or the next. He felt betrayed and he
felt foolish. Her kisses had meant nothing, it
seemed, bestowed without thought, for the
pleasure of the moment. She had responded

to his lovemaking, but it was his body, not his heart, that she wanted. She was no different, after all, from any other woman. For once he had chosen to ignore the lesson life had taught him and he was well served. He had allowed himself to contemplate love, dared to imagine a future lived together. What an idiot he had been! To think that he might have followed in his father's footsteps! That poor man's fate should serve as the greatest of warnings. Justin's mouth set in a forbidding line. If nothing else, he owed it to Lucien Delacourt to save himself, and he would.

## Chapter Nine

Lizzie had not thought it possible to stay so unhappy. But as each morning dawned her misery, if anything, increased. She longed to see Justin, but she knew that she must not. She had not replied to his invitation and now four days later he would have given up on her, she was sure. No doubt he felt aggrieved, even angry, and was certain never to renew his welcome to Chelwood. Keeping her distance had to be the right course, but why then did every day seem longer than the one before? For a while Mrs Croft required constant attention, but once her employer began to recover, Lizzie found it impossible to fill every minute of the day. She tried and failed to find solace in her drawing, she read every newspaper in

the house to Mrs Croft and then pestered her
for extra errands she might run, until the poor
lady pleaded to be allowed to sit quietly without interruption. She attempted to help Hester in her chores, but the maid told her firmly
that Lizzie was hired as a companion, not a
maidservant, and though she appreciated the
offer, the girl was simply getting in her way.
Cook was moved to suggest politely that the
kitchen was best left to her, after Lizzie had
burnt two loaves of bread and undercooked a
particularly succulent joint of beef being prepared for Mrs Croft's supper.

She felt wretched and restless and could
attend to nothing for more than a few minutes, dashing from one chore to another without pause. Even walking gave her no cheer.
Whenever she ventured out, she was careful to stay this side of the marsh and well
away from Chelwood, but with every step
she remembered Justin: his smile, his beautiful voice, his strong hands wrapping hers
in their warm clasp. Nights were even worse;
she would toss and turn endlessly until finally
she drifted into sleep, only to wake within the
hour. After four dreadful days, she looked at
her reflection in the mirror, pale and hollow
eyed, and knew that she must rescue herself.

She would drink some gooseberry wine, she decided, a potent brew kept under lock and key in the kitchen, and then read and read until she could no longer see the words on the page. Then she would be certain to fall into a deep and dreamless sleep.

That, at least, had been the plan. But either the wine was not as strong as she'd hoped or her reading was too absorbing, for it was many hours before her eyes closed and the book slid slowly to the floor. Two o'clock was striking in the hall below when a small sound roused her from the light sleep she had fallen into. She turned fitfully in the bed. Her covers were crumpled into a heap and the book she had been reading was somewhere wrapped in her pillow. She lit the candle to put herself to rights and then she heard the noise. That was what had woken her. It was the slightest murmur of voices, the smallest sound of crunching on stone.

She extinguished the candle and went to the window. A fingernail of moon floated amid the inky blackness, its muted light revealing only the hazy contours of the garden. For a moment she watched the shifting silhouettes of trees and bushes and through them, straight as any arrow, the path leading

to the cove. Had the noise she'd heard come
from the garden? She remembered the fate of
Mrs Croft's unfortunate granddaughter and
quailed, then scolded herself for cowardly
thoughts—*her* heart was not weak. What kind
of soldier would she make if she jumped and
ran at every small sound? She would investigate. Pulling a thick cloak and boots from the
wardrobe, she sped silently down the stairs
and out of the back door. She was on the
path now, the cloak wrapped tightly around
her nightdress, and noiselessly passing the
stone bulk of the folly. With each step she
stole closer to the beach and with each step
the murmurs grew louder. It was the still-
est night at Brede House that she had so far
known. That was why the noise had carried,
she thought, and she must take the greatest
care not to alert whoever was in the cove.

The gate creaked under her hand and she
held her breath, but the sounds below continued. She crept forwards to the head of the
wooden stairway and peered into the dark.
The river flowed softly, hardly a ripple maim-
ing its surface and the slither of moon played
along the beach. Gradually her eyes adjusted
to the gloom and she began to make out figures. Men? Were they men? If so, they were

the strangest creatures. Walking beehives was
the only way she could describe them. There
were some eight or ten of them dressed in
long black top boots, dark tunics and torn
leather jerkins, but it was what topped this
ensemble that sent a shudder up her spine: a
hive of coiled rope with three small windows
cut out of the front, two for eyes and one for
a mouth. It was a disguise that would ensure
the men were safe from recognition, but was
designed, too, to frighten away anyone un-
lucky enough to meet them.

She swallowed hard and tried to look beyond to a small boat standing offshore. The
faint strand of moonlight allowed her to make
out its shape, though the vessel itself showed
no lights. The voices she'd heard had fallen
silent—an occasional muttered oath, the
sound of water washing around the men's legs
was all that reached her. Several of them were
wading between ship and shore with what
appeared to be barrels strapped to their front
and back. Once they reached the beach, they
dropped their cargo and returned to the boat
for more. A second group hefted the barrels
one by one on their shoulders and crunched
their way across the shingle to the foot of
a path which climbed steeply upwards. She

stood on tiptoe, but could see no more than its very beginning, for a tall hedge ran down the west side of the garden. Then through the clear air, the rattle of a harness—there were horses on the cliff above! The illicit cargo was about to make its final journey. Her heart contracted painfully. This gang of smugglers—for they could be no other—was responsible for Gil Armitage's disappearance, she was certain, but where were they taking their haul and might it lead eventually to Gilbert himself?

If only Justin were here…but he wasn't and she must do what she could. She must follow them, see where they were taking their cargo and, if possible, discover where Gil was being kept. If she succeeded, she would make sure that Justin learned their direction. The last barrel was being carried up the pathway; she heard the sound of a whip and the slow creaking of carts. Cautiously she made her way down the staircase to the beach. The boat had disappeared and with clouds now obscuring the moon, it was hardly visible as it made its way downstream to the open sea. There was nobody left in the cove and she raced across the beach to the path which would take her to the clifftop. She dared not let them get too far ahead.

But once on the cliff, she came to a dead halt. The men appeared to have vanished and in their place a terrifying luminescence hovered in the air. The tales she'd heard from Hester returned with paralysing effect. The maid had tried to convince her that the marsh was haunted and that travellers who lost their way and disappeared had been taken by the marsh witches. Lizzie had laughed scornfully, but at this very moment she did not feel at all like laughing. Instead she stood stock still, quite unable to move. Had the witches decided to come to town this night? Then her wits returned and she realised that the shimmering cloud was moving forwards in a deliberate fashion, accompanied by the rattle of harness and the sharp, quick step of hooves. Silvery shapes showed faintly against the horizon—the ghosts, it seemed, were pack ponies! The animals must have been painted with a strange, phosphorescent mixture in order to terrify all that saw them. Newly brave, she squared her shoulders and began to follow.

Always careful to keep a distance, she walked swiftly in the wake of the convoy.

For a moment the moon floated free again and she could see in its frail light that she was following two—no, three carts, each one piled high with barrel upon barrel. By their side walked the black clothed figures, one or two holding the dimmest of lamps. For some half a mile they trudged along the coastal path, then abruptly swung to the right and began to move along a smaller track—one she had not known was there—winding their way around the base of the town until they reached a wooden bridge which forded the river at its narrowest point. Over the bridge, a bleak flatness loomed out of the dark. They were headed for the marshes!

It was desolate country, the bushes, when they grew at all, bent and crippled by the scouring of Channel storms. It had been windless in the cove, but now the first chilly gust was cold enough to penetrate her woollen cloak. She hardly felt it, though, for her heart was beating so fast that the blood ran warm in her veins. Here and there a thick mist, feet high, hung like the web of a thousand spiders over the dykes which zigzagged across the marsh. The moon had once more disappeared behind banking clouds and she could see little beyond the surrounding darkness.

From time to time she was startled by the huge dyke sluices which reared unexpectedly out of the night, rising it seemed out of nowhere. She must keep to the path at all costs for where there were sluices there was water as black as pitch.

The carts were picking up speed now and she had almost to run to keep up. Every so often she lost sight of the dim shapes ahead, but soon she would hear the trundling of a vehicle on the stony path and see a pinprick of light from one of the small lanterns the men carried. Then the convoy disappeared completely. It happened in an instant; she looked to her right and then to her left, but could see nothing. She strained to catch the clink of harness, but could hear nothing. It was as though the men and their horses had been swallowed by the night's blackness. The clouds above had darkened further and she could no longer even see her feet. Cautiously she took a step forwards and found the path. With relief she began to walk again, hoping she might soon discover the convoy. They could well have made a sharp turn from the track, she thought, in order to head to their final destination. The idea sent her blood thrumming. Perhaps she was near to finding Gilbert for they must be miles into the marsh by now and this lonely, isolated place would hide a captive admirably. A surge of energy and she began to quicken her pace.

But in one instant she lost the path. Somehow she had veered into mud that squelched and sucked around her feet. Hastily she tried to regain firmer ground, but once more mistook her footing and found herself cold and wet, her nightdress a forlorn, floating shroud and her cloak a sodden blanket dragging her downwards. She had fallen into a dyke and was plunged knee deep in water! She took a deep breath. She could get out of this, she must get out of it. Overhead the flap of a prowling bat breaking through the mists caused her to jump and she felt herself sink further into the quagmire. Fear screamed through her, but she told herself that she must keep calm, keep still until the moon swam free of cloud again and she could see her way back to the bank. If only the moon would shine! Nothing but blackness surrounded her, no sound save the tickling bubbles that rose from the mud bed to burst amid the bullrushes. Despite her best efforts at keeping still, she knew that she was sinking further into the mud. She tried again to reach out for the bank, but only succeeded in plunging deeper. Panic triumphed and she began threshing wildly in the water, crying out in terror, though there was no one to hear.

A hand grabbed her arm. She gasped. Could this be one of Hester's marsh witches? How very stupid, but on this night anything was possible. The hand was warm and firm and was pulling her to her feet. Hardly able to breathe, she regained the bank. Then she saw it—the horrifying beehive. Her rescuer was a smuggler! He must have been walking at the rear of the convoy and heard her struggles. But the gang was thoroughly ruthless, so why had this man saved her? Did smugglers have consciences? More like he had scented an opportunity to make money through kidnap or blackmail. She would be another victim like Gil Armitage! At the thought she almost threw herself back into the water. The gust had become a wind now, rising from the shore and scattering the mist towards the sea; through the lifting haze she saw him take off the dreadful headdress of coiled rope and when the fragment of moon sailed finally into clear skies, the two figures stood revealed, naked to each other's gaze.

* * *

'Lizzie, what on earth!' It was a familiar voice. 'What on earth are you doing here?'

She struggled into speech. 'But you, you're a smuggler!'

'A very bad one, as you see.' The joke made no impression, for her worst suspicions had come true. Justin Delacourt had joined this terrifying gang of men!

He seemed unperturbed at being discovered. 'Here—walk with me a little further along the track. It is safer where the path keeps well above the marsh. We must talk quietly for they are not far away.'

'They? Then you really are a member of Chapman's gang?' She was desperate to have judged him wrongly.

'A very temporary member. I promised you I would speak to Rosanna again, but when I considered the situation, I felt it unlikely she would be willing to tell me more. This seemed a better way—to gain the gang's confidence and hopefully discover what has happened to Gil.'

'But becoming a smuggler...' She was struggling to take in the enormity of what he had done.

'I could think of no other way of getting

their trust. Even so, they do not trust me. I am useful for the moment, no more.'

'How did it come about?' she asked in a dazed voice.

'I sauntered down to the Mermaid and let it be known through the rascally landlord that I was bored with life and a trifle resentful. I made out that I had been forced from the army and had a grudge against authority. I was finding it difficult to settle into civilian life and was desperate for some excitement. Sure enough when I returned the following night, one of them sounded me out. The gang was looking for a likely man, someone with my height and strength. I told my story again to one of the gang leaders and must have sounded believable enough for they took me on immediately.'

'So that was who you were meeting on the cliff!'

'That was who I was meeting—you can see why I could not tell you.'

'But it is so dangerous, Justin.'

'Not half as dangerous as a battlefield, believe me. I had to do it, Lizzie. It was our only chance of finding out what happened.'

She heard the 'our' and loved him for it. 'But do you not think they suspect your mo-

tives? They must know who you are, a man
of means, the owner of Chelwood.'

'They know, of course. But they also know
that I have been a soldier and they can imagine that I miss the thrust of battle. I have told
them that I left the army and Spain under du-
ress and was angry with my father for having
died so inconveniently—yes, I had to perjure
myself and I feel most badly.'

She thought for a moment. She imagined
that Justin could be highly plausible when
he chose, yet… 'Taking you into their confidence still appears a great risk on their part.'

The moon was shining more brightly now,
bleaching his halo of hair almost white and
catching the glint of a signet ring as his hand
harrowed a path through ruffled locks. He
smiled down at her, a rueful expression on his
face. 'To be truthful, I don't think they would
have taken the risk if they had not had this
cargo coming in so soon and been in great
need of another man. Two of their number
have been apprehended by the customs authorities down the coast at Chichester and
they have spoken of others leaving them in
a hurry.'

'Gilbert! Do you think they might mean
Gilbert?'

The grin had gone and he looked much older. 'I suspect that might be the case, but I cannot ask. All I have been able to do is join them this night and hope that they will lead me to their hiding place. I have heard them talk of a barn, one they have taken by force from some poor unfortunate who farms in the middle of the marshes, but I've been unable to learn its exact location. I believe them to be on their way there now and if they have kidnapped Gil, this must be the place they are keeping him.'

'It sounds as though you are still doubtful.'

'On the contrary, Lizzie, I think you are right and that Gil is a prisoner. Whether he was a member of their gang or not, he knows too much. They must prevent him from going to the authorities—at least until they have finished their work along this coast—and before they move on, they will no doubt demand a ransom for him. But for how long they intend to hold him or what his condition may be, I have no idea. All I know is that I must get to him.'

Her hands went to her face in despair. 'But you have lost their trail now. And it is my fault.'

'Should I have left you to drown?'

She shook her head sadly. 'I should never have followed them. I have ruined your plan.'

He put out a comforting hand and she took it. 'All is not lost. If I move swiftly, I should be able to catch them up. But I don't wish to leave you here alone—you are wet and cold and should find shelter immediately.'

He reached down for the small lamp he had been carrying and held it aloft. 'Dear God, is that a nightdress you are wearing beneath your cloak?!'

'There is no time to explain,' she said hastily. 'You must go and go now. I can perfectly well find my own way back.'

'No one's goin' anywhere, me laddies.' The voice had come from behind them and together they spun round to face this new threat. Their whispers must have carried across the marsh, Lizzie thought, and one of the smugglers had heard and come to find them.

The man cleared his throat and spat into the dyke. 'Whatever yer game, it ain't goin' no further. You be comin' with me', and very deliberately he pointed a large pistol at them. There was a loud click as the trigger engaged.

Justin's hand closed on hers and he nudged

her leg. She was alert to every hint from him, but was he really wanting them to flee and with a pistol pointing at their heads? The man began to move to their rear, keeping them covered on the march to join his companions, but as he drew level, Justin lunged forwards and caught him unawares. He dived at the smuggler's legs and upended him. The man hit the ground with a thud and before he could get to his feet, Justin had grabbed him by the jerkin and lifted him off the ground. The smuggler fell backwards with a loud splash—he had landed into the water from which Lizzie had so recently been rescued. As he fell, the pistol went off, the bullet travelling harmlessly above their heads and into the air.

'Quick, run!' Justin instructed. 'The shot will have alerted the others.'

They could hear the man wallowing in the water, his arms carving a passage to firmer ground. In no time he would be on them again. Justin threw the lamp into the dyke and once more they were plunged into darkness. Hand in hand they ran, he a little ahead, leading the way along the path she had just traversed. She followed him blindly into the night, hoping that he had more idea of the marshes than she.

* * *

They had run at least a mile when she was forced to stop, unable to continue. Her legs were reduced to jelly, a searing pain swept through her lungs and her breath was coming short and jagged.

'I can't... You...go on... He will not find me now.'

'You are quite mad, Lizzie Ingram. You cannot think for a minute that I would abandon you here.'

'But...'

He scooped her up in his arms as though she were no more than a child and walked swiftly onwards. They were soon at the bridge and making their way along the narrow path which edged the outskirts of the town, then swinging left again and back on to the coastal path she knew so well. At her insistence, he set her on her feet and together they made their way down the slope to the cove below Brede House and finally up the wooden staircase to the safety of its garden.

'Let us rest here.' Justin opened the door to the stone folly and together they collapsed exhausted on the cushioned seat, their hands momentarily entwined. In the turmoil of escape, they had forgotten their estrangement, but slowly remembrance came to rest between them. Justin rose and walked towards an old chest which squatted toad-like in one corner. Several neatly folded blankets lay on its top.

'Here, take off that waterlogged cloak and let me wrap you in these.'

She felt his hands tucking the warm wool around her, skimming her body, sending it into tingling alertness. The instant she regained her strength, she thought, she must make her way back to the house.

They sat in silence for some time. 'Why did you not answer my note?' he asked at length. She tensed, aware that she could not tell him the true reason.

'I have been a little busy,' she hedged, and then scolded herself for such a feeble response. 'Mrs Croft has lately needed my full attendance,' she tried again. That was hardly an improvement and he swooped on her words.

'How long would it have taken to pen a simple yes or no, I wonder?' His voice was harsh and she felt close to tears. Tonight she had felt herself part of him, sharing the adventure, sharing the peril, neglectful of the fact that he did not know the worst about her.

'I'm sorry,' she whispered brokenly.

'Lizzie!' He turned to face her, holding her by the shoulders and forcing her to look into his eyes. 'All I want is the truth. If you find my attentions distasteful, you must say so.'

The tears began to fall in earnest then and she could do nothing to stop them. 'No,' she sobbed, 'no, I don't.'

'Then what is going on?'

With a struggle she regained sufficient mastery to say in a quiet voice, 'It was discourteous not to have replied to your note and I am sorry, Justin, but it would not have been right to come to Chelwood. It *isn't* right.'

He shook his head, baffled. 'Why this sudden qualm? You have not minded visiting me in the past.'

'That was before...when we were just playing...but now.... you should not know me.'

'What nonsense is this?'

'I wish it were nonsense. If you knew...'

'But I don't know. That is the problem.'

She must put an end to this painful conversation. 'You must believe me when I say that if you knew the truth, you would not wish to be with me.'

He moved closer and before she could stop him had put his arms around her. 'Nothing you could tell me would make me wish that.'

He gave her a little shake. 'Now, what exactly is keeping you from my door?'

She fixed her gaze on the sodden edges of her nightgown, but did not disentangle herself. 'I have done a very bad thing.'

'Why don't you let me be the judge of that?'

'It was bad. You see, I was most anxious to find my father.'

'And you joined the circus.'

'No. Yes. I did, but this was later.'

His eyebrows were raised in question and she found the sentences tumbling out, staccato and unstoppable. 'It was when I was fifteen. I met this man. He was a soldier, too.'

'Aren't they all,' he groaned.

'I met him at a dance in Bath.'

'I take it that Miss Bates was not your chaperon.'

'I had no chaperon. None of the girls was allowed to attend dances—the teachers said we were far too young. But we all knew that there was a ball at the Assembly Rooms that night and that the 11th Foot were on furlough in the town. There would be soldiers aplenty to partner and everyone was desperate to attend. But it was impossible. Then Sophie Weston bet me that I couldn't get there—so I did.'

'Of course you did,' he sighed. 'That was inevitable. Dare I ask how you got there?'

'I climbed out of the landing window. It's on the first floor and the porch roof is directly beneath. I managed to jump down without harming my best frock or making a noise— and then I simply walked to the Assembly Rooms.'

'That could not have been easy.'

'I wore my boots and carried my evening slippers. It took me an age to get there—the Seminary is on the outskirts of Bath—but I like walking.' She saw him smile at this naivety and wished it were possible that he would go on smiling, but her revelations would change everything.

For a moment her breath caught in her throat. 'The return was much easier. Victor— he was the man I met—brought me back to the Seminary in a carriage he'd hired.'

'You should never trust a man called Victor.'

She knew he was joking, but said seriously, 'No, I should not have. But he looked so splendid in his uniform and spoke so convincingly. If I'd had one sensible thought in my mind, I would have known that a serving soldier could not simply disappear for weeks.

But I was desperate to find my father and Victor said he would take care of me, keep me safe from harm if I went with him.'

'You most definitely should not have trusted him.'

'To be honest, he should not have trusted me either. I told him the most terrible untruths. That my father was very wealthy but lived abroad and that I wanted to go to him.'

'That was not so untrue,' he said soothingly.

'The wealthy bit was. I made him believe I was a great heiress and that if he helped me travel to Spain, he would be well rewarded.'

'As you never got to Spain, I take it he did not help you.'

'No.' She shook her head miserably.

'So what happened?'

'I don't wish to tell you, after all. It was too terrible.' Her voice had sunk to a whisper again.

He grasped her hands. 'Tell me, Lizzie! At the very least, I am your friend.'

There was a long silence, then she swallowed hard and began in a wavering voice. 'We stayed at an inn—he said that Dover was a very long journey and that we would need to rest. I expected him to ask for two rooms, but he said we would have to share the same room as he did not have sufficient funds. I couldn't argue with him. I had no money myself and all I could think of was how much I wanted to get to Spain.'

Her voice grew smaller. 'He said he would be the perfect gentleman. I was not to worry. There was a sofa in the room and he would sleep on that. I was greatly fatigued from the dance and from the journey and I fell asleep almost instantly. But then—I don't know how long afterwards—all of a sudden I was awake and he was beside me in the bed.'

'My God, Lizzie. Did he not know how old you were?'

She studied the hem of her nightgown intently. 'To be fair to Victor,' she said in the quietest of voices, 'he thought me eighteen.' And when her companion said nothing, she added unnecessarily, 'I lied to him.'

Even in the fragmented light of partial moon and cloud, she saw Justin's expression was severe. When he spoke, his voice was equally so. 'You need tell me no more. I have understood perfectly.'

'No, no!' she exclaimed, desperate that he did not think the very worst of her. 'You haven't understood. When I found him beside me, I screamed. He tried to hush me, then he put his hand over my mouth to keep me quiet. But the more he tried to silence me, the more I struggled and the louder I screamed. It brought the landlady to the room. I remember that she stood in the doorway with a candle and just stared at us.'

Lizzie's eyes were wide with frightened memory, but she forced herself to go on. 'I thought I was saved then but she turned to go—she assumed that we were newly-weds and I was simply a scared bride. But when I called after her that I was fifteen and a schoolgirl, she stormed back into the room and wanted to throw us both out of the inn. It was only the fact that her husband interceded for me that I was allowed to stay the night.'

'And Victor—what happened to him?'

'He *was* thrown out and as he'd spent all his money on the coach and his shot at the inn, he had to walk back to Bath.'

'I am gratified to hear it. And did you have to walk back to Bath too?'

'No, indeed. The landlord sent a message to Miss Bates and she travelled to fetch me. I was in the most terrible disgrace. She said she did not know what she was to do with a girl who had no morals and was bold beyond belief. She was so disturbed that she sent a message to my father and demanded that he come home to discipline me.'

'I imagine he did just that.'

'Yes,' she said unhappily. 'He was furious. He never stopped berating me—though I think it was more because he had been called from his regiment than because I had run away. He never really knew what had happened, for Miss Bates could not bring herself to speak of Victor. But what I had done was bad enough for him to come close to washing his hands of me for good. All the girls in school were told to ignore me and nobody spoke to me for months. I was a pariah.'

'That seems very harsh.'

'Perhaps, but I think my punishment was just. It was a very bad thing I did.'

Justin looked into her eyes and she could see sympathy. 'And your father—did you manage to part friends when he returned to Spain?'

Her eyes shadowed at the remembrance of their leave taking. 'He bought me a dress,' she said sadly.

'And that was it?'

'He said that he never again wanted to be called back to England in such a fashion and that I must obey Miss Bates in all things, even after I finished my schooling.'

'So that is why you are in Rye—Miss Bates decreed it your fate.'

'She gave me a choice, although not much of one,' Lizzie said, sucking in her cheeks. 'Piers—Piers Silchester was the alternative. He is the beau Miss Bates would like me to marry.'

'You had the chance of marriage and yet you preferred to be companion to an eighty year old?!'

'Why should I jump at being wed?' she demanded. 'A husband would be the dullest thing.'

'You judge men severely.'

'*You* haven't met Piers.'

'I now have a lively interest in meeting him. Is he so bad?'

'No,' she wailed, 'he's so good—that's the trouble. He is most soulful. He teaches music at the school and has unimpeachable morals.'

Justin burst out laughing and she slipped from his side and rounded on him. 'It is all very well for you to laugh, but can you imagine being married to someone who never says a bad thing about anyone, ever. Someone who is always fussing around you, someone who thinks you a goddess.'

'I doubt that I would ever marry anyone who thought me a goddess—' he grinned '—or even a god. But don't you want to be worshipped, Lizzie?'

Her response was fierce. 'Only if I can worship equally!'

She was shivering and his arms were back again where she liked them most. She felt their strong clasp through the thin nightgown and shivered again, not from the cold this time, but from the sheer delight of feeling him so very close to her.

'And is the Victor story the only reason you refused to accept my invitation to Chelwood?'

'It was a very bad scandal—Miss Bates said that I had ruined myself and the best I could hope for was to meet a man who lived retired from the world and knew nothing of such doings. That's why she champions Piers so strongly.' There was a pause before she continued in a voice that wobbled very slightly, 'I think she spoke truly. I didn't think—I don't think—that your friends, your neighbours, would judge me a suitable person for you to know.'

'Yet somehow, I have got to know you. You

were little more than a child when this happened and you were blameless.'

She shook her head vigorously. 'Not blameless, Justin. I behaved abominably. I used Victor and deceived him. He spent all his money on me and I left him penniless.'

'It was only what he deserved. Indeed, he got off lightly. He could have been dismissed from the army and put into prison for abducting a girl of your age. He should think himself lucky that his only punishment was to walk back to Bath with his pockets to let.'

She nestled up to him. 'Does it really not bother you that I have been a wicked girl?'

'Dear Lizzie, you have no notion of real wickedness. What you have is a very small skeleton in a very young cupboard.' His lips brushed against her hair and came to rest on her cheek.

'I thought if I told you, you would never wish to speak to me again.'

'How could you misjudge me so badly?'

'For a long time I did not think you even liked me,' she said shyly. 'Not until that evening at Chelwood. Before then you seemed so cold and indifferent.'

'I was a fool. I liked you too much. But I couldn't cope with the way you disturbed my peace of mind—and much else besides! You're not the only one to have skeletons.'

She had an inkling where those skeletons might lie, but her question was tentative. 'Did your mother's friends perhaps cause you distress?'

'One of her friends certainly. I hated her crowd, Lizzie. Hated them with a passion. I loathed the way they descended on Chelwood, even after my parents' marriage had ended, polluting everything they touched, everything that was dear to me.'

'You feel very strongly,' she remarked gently.

'I have good reason. I was little more than a stripling the last time she visited the estate. She brought with her a group of so-called society women and their husbands. One woman—she shall remain nameless—arrived with her cuckold of a husband and decided that I would make for pleasing entertainment. She came to my room. I imagine I need say no more. But bear in mind that I was not yet eighteen and that her husband was doubtless snoring in the next room. Some young men, no doubt, would be gratified by the attention. But I was not one of them. I was an innocent and deeply shocked. I would know how to deal with her now, but not then. I agonised for days over whether it had been my fault, whether I had perhaps inadvertently suggested to her that I was attracted. At one point I was even going to confess to her husband! Instead I went to my mother.'

'And what did she say?' The wretchedness in his face drove her to ask.

'She told me that I should be grateful for what I could get.'

Lizzie felt quite sick. 'Now do you see why I do not want her here? She and her cronies are manipulative and immoral. That woman was happy—delighted—to pick on a vulnerable boy for her own base ends. She enjoyed the seduction. So did her husband. So did the whole company who she lost no time in telling.'

'How very, very dreadful,' she said in a half-whisper and meant it with all her heart.

For a long time he was silent and when he spoke his voice was filled with regret. 'I'm sorry, Lizzie, I should not have told you such a thing. That was selfish of me. I have kept it to myself all these years and should have continued in that way.'

She nestled herself more deeply in his arms. 'Don't be sorry. I'm glad you told me—

it means that you care enough to trust. I've been telling myself that I was an idiot to think you *could* care for me.'

'I care a great deal and we have both been idiots, have we not? Maybe we can start again.'

'I do hope so,' she murmured.

He tipped her face upwards and smiled down into her eyes. 'Shall we make a beginning? Right now?'

## Chapter Ten

She tangled her arms around his neck and pulled him close. Her mouth softened, waiting for his kiss, and when it came, it was warm and inviting. Then more kisses—showering down on her, growing harder and hotter, gathering in intensity until her lips were bruised and swollen from his touch.

Finally they pulled apart but looked longingly at each other. 'One more kiss,' he whispered, 'and you must go. It is almost dawn.'

'One more kiss,' she whispered back. 'Make sure it is a good one!'

His tongue traced the outline of her lips and now she was opening her mouth to his probing, allowing herself to fall deeper and deeper into the delightful haze that was taking over her body. She pressed him even closer, feeling the hard outlines of his form shaping themselves against her softness. He kissed her eyelids one by one, nibbled at her ears and then his lips were moving down her neck and pressing kisses into the delicate skin of her chest. She took his head between her hands and pulled his mouth down to her bosom. This is where she wanted his lips. He parted the nightgown and found her breasts, kissing them gently at first, one at a time, but then more urgently until she was straining against him, her hands feeling his hardness, her stomach churning in pleasure. The most exquisite ache shot through her whole body as they clung together, hot, liquid, overwhelmed by the waves of desire washing over them.

'We should…' he began, but he never finished the admonition. With a groan he threw the blankets down on to the wooden floor and rolled her off the seat to enmesh his body with hers.

'Are you sure, darling Lizzie?'

In response, she tore at his shirt, desperate to feel his naked skin against hers. She was sure, of course she was. Convention could beat its empty drum for she loved him too much, she wanted him too much. And he wanted her—badly. His hands were caressing her legs moving upwards in gentle, stroking motions until she thought she would die of this new-found pleasure and harbour no regrets. Her nightgown was cast aside, his breeches and shirt joined it, and they were naked at last, body on body. She felt herself carried aloft on a torrent of such intense feeling that the whole of her being sang with passion. Surges of pleasure, one after another after another, until she felt that she could bear no more. Then a crescendo of desire and they were together at last, trembling, ecstatic, two bodies melded to one.

For long minutes they lay locked together, their passion spent, their bodies adrift and unable to move. Then Justin rolled to one side and reached for the nightgown so carelessly discarded.

'You must not catch cold else I shall be hearing from Mrs Croft that you have contracted pneumonia,' he warned, covering her carefully with one of the blankets. 'If you fall ill, she will fuss endlessly, I know, and insist that you keep to your bed.'

'That would be hateful. Imagine being confined to the house—even more than I am already!' She smiled up at him.

'In time she might allow you a gentle saunter in the garden,' he teased. 'Or perhaps not. I think she has a dread of this place. I've noticed that she never walks here herself.'

'There could be reason for that.' Lizzie was hazed in pleasure still, but his words had brought back the terrors of the night. 'Do you think that it was a smuggler who disturbed Mrs Croft's granddaughter and caused her death?'

'I'm beginning to think it might have been,' he said sombrely. 'That gang has much to answer for. It would be splendid if we could bring them to justice, though at the moment I cannot see how.'

She could not either, but as she gazed through the small window set high in the stone wall and watched rags of clouds pass across the face of the moon, a tremor passed through her. A thought had arrived, but one that trailed malevolence. 'Justin—' she clutched at his arm '—they will know now that you are not one of them. They will come looking for you.'

'It's possible.'

His tone was too careless. 'But don't you see, you will be in danger. They are quite, quite ruthless.'

'I am a pillar of the community, Lizzie, and I doubt they will lay a hand on me. Nor on any of my people—I made sure that I acted alone. They would be foolish to do so, for they would be very quickly found out and hanged for their trouble. If they come calling, I will simply tell them that I have changed my mind and that I find the undertaking too dangerous for my liking.'

'But if they tell tales—spread rumours about you?'

'If they threaten to expose me—though I doubt they will, since that would make clear their own wrongdoing—I shall deny all knowledge of my involvement. And who is likely to gainsay me?'

'But how are you to explain me? The smuggler with the gun—he saw me.'

'He saw only a woman in night attire. I shall say that I was followed from my house by one of my maidservants who has a tendency to sleepwalk.'

She burst out laughing. 'That sounds as far-fetched as anything *I* could concoct.'

'It's pretty good, isn't it? They did not see your face and can have no idea who the mad woman in the cloak and nightgown might be.'

He scrambled to his feet and began quickly

to dress. 'Come, Lizzie, we should go. It must be nigh on six in the morning.'

She glanced towards the window again. Even through glass streaked with the dirt of recent storms, she could see that the faintest rays of light were already filtering through the clouds. It really was time to go.

They walked together up the garden path, hand in hand, Lizzie no longer caring who might see them. 'Your disguise is no more,' she said sadly, as they reached the back door of Brede House, 'and the risks you took have all been for nothing. Gilbert is still missing and we have no idea where he is.'

For a moment Justin's shoulders sagged. 'I hate to admit failure, but at the moment there seems little more that we can do. I dare not even tell the Armitages what we have discovered so far. It is only suspicion, after all, but it would kill them to think that Gil might have been involved with such a gang and with a woman like Rosanna.'

She tried the latch and it opened to her touch. 'I left by this door and thank goodness Hester has not come down during the night and turned the key. I may even gain my bedroom without being discovered.'

'You should try to get a little sleep before

the household is up and about.' He bent his head and found her lips again.

'I will,' she said softly in his ear. She twined her arms around his neck and her breasts, rubbing against him, were tantalisingly erect. In response he pulled her roughly towards his hardening body.

'Go, you must go,' he said hoarsely. 'There will be another invitation on your doorstep tomorrow. Please accept it, Lizzie. I want to see you back at Chelwood.'

She turned and stroked his cheek. 'I will, Justin. I promise.'

He walked back to Chelwood through the dewy early morning, the sky gradually turning from ice blue to an undertow of the palest pink and then, as a majestic sun rose over the tree tops, into a wash of peach and apricot. The once-green lane had turned into a tunnel of dull golds and reds and walking through its splendour, he felt at one with the world. Great surges of happiness swept through him at the thought of what the night had brought. He hardly felt his fatigue though he was without sleep and had walked nigh on fifteen miles. Euphoria was keeping him afloat.

\* \* \*

The household was already up and at its work when he trudged through Chelwood's front entrance straight into Chivers, hovering in the hall. His butler's stare of surprise brought him up sharply but he was too tired to conjure a credible explanation for his long absence.

'I couldn't sleep, Chivers,' he managed. It was weak, but it would have to do. 'Problems with the estate. I thought it best to walk off my worries.'

'I hope you were successful, sir. Mellors is already in the office if you would care to consult him.'

The thought made Justin blench. 'Not just at this minute. The fresh air has tired me and I must try to get some rest.'

He could see the butler attempting to arrange his face to one of neutrality and knew that behind the façade, the man teemed with unsatisfied curiosity. It would have to stay unsatisfied for this was one secret his servants would not learn.

He started towards the grand oak staircase, his mind intent on hot water and a soft bed— he must close his eyes, if only for a few hours. But he had gone only a few steps when he became aware of luggage piled high in the furthest corner of the hall. He walked up to it and counted: three large trunks.

'What is this, Chivers?'

'They belong to her Grace, Sir Justin. Her Grace and her maid arrived late last evening and are still abed. Alfred will take the baggage to her Grace's quarters as soon as he is able.'

'Her Grace? What the deuce are you talking about, man?'

'Lady Lavinia has arrived.' The butler gratefully reverted to the name by which he had always known his late mistress. 'You were not at home, sir, but in your absence I instructed Mrs Reynolds to prepare the blue suite for her ladyship. I trust that meets with your approval.'

Justin slowly retraced his steps. 'Are you telling me that my mother is here at Chelwood?'

'Indeed, yes, sir. Lady Lavinia has come to stay for a while. I understand there has been a few problems in London.' Chivers coughed delicately.

Justin clamped his lips tightly together, but could not quite suppress a flicker of fury.

'I hope I did right, sir.' His master's unfamiliar anger was making the butler anxious. Justin recovered himself sufficiently to say, 'You could do no other, Chivers. I will see Her Grace later.'

Then more concerned than ever to reach his room, he bounded up the stairs two at a time. He had no wish to face the woman he so disliked, jaded and unkempt. His valet was waiting for him and he gladly gave himself up to the man's ministrations. When finally the door closed and he was alone, he tried to focus on this new problem that had sprung out of nowhere. Chivers had said his mother had come to stay for a while. That was annoyingly vague. He did not want her here for a while—he did not want her here for a week, for a day even. But he knew that he had no choice but to house her. There was nowhere else for her to go, that much was clear, for she would never have come to Chelwood unless she were desperate. The house must be the only refuge left to her. She would hate living in Rye and he would hate living under the same roof. He climbed wearily into bed—it was not a happy thought.

And just when life had seemed so right. Well, almost right. He was no nearer finding what had happened to Gil than he had been weeks ago, and he dared not contemplate Caroline's face if he were forced to tell her that he had discovered nothing. He'd had few hopes for tonight's plan, but while there had been a small chance of finding where Gil was incarcerated, he had thought it worth the risk. In joining the smugglers, he had exposed himself to danger and possible future reprisal. All for nothing as it turned out. If only Lizzie hadn't followed him...but she had. She was a courageous girl and she had done what she thought right. And how could he regret her arrival on the scene—had it not led to their reconciliation?

And what a reconciliation! His eyelids closed at the memory of her soft arms twined around him, the memory of her soft lips opening to him, their bodies moving as one, two halves made whole. It had been an extraordinary passion. He had never thought he could so completely surrender himself to a woman, give himself in the most exquisite way—and glory in it. But he had and he must cling to this new and wonderful knowledge whatever the difficulties ahead. As he drifted into the soundest sleep he had enjoyed for weeks, the face of Gil Armitage floated across his inner vision. From the start the image of his dearest friend had been entangled with that of the girl he had come to love. Why was that? he mused dreamily. They were both exceptionally dear to him, but surely there must be more to it than that. Was it that Gil had disappeared from his life at the very same moment that she had walked into it, that with Gil's eclipse he was saying a final goodbye to his childhood and to the unhappiness and prejudice to which he had been heir. Maybe. But he could not say goodbye to Gil just yet. He had to know what had become of his friend and Lizzie was as much involved as he in that quest. He fell asleep pondering the strange quirk of fate that had brought these two very different people together in his life.

His valet did not wake him until midday but he felt so well rested that he did not reprimand the man for leaving him to sleep. His unwelcome guest, it appeared, was this minute in the dining room and partaking of a light nuncheon. The thought of food roused him fully, for he had not eaten for hours and was extremely hungry, and though he did not relish joining his mother at the table, it clearly behoved him to welcome her to Chelwood. He might wish her miles away, but he needed to talk with her. Since he'd left Lizzie early that morning, he had been turning over in his mind an idea so shocking that it almost stopped his breath. It was hardly possible, he knew, but the idea would not quite go away, and whatever plans Lady Lavinia entertained might matter greatly for his future.

Despite the pangs gnawing at his stomach, he took time to dress carefully. A single-breasted blue tailcoat, a striped-silk waistcoat and pantaloons of muted grey were set off by a dazzling snow-white cravat arranged in precise and intricate folds.

In half an hour he walked into the dining room, complete to a shade. His mother had been making ready to leave and tripped prettily towards him as he entered, exuding a heavy, sweet perfume with every step.

'Justin!' She threw up her hands in an exaggerated gesture. 'At last, and how very good to see you!'

'Is it? It has been some years since you felt the need to see me, has it not?' His voice was bereft of all emotion.

'Years indeed, but you have changed little.' She could not quite conceal the sourness. 'It's true that you have grown—taller, broader. But that was inevitable, I imagine, for a soldier's life demands physical strength, does it not?'

He had no wish to talk about soldiering, no wish to converse on his army career. At this moment his mind was fizzing with doubt and possibility, and he had no intention of sharing those feelings. What he did intend was to talk about his mother's future and its likely effects for him and for Chelwood. Food would have to wait.

'Shall we repair to the library? An excellent fire is burning and we can discuss your situation there without fear of being interrupted.'

'And what situation is that, Justin?' she cooed, her tone at odds with the frown that furrowed deep across her brow.

'Come, let us go.'

He led the way out of the dining room and across the hall. His words were not for the ears of even the most trusted of his servants and he would not speak until the library door was firmly shut. Lavinia followed him unwillingly. She eschewed the comfort of a fireside chair and instead perched herself on the arm of the large, leather Chesterfield, as though ready to take flight at any moment.

'So, Mama,' he said abruptly, 'why are you here?'

'Why should I not be? Chelwood is your home and you are my son. There is no mystery to it.'

'That has always been the case, but you have not seen fit to visit before, or at least not for many years.'

'There were reasons, as you well know,' she said pettishly.

'I could point out that you divorced your husband, not your son, but that would be stating the obvious. What I wish to know is why you have returned now, having stayed away so long?'

He thought he knew the answer, but he wanted to hear it from her lips.

'It's quite simple.' She attempted an airy tone. 'Sufficient time has passed between now and the rather unpleasant events to which you refer. I thought it time to see you again.'

Surely she could do better than that? he thought derisively. He wanted to laugh out loud but instead schooled his face into a blank mask. 'So why did you not let me know you were coming? You have arrived out of the blue and no doubt sent my household into a flurry. I have little contact with polite society, but is it not still usual to announce one's arrival, even, dare I say, wait for an invitation.'

'Pooh!' She brushed aside his criticism. 'Chivers dealt with my arrival admirably. Really he has grown into an excellent butler— you would never have guessed it for he was such an awkward young man when Lucien first employed him. But where were you last night, Justin? I would not have thought country delights could have kept you out so long and so late.'

He had no intention of explaining his absence and neither was he going to allow her to change the subject. 'So why did you not write to me of your decision to visit?' he persisted.

'I did write.'

'Only to tell me that your esteemed husband had found himself more entertaining company.'

'Surely that was enough. It was hard to write even that.'

For the first time, her voice lost its false animation and for the first time Justin felt the stirrings of pity. She bowed her head and he noticed how frail her shoulders were, how the rich satin of her dress hung limply on the thin frame.

'I am sorry that things have come to this

pass,' he said awkwardly. 'But I cannot think that Chelwood is the answer to your problems.'

'What other solution can you offer me, Justin? I have nowhere else to go.'

And now he was staring into her eyes, wide and scared. Her face, so smooth and lovely when he had last looked upon it, had crumpled into lines of terror at the future she faced.

'Nowhere to go? You have friends, surely?'

'Friends!' She almost spat the word. 'I have no friends. They are hangers-on, fair-weather people who trim their sails according to the wind. And the wind is definitely blowing the wrong way for me. When I married the duke, my every move was dogged by a trail of admirers—flattering, effusive. They were always in the house, always with me. Of course, Dorian is so rich he could afford to support any number of fawning courtiers. But now that is over. I am an abandoned woman, a poor prospect for a social climber.'

Justin knew his mother's world sufficiently well to realise that this latest scandal would have rung out across London. There had already been too many scandals in Lavinia's life, he thought, and this time she would not survive. None of her so-called friends would offer sanctuary for fear of being tainted by association.

'I presume the duke has closed up the London house?'

'Naturally. His latest *inamorata* is an Italian princess and it is to Italy that he has gone. He intends to buy a large estate there, I believe. Bianca will require the very finest, you can be sure.'

'And he has left you with nothing? Can that really be the case?'

'It may be hard for you to believe, but it is the truth. When I entered marriage with the duke, I had no voice in the settlement. I was without family to oversee the negotiations and no money to afford a lawyer to protect my interests. And after all, I was bringing little into the marriage except myself—by the time I met Dorian, I had run through what small capital I possessed. It follows then that as soon as I became worthless to the duke, I was forced to leave with just as little.'

Was Lavinia suggesting that his father had left the wife he adored without means? That could not be so.

'I imagine you received a settlement at the time of the divorce,' he said in a colourless voice. He hated to talk about this wretched time in his life.

'A small settlement, Justin. Your father was not ungenerous, but neither was he very generous. And I am an expensive woman.' She gave a small, hesitant laugh. 'The money I received from Lucien ran out very quickly and a condition of the divorce was that I must never petition for more.'

It gave him a jolt to realise that his father could lack sentiment, even feeling, towards the woman he had loved to distraction. There were reasons, of course, but still, it did not quite accord with the picture of Lucien Delacourt that he held in his heart. In some agitation he strode to the window, drumming his fingers on the wood of the broad sill. He looked out at the grassy expanse still wet from autumn mist and in the distance the soft lines of trees, a faded blur on the horizon. This was a landscape he loved, a landscape he would defend with his life. His mother did not belong here and he felt a vague, anonymous threat gathering pace and stiffened himself to meet it.

'I suppose there is no question of a reconciliation between yourself and the duke?'

The question was crass, but he felt trapped, defensive.

Lavinia jumped up from her perch, twisting her mouth into a small, bitter shape. 'The *principessa* is twenty-five. Do you think he is likely to return to me?' She fixed him with an unflinching gaze and, when he did not respond, exclaimed in a voice which shook, 'Look at me!'

There was a long silence while they faced each other across the room. At length Lavinia took a deep breath and said quietly, 'Would you have me return to a man who has brought public shame on me? I have not been a good person, Justin, I think we are both agreed on that, but for the last seven years I have tried to be a dutiful wife. I believe that I succeeded— perhaps too well. What those years have taught me is that there is no greater comfort than an unspoiled conscience. I would never willingly go back to one who has sullied my life in such despicable fashion.'

'I understand your repugnance, but I cannot believe you will be happy living miles from the slightest gaiety or distraction.' He paused for a moment, unwilling even now to capitulate, but then forced himself to continue, 'However, for as long as you wish to stay at Chelwood, you are welcome to do so.'

His mother smiled faintly. 'Thank you. I will endeavour to be a conformable house guest. But there would appear to be far more distraction in the neighbourhood than you own. Do tell me, where were you last night?'

'I had business to attend to and it took rather longer than I expected,' he said shortly. 'If you will excuse me, I must leave you to your own devices. You will see that the estate has fallen into some disrepair and there is much to do. I have not seen Mellors for several days—he is the new bailiff—and I am aware that he has a long list of things he wishes to discuss.'

He nodded a brief farewell and made for the door, but then something prompted him to turn and say, 'I intend to invite one or two of my neighbours to Chelwood in the next day or so and you will most likely meet them.'

Lavinia raised her beautifully shaped eyebrows. 'They must be special people if you have invited them here. The place has always been well guarded against intruders, or at least it was under Lucien's rule.'

He was tempted to retort that she and her friends had frequently breached Chelwood's walls, but said instead, 'I will leave you to decide whether or not they are special. You may remember Henrietta Croft—she was a good friend of my father's. She has a young companion, Elizabeth Ingram, who will accompany her.'

'And I imagine it is Elizabeth Ingram that is the attraction,' his mother said shrewdly.

He did not answer her. 'If you are to remain at Chelwood, I would like you to meet them both.'

'Miss Elizabeth is evidently important to you. But why must I wait until she comes to Chelwood to meet her? Chivers tells me that today is Rye's annual fair and that it is magnificent. Why do you not send a note to Brede House—have I that right?—and ask them both to meet us there?'

'Mrs Croft is too infirm to attend any fair.' He was impatient to be gone and annoyed that his mother was taking so much interest in this very personal project.

'But the young woman would enjoy it greatly, I am sure,' Lavinia pursued.

Justin thought for a moment. He would have to introduce his mother to Lizzie, there was no escape from it, and it might be better that their first meeting took place informally.

'I would love to go, Justin. It is a very long time since I attended such an event.'

'You would not enjoy it.'

'You would be surprised. I have changed a great deal since we last met. For one thing, I have learned to find pleasure in simple things.'

He *would* be surprised, he thought. Simple pleasures and his mother were hardly bed-fellows. It was far more likely that she was already planning to summon to her side the detestable people she had earlier denounced.

'So you will not be expecting London society to keep you company at Chelwood?'

'Have you listened to nothing I've said? Or is it that you mistrust me so completely? You are too suspicious for your own good, my angel. You always were. I imagine that comes from Lucien. But you must not think so badly of me. There are always two sides to every question.'

She saw his sceptical expression and went on, 'I understand more than you think. I am aware of what you suffered in your youth. You are a grown man and yet you still flush when I talk of it. It pains you, I can see. The deed itself was nothing—a mere rite of passage—but the gossip, the innuendo, the husband who pretended he wished to call you out—my poor dear, that was a shameful humiliation to visit upon you.'

He was shocked to realise that his mother had guessed at his feelings. He had always imagined her indifferent, or worse, laughing with friends at his discomfiture. It seemed that was not so. She had not laughed, but had been powerless to prevent his humbling. And powerless to prevent the scandal that had dogged his young years and sent him hurtling into the army, desperate to escape the clutch of women.

She watched him measuringly. 'So will you escort me this afternoon and introduce me to this young lady? I am most anxious to meet her.'

He made a swift decision. 'I will send a note to Brede House.'

'Excellent. Meanwhile my maid can unpack my portmanteaux. The dresses will be horribly creased, but she can press the plainest one and we will sally forth to Rye together.' Her tone was almost carefree.

He bowed a farewell, but had gone only a few steps into the hall when Chivers approached him bearing a silver salver. 'A letter, sir, just arrived. I did not get sight of the messenger.'

Justin glanced at the hand without recognition. The letter had to be from Lizzie, he thought, though the writing seemed clumsy. Eagerly he tore open the envelope and found himself disappointed but intrigued—it appeared that someone else wanted to meet him at the fair.

## Chapter Eleven

Lizzie woke from a deep sleep. Hester was moving around the room, gathering the clothes she had thrown off when she fell into bed at dawn. Somehow she would have to explain the crumpled and soiled nightgown, but not now. She lay still and soundless until the maid went downstairs. A thread of excitement was tugging at her from the tip of her head to her smallest toe. Justin was her lover and she hugged that knowledge close. He had made love to her as she had always dreamed of being loved and a bleak future had turned rose coloured. True, he hadn't told her he loved her, but surely that would come. In all other ways he had shown her the depth of his feelings and she had been left tingling with happiness.

At the sound of Hester's retreating foot-steps, she opened her eyes. The promise of early dawn had been fulfilled and a hazy circle of gold now shone from a cloudless sky. It would be a beautiful day and with luck she would meet her lover. She scrambled out of bed and quickly washed, then donned the dress of primrose-floret sarsnet that she had not worn since its return from Chelwood, cleaned and pressed. Would she be visiting there today in this self-same dress, but this time not as a trespasser? She hoped very much so; she would make sure there were new slippers on her feet and a newly refurbished reticule in her hand. Anxiously she checked the mirror. Her complexion was smooth and clear, warm with happiness, her curls shining but hopelessly tangled. She should go to Mrs Croft, but first she must set her hair to rights. Standing before the glass, she carefully arranged her ringlets to tumble from a chignon atop her head and cluster about her neck and cheeks in wisps of silk. It was a style that would not have been out of place in a ballroom, but she did not care. Today she wanted to look as special as she felt.

Satisfied with what she saw, she tripped down the stairs into the small, square hall. A thick white envelope lay on the console table, her name clearly inscribed on the front. As long as Mrs Croft was willing, she *would* be going to Chelwood this very day!

Hester appeared from the kitchen and busied up to her. There was a doubtful expression on her face and her voice was just this side of querulous. 'Are you all right, Miss Lizzie?'

'Of course I am. Why should I not be?'

'There's a gown of yours in the laundry that looks as though it fell into the marsh,' she said accusingly. 'Yet this morning, you're looking as fine as fivepence.'

Lizzie laughed as naturally as she could. 'Now what would I be doing in the marsh? As for looking fine, I have dressed for the day—the sun is shining bright and there is not a cloud in the sky.'

Hester sniffed a little too loudly. 'That's as may be, but what's happening in this house is more important. Mrs Croft has been asking for you—the poor dear is feeling poorly again.'

'I am so sorry,' Lizzie said quickly. 'I will go to her this minute.' Hester sniffed once more.

She left the maid looking dubious and ran

back up the stairs to Henrietta's bedroom, clasping the envelope tightly in her hand. Mrs Croft's voice was slight and fading as she bade her enter. The old lady was sitting upright in bed, a mound of pillows behind her, and an empty tea cup nearby. Her face was tired and white.

'Forgive me for being late, Mrs Croft. I suffered a bad night and no one woke me.'

'I told Hester not to disturb you. You have been looking a little wan of late, my dear, and I do not want you to fall ill. One invalid in the house is sufficient.' The old lady gave her a penetrating look. 'But you seem much recovered this morning. Perhaps it was only sleep that you lacked.'

'It must have been,' Lizzie agreed, grateful that she need offer no further explanation. 'Now that I am here, what tasks have you for me? The newspaper has arrived if you would care to have it read. Or I could finish sorting your workbox while you watch—so far I have only tidied one layer.'

Mrs Croft shrank back into her bed. 'I think not, my dear. I shall spend the day very quietly and Hester will bring me whatever refreshment I require. But you have a letter.'

She pointed to the crisp, white object in her companion's hand.

If she opened it here, Lizzie thought, she might get the permission she needed.

She slit open the envelope. 'It is from Sir Justin Delacourt. An invitation, Mrs Croft. He wants me to...to meet him at the fair. Both of us are to meet him at the fair.' It was a surprise; she had expected a visit to Chelwood and here was Justin wanting to see her in a public place and amid a crowd of people.

'That will be the annual Rye fair. Hester mentioned it this morning and I told her she may go.'

'Then I had better not.' Despondency began to weigh on her.

'Of course, you must go. It is a marvellous occasion. Hester will be gone a few hours only and I do not need constant attention— at least not yet.' The jest was weak, but the pressure of her hand on Lizzie's arm was determined.

'You must write to Justin, though, and tell him that I am not fit enough to join you both. But give him my very best wishes and tell him there is always a welcome for him here.'

Henrietta was getting more tired by the minute and Lizzie could see that the old lady was waiting for her to leave so that she could once more fall into a doze. That was fortunate. There was only an hour before she was supposed to meet Justin and the walk into town was a long one.

'If you're sure that you will do well on your own…'

'Go, my dear, go!' Henrietta shushed her out of the room. 'Walk there with Hester and make sure that you both enjoy yourselves.'

Lizzie had expected a modest affair—Rye was only a small town, after all—and she was taken aback as she and Hester walked through the Strand Gate. A veritable cacophony of smells and noises greeted them as they reached the bottom of Mermaid Street, today as innocent and unthreatening as any other in the town. Hester linked arms with her and together they marched firmly up the infamous road to the square of streets above. Each was filled with noise and bustle and everywhere booths and standings spilled out over the thoroughfare, many of them crammed high with food. There were stalls for oysters, stalls for hot pies and sausages—disappearing at a rapid rate—and lines and lines of gilt gingerbread. Tables were set here and there for

people to sit and eat their fill. There were
stalls selling clothes and toy stalls for the
children, gay with decorative paint and coloured lamps. But the predominant interest
of the fair was entertainment. Lizzie saw in
the distance the Rector of St Mary's looking
somewhat aghast, and she wondered whether
he had given his approval to such wholesale
abandonment: horse riders doing tricks were
everywhere, tumblers, illusionists, even a
knife swallower. In the background a band
of itinerant musicians consisting of a double
drum, a Dutch organ, a tambourine, violin
and pipes were playing a selection of military
tunes. She strolled past food and toy stalls,
past the fire eater who was drawing gasps
from his captive crowd, past the puppet show.
By now she had lost sight of Hester, who had
lingered at several of the stalls. She would
leave the maid to choose new trimmings for
her hat, she decided, while she herself made
for the church, for it was almost two and Justin would be waiting.

Ever since she'd opened his message, she
had been puzzling why he had chosen to meet
her in such a public place. When they'd parted
early this morning, his invitation had been
to Chelwood and she had been cherishing

the thought that she would visit the home he
loved, this time as his sweetheart. She had
imagined them walking and talking together,
just the two of them, exchanging confidences,
exploring feelings. A tryst at Chelwood would
have been so much more romantic than the
hubbub that surrounded them here in Rye. An
uncomfortable thought sprang at her. Was that
why he had changed their meeting place—
because Chelwood was too intimate? Had last
night been too good to be true and he was already regretting their lovemaking? He would
wish to let her down gently by meeting as
promised, she hazarded, but he had chosen a
place in which to distance himself.

The chimes of St Mary's great blue-and-
cream clock rang out the hour. She looked up
as she passed beneath the tower and the slightest of shivers nipped at her spine. The clock's
stern message, *For our time is a very shadow
that passeth away*, seemed even sterner today.
There was no sign of Justin and she walked
quickly past the church door, impatient to be
with him and shake off the dreadful doubts
that had overtaken her. Rounding the corner
buttress, she saw with relief his figure in the
distance, the bright halo of his hair glistening beneath strong sunlight. Dressed in the

palest of grey, he could have been a classical statue dropped amid the dark lichen of the gravestones. But he was not alone! Lizzie stopped in her tracks. Had he been waylaid by an acquaintance perhaps and was even now being stopped from meeting her by the church door as he'd promised? She looked again. It was a woman, a young and shapely woman. A voluptuous figure curved itself from the clinging folds of the dress she wore and an abundant tangle of long, dark hair hung down her back. It was Rosanna!

The two of them had their heads together as though in intimate conversation. Whatever it was they were saying, it seemed to engage them to the exclusion of all else. Lizzie waited, half-hidden by the old stone buttress, her mind churning. What was he doing with a woman they both knew to be their enemy? Justin had said that Rosanna had nothing more to tell him and had sworn that he would have no further dealings with the smugglers. So why was he talking to her? Rosanna had sufficient charm to deceive any man, even Justin, but surely he would not trust her a second time—unless he was so fascinated that he couldn't help himself. The thought that Justin might be no more steadfast than any other man she'd known, made Lizzie feel suddenly unwell.

At last the conversation was ended and they were smiling a farewell. He was walking in her direction now and she moved out of the shadow of the church into his path. She thought she saw an expression of guilt flit across his face.

'Why were you meeting that woman?!' she demanded.

He looked shocked at her curt greeting, but answered readily enough. 'She asked to meet me, Lizzie.'

'But why? You said you would have nothing more to do with her or with the Chapman gang.'

'I agreed to see her because I've not yet discovered what happened to Gil and I thought she might provide a last chance.' His voice was quiet, but she sensed his growing displeasure. It made no difference. Inside her a fiery ball was unfurling—a ball of misgiving and anger.

'She will tell you nothing—you said so yourself. She simply wants to dupe you again.' And lead you into danger and misery, she thought.

'Things may have changed,' he said evenly,

trying, it seemed, to defuse the tension. 'Rosanna learnt today of my attempts to infiltrate the gang and reasoned that if I was prepared to go to such lengths, the matter must be far more important than she'd previously thought. After all, the gang boasts some very dangerous men—she, herself, is fearful of them.'

Lizzie's laugh was short and scornful. 'Fearful? Rosanna? She is Thomas Chapman's lover and hangs on his every word.'

'She *was* his lover,' Justin corrected, 'but she is disenchanted with Chapman and regrets keeping company with his gang. Above all, she is desperate to be free—of them and all their doings—and has promised to aid me in return for helping her to settle elsewhere.'

Lizzie wanted to hit him and hit him hard; she could not believe that such a clear-sighted man could be so badly taken in.

'And how precisely does she propose to aid you?'

'She knew Gil a great deal better than she admitted to me when I last spoke to her.'

'Of course she did. That has always been evident—at least to me. But she has not previously been forthcoming, so why is she talking now?'

'I told you. She knows I was in the gang. It has made her realise how important the matter is to me—and it has given her the chance to break free.'

'And you believe her?'

'Why are you so suspicious, Lizzie? I had not thought you would fall into jealousy.'

The remark served only to stoke the fires of her anger. 'Jealous of Rosanna? No, indeed! But I am a woman and not so easily deceived.'

He glowered, but she went on, 'You did not see her with Thomas Chapman. If you had, you would not believe she would ever leave him, let alone work against him.'

'It's possible for people to change,' he said slowly. 'She may well have been infatuated, but she has come now to see his true nature and she doesn't like what she has discovered. I believe her—and my judgement must prevail.'

She raised her eyebrows. 'Your judgement of Rosanna has proved faulty in the past. Why can you not trust me when I tell you that she is still deceiving you?'

'I believe your woman's heart is leading you astray—what, after all, has she to gain by deceit?'

'*You*, for whatever reason. Rosanna is a female who gets her man. And you are now the man in her sights. She is aiming for you, Justin, even if you don't or won't see it.'

'This is utter nonsense.'

'Is it? Then consider—why did the gang decide to recruit you? You were a most unlikely candidate. The story you spun would not have stood up to any close inspection—unless, of course, Rosanna was urging Chapman to employ you and, to please her, he agreed.'

'What!'

'And you agreed as well, didn't you? When they approached you, you accepted their proposition without hesitation. Was it in order to get closer to her? Did you become a smuggler because of her?'

'Lizzie—' he grabbed her by the arms '—I can't believe we're talking like this. I joined the gang because I thought they would lead me to Gil and I have no reason to believe Rosanna had anything to do with it. I can't know, of course, if she suggested it to Thomas Chapman, but my motivation was clear. Just as it is now—Gil's story is unfinished. I want to complete it and not just for my sake. Remember that his parents are living a nightmare. I want to be able to tell them the truth of what happened to their son. And if Rosanna can help, then I will take that help.'

Lizzie struggled free of his embrace and planted herself firmly in front of him. 'If she is so keen to help, why did she not tell you today the information she has? You were speaking for long enough.'

'We spoke for a few minutes only and she said that she dared not be seen talking to me. Whether she is still with Chapman or not, she is frightened of him. He is a very dangerous man and I was not willing to expose her to risk by keeping her here.'

Lizzie began to pace up and down, weaving backwards and forwards between the gravestones, only stopping when her shoes were dark from the damp of the long grass. He was wrong, utterly wrong, and she feared his refusal to believe her would one day return to haunt him. But it was the knowledge that he would rather trust Rosanna's words than her own that filled her with despair.

But her voice when she spoke was level, almost indifferent. 'So what now?'

'She has promised to arrange another meeting at a time and place where she will not be seen.'

'A lovers' assignation?'

She could almost hear his teeth grind. 'I would like to shake some sense into you, Lizzie. You must know how I feel about you.'

Did she? Did she really know how he felt? When it came down to it, all she knew was that he found her enticing and that he was a wonderful lover. There had been no vow of enduring love, no vow that they had a future together. She had come to meet him today, hoping to hear those words. Instead she had seen him talking secretly to another woman. And what a woman! Made desperate by the idea, she was stung into unrestrained speech.

'I hardly know how you feel, but I am beginning to understand and that is my misfortune. Last night—' and she broke off, struggling to keep her voice steady '—last night, in those moments that we lay together, not one mention of love passed your lips. Instead it would appear that you merely completed what Victor failed to.'

Her sentiments were bitter, but she wanted to hurt him. Perhaps she had; she had certainly enraged him for she had never seen him so angry. His hands clenched into fists, his eyes blazed dark and beneath the tan his face was deeply flushed. Even the golden halo of his hair seemed on fire.

'You liken me to that man!'

'Why not? He was a soldier and so are you.'
She was in the thick of it now, so why hold
back? She was hurt, bleeding, and she lashed
out indiscriminately. 'Women are incidental
to military life—I have always known that.
My own father cannot be bothered with me.
The focus of his world is elsewhere. Yours,
too. I have been an entertaining interlude for
you and that is all.'

'I cannot believe you would say such a
thing.'

'But why not? A few hours ago I gave myself to you, yet I find you conversing intimately with a woman who has had half the
men of this town. And not content with that,
you intend to meet her again. And your reason? That she might just help you—another
meeting, another delightful *tête-a-tête*,' she
mocked. 'What else am I to think?'

'If you value me so poorly, think it then.'

'Is this the young lady, Justin?'

Startled, they turned to glare at the new-
comer. Lady Lavinia rustled delicately up to
them, looking interestedly from one inflamed
face to the other.

Justin compressed his lips and said in a
voice tinged with arctic cold, 'Mama, this is

Miss Elizabeth Ingram. She is companion to Mrs Croft—as I told you. Miss Ingram, allow me to introduce my mother, the Duchess of Alton.'

Lizzie curtsied briefly and received a nod in recognition. There was an uncomfortable silence while the duchess pinned a bland expression on her face and waited for one of them to speak. It fell to Justin.

'If there is nothing further, Miss Ingram, Mama, I hope you will excuse me. A great deal of work awaits me at Chelwood and I should be returning there.'

And with that he strode off, his feet beating a tattoo on the uneven pathway. His mother looked thoughtfully after him and then turned to Lizzie, who had been shocked into speechlessness by the disasters of the afternoon.

'Well, my dear, hats off to you. In all my misdemeanours, I have never managed to make Justin quite so furious—cold and unforgiving certainly, shocked and determined, too—but never quite so angry.'

Lizzie's face had paled, but the duchess's speech caused her to flush with embarrassment. 'I do not take that as a compliment, your Grace. The conversation…I had not meant, you see…'

'I do see. No one better. In the heat of the moment words have a habit of running away with one, do they not?'

For the first time, Lizzie looked properly at the woman who had interrupted their bad-tempered tirade. The richness of her clothes was overwhelming, the perfume she wore expensive and the jewellery which clasped her neck and her arms surely worth a queen's, if not a king's, ransom. But though she exuded wealth and ease, behind the façade Lizzie sensed that she was looking at a lost and lonely woman. It made her more candid than she would otherwise have been.

'I cannot help but feel as I do,' she responded, 'but I should not have said some of the things I did.'

Lavinia's gaze was shrewd. 'I am sure you will not relish my advice, but I will give it anyway. A simple adage only—do not let the grass grow beneath your feet.'

'Whatever can you mean, ma'am?'

'I have a difficult relationship with my son, Miss Ingram, but I am quite aware that he is a man worth winning and keeping. The winning I think has been easy for you, but the keeping…ah, that is a different matter entirely. And as a woman who has managed in her time to win the most appalling of men, and lose one of the best, I know what I am talking about. Don't allow the wounds to fester—go to him as soon as you can!'

Justin had been sitting at his desk without moving for at least an hour. He had returned from the fair to work, but it was work that he could not do. The encounter with Lizzie had been short, sharp and devastating. It had never for one moment occurred to him that she would challenge his decision to talk again to Rosanna or misinterpret the woman's presence in the churchyard. When he'd received Rosanna's note, it had seemed sensible to name the same meeting place so that he might tell Lizzie what had been said. The meeting had gone to plan, but with a result far different from his imaginings. Lizzie had accused him of poor judgement and, even worse, the grossest conduct. She had refused to believe his denials, no matter how vehement. Instead she had chosen to believe her own fabrication and to accuse him of playing with her affections. It sickened him to think that she could believe he cared nothing for her, that last night he had been intent only on physical pleasure. She had accused him of not speaking one word of love and he had to plead guilty. Their lovemaking had been sudden, passionate, coming at the end of a night of turmoil and danger and he had been too astounded by the feelings she had released in him to find the right words.

But he had been right to keep silent. If he spoke words of love, she was entitled to expect more. For a while the dream of a different future had hovered before him, but he knew that it could not be. Chelwood might survive without him but a wife would not, especially not a wife such as Lizzie Ingram. He could not marry and then abandon her to go to war. She would not sit quietly and wait for his return from Spain, and he could not expect her to. God knew what mischief might ensue: marriage could be a disaster for them both. He was trapped, he thought, trapped by the allegiance he owed elsewhere, to the army, to his father.

And what if he were to lose all sense of duty, as he had been so badly tempted to do in the hours since he'd last seen her, would that result in happiness? For him, for her? How happy would he make her? She was a restless spirit constantly seeking distraction. She had poured scorn on marriage and no wonder, for she would find it a straitjacket.

A sudden thought made him grasp the pencil he'd been holding, so fiercely that it snapped clean in two. She would find marriage a straitjacket! She had no serious thoughts of a future with him, that was the truth. Why was he allowing himself to be torn apart by opposing loyalties when she could be the one who was guilty—guilty of playing with *his* affections? He was stunned by the notion, but their quarrel had come out of the blue, springing it seemed from nowhere. She had deliberately set her conviction against his, insisting that Rosanna was deceiving him, yet she had offered no sensible reason why that should be. Her accusations were ridiculous and she could not seriously believe them. They must be a ploy for detaching herself, a convenient ploy if she were regretting her indiscretion of the previous night! Was her outrage over Rosanna then simply bluff? If so, he had misjudged her utterly. He had thought her different from the society women he disdained—innocent and free spirited—but today's bruising encounter had left him wondering how different. Was she just as manipulative, just as unfeeling, simply able to disguise it better?

That must be the case. It was clear to him now that she feared her freedom might be compromised and she was running from any serious commitment. His soldier's life no doubt made him attractive to a girl who craved adventure, but what if he were no longer a soldier—he would bore her as thoroughly as the hapless Silchester. To think that he had opened his heart to her, confessed a vulnerability that he'd buried so deeply and so surely years ago. How could he have done that? Worse, how could he have allowed himself even for a second to contemplate relinquishing the army? He must have run mad. If he should ever doubt her need for excitement, he had only to remember the past. A child's wish to find her father was forgivable, but did her uneasy relationship with Colonel Ingram make any soldier she met fair game? The incident with the wretched Victor—how forgivable was that? She had presented herself as the wronged innocent, but she had also admitted that she'd made up stories to deceive him, or to put it plainly, had told lies. Of course, the man was an unscrupulous philanderer and deserved all he got. And how dared she utter their names in the same breath!

There was a knock at the door and he lifted his head impatiently. He knew Mellors to be riding to a far distant tenant and had hoped that he would not see his bailiff for many hours.

'May I come in?'

His mother stood on the threshold, her aubergine satin incongruous amid the rough furnishings of the estate office. He stood up as she walked into the room, but did not invite her to take a seat.

'I will not stay long,' she said, having understood his mood exactly. 'I have come to speak to you of your young friend.'

He stiffened. 'What of her?'

'She is a lively young lady, is she not? Intelligent, sharp. Beautiful, too. You could do far worse if you should be hanging out for a wife.'

'I am not,' he said shortly.

'That is a pity. I think she would suit you well.'

He shifted irritably on to one foot. 'Cut to the chase, Mama, what is it you want?'

'For once, dearest Justin, I want nothing. But you do, I think.'

He did not pretend to misunderstand her.

'Forgive me for being blunt, but your knowledge is imperfect and I would ask you not to interfere.'

'I have no intention of doing so. I have come merely to remind you that intransigence is like to lose you what you most want.'

'I thank you for your concern, Mama. However, there is no need for you to bother yourself further.'

'In other words, mind my own business. I will, I promise, but it seems to me that the pair of you are behaving rather stupidly. Like star-crossed lovers. But you are not in a play, my dear, this is real life, and as an old hand at it you should take my advice and not play too long.'

'Is that all?' He was wishing his mother at the other end of the world.

'It is all—a simple message. You love her—I can see it in your eyes, hear it in your voice—but you wish to deny it to yourself.'

He refused to look her in the eyes, fixing his gaze some distance away at a broken floorboard.

'You love her,' his mother continued inexorably, 'and love does not come easily or often. Do not let it slip through your fingers.'

Her skirts swished through the doorway

and she was gone. He closed the door loudly behind her and grabbed a cluster of files that had been gathering dust on a nearby cabinet. He would work on these, he decided, anything to keep his mother's voice at bay. If *he* knew Lizzie so little, how could Lavinia be an expert? Whatever she might claim, his mother was simply interfering and no doubt enjoying it. She must already be bored with Chelwood and looking for something to enliven her day. He opened the first file.

But what if she were right and they were both of them behaving as stupidly as she said? What if the fears that had been tormenting him for the past hour were will-o'-the-wisps? A heaviness sapped at his spirits—it would change nothing, he thought. He had flirted for a short while with the idea that his future might be different, yet he knew that it could not be. He owed too much—to Lucien Delacourt who had been both mother and father to him, to his army comrades who had supported him through thick and thin. He must keep to the path he had chosen. His mother had advised him to marry, but she took no note of loyalties, of duties that must be met. To Lavinia, the military was what men played at until they found something better. She had nagged his poor father to distraction until he had given up the world he loved, and for what? He closed the file and returned it to the pile with a loud smack, sending clouds of dust rising thickly into the air. Yet in one thing she *was* right, damn her. He had never felt so deeply for any person on earth as he did for Lizzie Ingram, and he knew that he never would.

But he must forget such feelings, he thought grimly, put behind him the role of lovesick swain, and return to the life he knew. Chelwood was in better shape than it had been for years and he need tarry no longer. In the next few days he would hand the reins to Mellors and say goodbye to his neighbours. They would not be surprised for he had already hinted at his departure. A few hours more and he would be packed and ready to leave—back to a man's world. That's where he belonged and where he would stay.

A sudden squall of rain beat at the window. The weather had turned and a storm was setting in. He sat for long minutes staring through the glass, then, irritated by his lack of action, he picked up the piece of paper lying crumpled at the side of the desk and smoothed it out to read again. Rosanna had been swift to keep her promise and their meeting was already arranged for this very night. But there were hours yet to pass before eleven struck and he did not know how he was to fill them. He must put aside his warring emotions and hold to the fact that tonight at last he would discover Gil's fate and tomorrow he would brave one last encounter with the woman he had loved.

Once again he sat down at the battered desk and this time took up his quill. His note to Brede House took some time to compose and several wasted sheets lay in the paper basket before he was satisfied with the result. He kept the note crisp and neutral, merely informing her that he had heard from Rosanna and that their meeting was tonight. If it was convenient to Miss Ingram, he would be at Brede House at midday on the morrow when he would convey whatever information he had garnered.

## Chapter Twelve

Lizzie turned the note over again and for the hundredth time read its cold, unfeeling message. It was clear now that when Justin called tomorrow, it would be their last meeting. In a short while she would hear through acquaintances no doubt, that he had left Chelwood Place to return to Spain and that would be the end of everything. How had it come to this? Twenty-four hours ago she had lain within his arms, deliriously happy, yet now... She let the note drift to the bed and wandered to her window. The rain had stopped, but mists were already stealing out of the twilight and an ice-cold moon was rising in the sky. Winter had arrived and all she had to look forward to was this quiet house and the narrow, love-

less life that went with it. A sheaf of draw-
ings was laid on the window seat and she
flicked idly through the pages, stopping at
one that she had hidden well from sight. The
sketch had been done only that morning, just
before she set off for the fair—she and Justin entwined in each other's arms—and she
could not tear her eyes from it. Slowly, over-
whelmingly, waves of sorrow built and toppled within her. But then Hester's voice was
sounding from below, calling on her to attend
Mrs Croft, and she hastily stifled the sobs
that threatened.

'You called for me, Mrs Croft. Are you
ready to retire?'

Henrietta was propped upright in her favourite fireside chair, her feet raised on an
old brown-velvet stool. A bright fire burned
in the grate and, despite the gloomy furnishings, the room looked warm and welcoming.

'Not quite ready, my dear. I shall read a little while longer I think, but I have news for
you. Good news.'

Lizzie was quickly alert. Had Justin regretted the cold note and sent another message,
one that sought to make amends? A ripple of
joy spread itself outwards, radiating through
her whole body.

'A message has arrived,' Mrs Croft continued. The rippling grew intense and she looked eagerly across at the old lady. 'Two messages, in fact. They came this morning, but in some strange fashion became entangled with my books from the circulating library. Hester has only just this minute found them.'

If they had come this morning, neither could be a message from Justin. Lizzie's joy died as instantly as it had flamed.

'Who are they from?' She tried to infuse her voice with interest.

'From Clementine, my dear. She promised to pass on any news she had of your father, and she has done exactly that.'

For a moment, Lizzie was stunned. 'How is he?' she stuttered. 'He is not…'

'Don't be alarmed, Elizabeth, he has suffered no harm. On the contrary, he has been given leave. And from what you say, it is not before time—the poor man has had little respite from the fighting.'

'My father is returning from Spain?' She was still trying to grasp the news.

'He is. Is that not wonderful, my dear? And Clementine writes that she has given him our direction and he will be with us as soon as he can make passage across the Channel. I must get Hester to clean and tidy the large room next to yours,' she muttered, a little flustered at the thought of this new housekeeping. 'At the moment it is full of odds and ends and we must make sure it looks a deal more inviting for Colonel Ingram's arrival.'

Lizzie could not bring herself to speak. For years she had been longing for this moment and now it had come, she was struck dumb. Somehow the Colonel's homecoming was not as welcome as it should be. She felt a traitorous guilt. She should be ecstatic and she wasn't. She knew why, of course. Her heart was broken and she wanted no one to know, least of all her father. He would be unsympathetic. He might even be angry with her that she had become involved with a fellow officer. He would think that she was up to her old tricks again and still could not be trusted. And she would have to put on a shiny face, a façade that pretended she was whole and that whatever she had enjoyed with Justin Delacourt had been a silly diversion.

Henrietta was looking at her thoughtfully. 'It is good news, I hope, Elizabeth?'

'Yes, of course. It has taken me by surprise, that is all.'

'Naturally it has, my dear. But you will

have a few weeks, I imagine, before your father is here, a few weeks to plan how you will spend your time with him. While he is with us, you are to have a holiday.'

'I cannot do that, Mrs Croft.' Feeling the way she did, to be always with the Colonel would be torture.

'You can and you will. I insist.'

'You are most kind,' was all she could murmur.

'Now tell me about your afternoon.'

It was the last thing she wanted, but she had already allowed her feelings to show too much. She sensed the old lady's sharp eyes on her and wondered if Hester had been telling tales. The maid had returned early from the fair and, when Lizzie had come through the door, had stared in surprise at the young woman's flushed face.

'It was a very large event,' she began, 'but then I imagine you know that—I was surprised at its size…' Her voice trailed off. Really, she could not bear to think of the afternoon.

'And Justin? He was there to escort you—escort both of us, if I remember rightly. I trust he proved a helpful guide.'

'We met as arranged.' It was inadequate,

but even so Lizzie could not keep the quaver from her voice.

'I have always found Justin excellent company and today is likely to be one of the last times he can play host,' Mrs Croft said carefully. 'James Armitage called while you were out. His wife is still deeply distressed for there has been no news of their son. And now James thinks there never will be. He mentioned that Justin is preparing to return to the Peninsula very shortly and when he goes, Caroline's last hope will go with him.'

'Sir Justin is to leave Chelwood so soon?' The lump in her throat was so large that she felt sure she would never again be able to swallow.

'Why, yes, my dear. He was always set on returning to Spain once Chelwood was on its feet. I fear that we must get ready to say goodbye to him.' Her voice was kindly, but firm. *She is telling me to abandon any foolish hopes I may have cherished*, Lizzie thought.

Mrs Croft settled herself more comfortably. 'Could you pass me the newspaper, Elizabeth? I will read the political columns. They are bound to make me sleepy, but you need not see me to bed this evening—Hester is on hand to help.'

Lizzie could only nod miserably and walk towards the door, but her hand had barely turned the doorknob when Mrs Croft said abruptly, 'Stop! I had almost forgotten', and began to rummage in the folds of the bedspread.

'Here, my dear, here it is—the other message.' Lizzie walked back to the bed and took the proffered envelope. 'Clementine enclosed it with her letter. It must be important for she paid extra for it to be delivered. You must read it immediately!'

Once in her room, she tore open the envelope and drew out three closely written sheets. The handwriting was vaguely familiar and when she flicked the pages to find a signature, she knew why. Piers, Piers Silchester! She skimmed his hundreds of words, sentence after sentence, hoping she was happy, feeling sure the sea air must be bracing, imagining her employer to be a woman of generous spirit. She frowned, trying to find a purpose. And there it was—on the final page.

…But even the most benevolent employer, Miss Ingram, must leave you wishing for your own establishment and it is for that reason that I have dared once more to approach you. Miss Bates has given me kind permission to write and ask if you might now be willing to consider my offer of marriage...

She dropped the letter on the floor, too agitated to read more. At this lowest ebb of her fortunes, nothing could be less welcome than the renewed attentions of a man for whom she felt so little. She would rather stay a companion until she was eighty than agree to Piers's proposal. He was offering her an establishment, he said. She did not want an establishment, she wanted a home. He was offering her affection, but she did not want this cautious, tepid love. She rejected the limp sentiments, the mediocre emotions that filled the pages before her. She wanted fierce love, words that scorched the very paper they sat upon. She wanted Justin's words of love, only Justin's.

But she would not get them, ever. Listlessly, she sank down on to the window seat, a shawl draped around her shoulders to keep warm. There was no point in going to bed for she would not sleep. All she could do was sit and think. The letter was soon forgotten, her mind too busy replaying the angry exchanges with the man she loved, too busy questioning why they had quarrelled so badly. But why question the unreasoning fury she'd felt? He was a soldier and she did not trust him. Experience had taught her to doubt: her father had abandoned her, Victor had taken gross advantage of her youth and now Justin. Perhaps, she thought mournfully, she did not deserve a man who was true, who would take her heart, but keep it safe. She might be pretty and lively and spirited, but that had not been sufficient to keep her father by her side. So why should it be any different now she was a grown woman? If she were honest, she had never quite believed it would last, never quite believed that a beautiful man such as Justin could be hers. And it appeared she had been right to doubt him, even if she'd jumped to conclusions and was wrong about Rosanna. He was planning to leave Rye and very soon, yet he had said nothing of it; she'd had to learn the news from her employer. Justin had enjoyed her and was moving on, that was the sum of it. Their quarrel today had given him the perfect excuse to walk away.

She heard the clock in the hall strike eleven. Two hours had passed, yet she'd hardly noticed. The house was deathly quiet and she wandered over to the bed and lay down on the coverlet. There was no possibility of sleep, but she must rest. She would need to have herself under control when Justin came calling. Something scratched at her neck and she extracted his abandoned note and held it up to flickering candlelight. Three letters in one day and not one of them had brought joy. His words seemed even more coldly indignant than before. If he were going to meet Rosanna, might it really be true that she had new information? But why then had the woman chosen to meet him at night—because she was as scared of Chapman as she'd said or because she hoped to make Justin her lover? But what if Rosanna really *were* scared? One thing was certain: the tow-headed man was villainous and if he knew his lover was confiding a dangerous secret to Justin, he would not hesitate and—what?—would he kill her?

The nape of her neck prickled. That man was capable of murdering anyone. She had always hoped, Justin, too, that somewhere Gil was a prisoner, kidnapped and kept out of sight until the gang had finished their smuggling operations along this stretch of coast. But what if Chapman had not kidnapped Gil, what if he had killed him? The idea had lurked at the back of her mind for weeks and she suspected similar thoughts had plagued Justin. Neither of them had ever spoken of it, unwilling to give life to such a dreadful outcome, but they both knew that if the gang had killed the excise man, they would not hesitate to kill Gil if it was necessary. He would be costly to guard all these months and any ransom money was uncertain. Why, in fact, would they not kill anyone who knew too much—including Justin?

Justin had been part of Chapman's gang. It was all very well for him to say that he was a pillar of the community and safe from retribution, but had not Gil been such a pillar? Her thoughts were now roaming the darkest of alleys. Suddenly it seemed more than possible that Justin was in danger. If Chapman had decided that his erstwhile gang member was too much of a threat, how would he kill him? He could hardly storm Chelwood Place or accost his victim in full view of the town. No, he would lure him to a lonely spot where his cries would go unheard and his body never found. She began to feel very uneasy. Might that actually happen? Of course not, she scolded herself, Justin was far too good a soldier to fall into such a trap. Unless…Rosanna. Of course, Rosanna. Chapman would get Rosanna to lure him, either with her beauty or by dangling the hope of more information. Her stomach lurched as the thought scissored its way through her. The meeting tonight, the meeting that Rosanna had arranged—and in an instant she knew that Justin would learn nothing, only that he had been betrayed.

She scrunched the note into a fierce little ball. He was facing death! She was almost sure of it and she could do nothing to help him. She had no idea where they would meet or when—it was pitch-black now and they could be anywhere. Perhaps on the marshes? From her previous experience, she knew it would be hopeless to try to find them there. But after what had happened last night, would Justin return to the marshes? Surely he would be suspicious of any suggestion by Rosanna that they meet there. No, it was not the marshes, but where? Her gaze intensified as though she could break through the uncurtained window and fly on wings to his side. The cove! The thought dropped into her head out of nowhere. The cove beneath the garden of Brede House. It had to be. She knew it for a haunt of the smugglers and she knew that no one else visited. Mrs Croft and Hester hardly ever ventured into the garden, certainly not once darkness had fallen, for it held such bad memories for them. So what better place to commit foul murder than a quiet cove below a deserted garden with a convenient river running by.

In an instant she was off the bed and grabbing her cloak from the wardrobe. Whatever stupid mess she had made of knowing Justin Delacourt, she would move worlds to keep him from harm. Silently she stole downstairs in her stockinged feet. Mrs Croft would be long asleep, but she was wary of meeting Hester. The maid might still be up and about, clearing dishes or setting the table for breakfast. Lizzie craned her head around the kitchen door and saw with relief that she was alone. Light from a half-moon was shining through the window and, by its muted sheen, she found her boots tucked neatly behind the great black range. Then slowly and carefully she unlatched the door which led into the garden. Moonlight glistened off the winding path, guiding her onwards, past the folly to the wicket gate. The wind had fallen away and above her an enormous sky shone a dark-blue enamel. She flitted along, her black cloak seeming to meld her into the darkness. No sounds reached her, no sights disturbed her. The garden lay quiet and unmolested. But her heart began to thump louder when she passed through the gate and started down the stairs. The beach lay still and empty in the moonlight. The whole world was still, it seemed, the mirror surface of the river blurred only by lowering mists. Not a movement. She looked upwards along the path that led to the clifftop, the path she had taken only last night in pursuit of the smugglers. But again there was no one. If the gang had ever been here, they had dissolved into thin air; wherever they planned to attack Justin, it was not on this beach.

She turned to go, feeling a leaden disappointment. She had been so sure that she would find them here, but she'd been mistaken. And what a mistake! Even now in some unknown place Justin could be suffering pain, torture. The thought was anguish, but she could do nothing. All that was left was to return to the house and pray.

She had reached the second step of the wooden staircase when a slight sound caught her ear and she stopped to listen. In a second a whirlwind had descended. A large hand covered her mouth and another thrust

an ill-smelling gag between her lips. With
her arms pulled painfully behind her back,
she was pushed roughly down the stairs and
on to the strand.

'What 'ave we 'ere, then?' A man emerged
from the shadows and it was Chapman. The
bleached hair and colourless eyes were almost
invisible in the moonlight, but she could read
his expression clearly.

His smile jeered at her. 'Were yer lookin'
for someone? I wouldn't want to disappoint
yer, not when yer such a pretty little miss.'

This man was truly evil and she had fallen
into his hands. He came closer and thrust her
chin upwards. She felt his sour breath hot on
her cheeks and told herself that at all costs,
she must not faint.

A circle of men surrounded her, dark-
looking cut-throats, salacious smirks on their
faces. 'What d'yer want us to do with 'er?'
one of them dared to ask.

Chapman spat. 'All in good time. I might
just have a little bit o' fun first.'

The man who had spoken jerked his head
towards the clifftop and Lizzie could see the
faint outline of a woman. Rosanna! So Justin
was not with her and she had been mistaken
again. Whatever had made her think she was

cut out for adventure? If she escaped this nightmare, her life must change. Her longing for adventure had done nothing but lead her into danger and upset those she loved. It was time to stop—if only she had not left it too late.

Chapman shrugged his shoulders and walked away. 'Tie 'er up proper. Get rid of 'er.'

The words were barely out of his mouth when two of his comrades lunged forwards and grabbed her. A rope was tied around her wrists so tightly that she felt her skin break and bleed beneath its force, and then she was forced to the ground. *Don't give up*, she told herself, *don't give up*. Struggling fiercely, she kicked out at them, managing to land the occasional blow, until a third member of the gang arrived at their calling and sat down heavily on her legs.

'Yer shouldn't do that, missy. We can git narsty,' he said, pantingly.

Another length of rope was round her ankles and then two of them were lifting her horizontally in the air.

A fourth man who had stood looking on, silent and motionless, let out a hoarse guffaw.

'Nicely trussed, lads. We'm gettin' good, ain't we?'

''Old the lantern, Nat. 'tis black as pitch.'

For the moment the moon had disappeared into a basket of cloud and in near obscurity she was carried across the shingle towards a dark wound in the cliff. The light from the lantern swung back and forth in an erratic arc, but when they drew nearer she could see that it was the opening to a cave. They were going to leave her in a cave. She felt a draining relief. They were not going to murder her, after all—or worse. But why leave her here? The answer was swift and stomach-turning.

'Take her gag orf, Jack. She can yell all she wants, but no one will 'ear 'er.'

'You sure?'

'Yeah, that way she'll drown quicker. We'm compassionate, ain't we?' Again that rough guffaw.

She lay rigid as they carried her deeper into the cave. A terror had overtaken her and she was numb with despair. This was the end, after all. She would die alone in this wretched place and no one would ever find her. Mrs Croft would think she had left without notice, her father when he arrived would decide she had gone off on one of her mad adventures and wash his hands of her for good. And Justin, what would he think? Certainly not that she had tried to save him from a fate he did not even face. More likely he would imagine that she had left Rye as swiftly as she'd arrived and then dismiss her from his mind.

She was dumped unceremoniously on the shingle floor of the cave amid a huddle of large rocks. The sound of retreating footsteps and then she was alone. Gradually her eyes adjusted to the dark and in the distance she made out a shard of light. The moon must have broken free of its prison of cloud and she was looking back at the cave's entrance. She wondered if it were possible to roll herself towards it, but rocks and stones littered the path and what if she succeeded—the tide was already rising, and instead of dying here, she would simply die on the beach. She shuffled her body around, trying to get more comfortable. What a ridiculous notion! How comfortable could you get with hands and feet tightly bound, waiting for certain death? In her squirmings, the slightest trickle of light caught her ruby ring. She fell to wondering why the smugglers had not stolen it, when a voice came out of the dark and punched the breath from her.

'Lizzie? Is that you? Is that really you?'

'Justin?'

'I saw the glint of your ring—but what are you doing here?'

In the circumstances it seemed the strangest of questions, yet the entire day had felt surreal, unfolding in fits and starts like the worst possible nightmare.

'I came to look for you,' she stammered.

'But why? I thought...' He did not finish, but she knew he was remembering their dreadful quarrel. Didn't he realise it made not a scrap of difference? When you loved truly, you had no choice but to love for ever.

Aloud she said, 'I was sure you were in danger.'

He seemed to be pondering her words and for a while they sat in silence, the only sound the slow wash of river water. 'Have they bound you?'

'They have—my hands and feet.'

She felt an uneven movement to her right and the warmth of his body coming closer.

'What happened to you?' she asked, though she didn't really need to. She knew exactly what had happened for, hadn't she foretold it in her darkest imaginings?

'Chapman used Rosanna to get me here,'

he said bitterly. 'She betrayed me—she never intended to tell me a thing.'

Lizzie said nothing. It was cold comfort to have been proved right.

'We must get out of here,' he continued. 'The tide has turned and it will not be long before the river reaches us.'

'But how? These bonds are so tight, it's impossible to get free.'

'It has to be possible,' he said with a fierce determination.

She sensed him striving to stand upright on the uneven floor, but the rope binding his ankles caused him to lose balance and crumple painfully downwards on to the pebbled floor. In the distance she heard the sound of water growing nearer, its thunder filling the rocky bay and echoing eerily around the hollow space of the cavern. She fought down panic. The water was still some way off, she told herself, and closer to hand she heard Justin moving again, then a few suppressed curses and somehow he had managed to wriggle himself into a sitting position beside her. There was something immensely comforting at having him by her side. They would at least die together.

'We're not going to die.' He had read her

thoughts with uncanny accuracy. 'I'm going to rub my wrists against the rock behind me and try to fray the rope. The surface feels sharp enough. It will take time, but it's the only thing I can think to do.'

'But you will damage yourself badly.'

'I'll be a lot more damaged if I don't get free,' he said, with an attempt at humour.

A moment later she heard the slightest sound of chafing rope. She could not bear to think of the rock cutting into his wrists and hands, as surely it must. She felt his body tense beside her and she knew that he was in pain.

'What made you come to the cove of all places?' he jerked out, trying, she thought, to distract himself. 'You should be safe in your bed.'

'I wanted to warn you. I was sure that the meeting was a trap and that you were in danger. The cove seemed the most likely place for the smugglers to lure you.'

There was another moment's silence. 'You should not have come, Lizzie.' Then, when she said nothing, he went on, 'But how? How did you know I was in danger?' He stumbled on the words as the rock cut deep into his skin.

'I didn't trust Rosanna. I never have. She could easily have told you what you wanted to know in the churchyard. Instead she arranged to meet you at this late hour.'

'She is still with Chapman,' he said bitingly. 'You were right and I was wrong—very badly wrong.'

'You didn't see them together. If you had, you would have known that she would never betray him.'

'So even women like Rosanna have their principles?'

'She loves him,' Lizzie said simply.

There was a loud exclamation as Justin's wrists once again hit rock. 'Stop!' she cried out. 'I cannot bear that you hurt yourself any more.'

'Would you rather that we drown?'

She wanted to say that, yes, she would rather, for at least in death they would be together.

'You are not going to end like this, Lizzie,' he said urgently. 'You are far too precious', and he set to rubbing again with even greater energy.

The hissing of water over shingle was growing ever louder, but it was the sound of sawing that filled her ears as the rope gradually began to fray under Justin's pressure. The rhythmic echo sent her eyelids closing and, despite her discomfort, she had begun to doze when she felt the first trickle of water nip tentatively at her toes.

'The river is rising fast,' he said grimly.

'Does it fill the cave as those men suggested?'

'At high tide it does and we are not so far from that.'

'Should we try to move further back?'

'With boulders strewn everywhere, it will be difficult, if not impossible. And it would gain us only a little time. I need to stay here— I think the rope is becoming slacker.'

'Then we will stay here together.' She felt his thigh nudge warmly against her.

'Did you really think that I was Rosanna's lover?' he asked out of the blue.

'Yes…no,' she said confusedly.

'How could you think that?'

'I didn't—not really. But when I tried to warn you, you wouldn't listen. You preferred to put your trust in an untrustworthy woman.'

'If only we had not quarrelled…' he began, and then let out a loud groan. There was a thud as a length of rope was hurled into the distance. 'I've done it, Lizzie, I've done it!'

His legs freed, he moved quickly towards her. She felt his hands on the rope securing her feet and at the same time a splash of liquid on her bare limbs.

'The river, it's coming in more quickly than ever.'

'Not too quickly, I hope. The water is still only ankle deep.'

'But...' Then she realised that what she was feeling was not water, but blood. Justin was bleeding profusely.

Shaking her limbs to get rid of the numbness, she reached down to her skirts and tore a strip of material from her petticoat. 'We must bind your poor wrists or you will lose too much blood.'

She bound his wrists as tightly as she could in the near impenetrable darkness and hoped against hope that the makeshift bandages would be sufficient. If he continued to bleed—she blinked back the tears.

'You are crying, Lizzie. Please don't.'

And his arms were around her and he was kissing her full on the lips. It was madness. If they had any sense, they would be scrambling to their feet and running for their lives. Instead they clung to each other, locked fast in an embrace, unable to let go. The cave, the rocks, the sound of the approaching river retreated into nothingness and all she could think of was that she was in his arms again. He was kissing her over and over, deeply, tenderly, when a sudden rush of water soaked them to the skin.

'You were right, the river *is* rising quickly.' His voice assumed a deliberate calm. 'The only way out is through the entrance to the cave, but the water is too deep now. We would have to swim and that's dangerous—the currents are very strong.'

'And I cannot swim.' Her words were barely audible.

'Then we must think again.'

'There is nothing to think about. *You* must escape, Justin. You can swim out into the river—I am sure you are strong enough to manage the currents—and then you can bring help to me.'

'By the time I could do that, you would be swimming with the fishes. There must be another way.'

But she could not see how. She did not want to die; she wanted to live, wanted once more to taste his love to the full. But if that was not to be, then he must save himself.

'You must go!'

'*We* must go,' he corrected her. 'We must climb to the back of the cave. There are passages linking one cave to another. When Gil and I were boys we would dare each other to travel as far along them as we could, before we reached the sea. And if there are passages running parallel to the river, there should be at least one leading inland.'

Another great rush of water had them scrambling to their feet. From behind came the sound of the river filling the space they had occupied just minutes before.

'Come, we must move quickly!'

He clasped her hand in his and together they began a perilous climb in the dense gloom over rocks and rough stones towards the rear of the cave. The further they moved from the entrance, the darker it grew. Lizzie could not share her lover's optimism that they would ever find their way out.

Justin's cheer seemed to be waning, too. 'It looks as though we will have to swim, after all.' They had come to a full stop at the very rear of the cavern and before them stretched an enormous lake of water, left by the retreating tide.

'I can't,' she protested, aghast.

He squeezed her hand tightly. 'We'll go together, Lizzie. It may not be as deep as we think.'

She stood on the brink of the pool, unable to take the first step. Behind them the roar of river water grew louder, tumbling itself through the narrow entrance and crashing through the barrier of rocks. 'We must at least try,' he said into her ear. 'It is our only hope. Hold very tight to me and all will be well.'

She did as he told her and walked forwards. Almost immediately she was plunged waist deep in water and had to smother a terrified cry. She had wanted adventure to knock at her door, hadn't she? Well, here it was and knocking loudly. Frantically she clutched hold of his hand and, though the water rose breast high, she continued to walk beside him. Something knocked against her left side and she put out her hand to fend it off. It seemed like clothes, but what were clothes doing floating in this horrible, murky pool?

'Justin…' She curled her fingers into the palm of his hand. 'There is something odd.'

'Odder than us trying to wade through we know not how much water, fifty feet into the cliff?'

Her voice grew strained. 'There is definitely something wrong—I can feel it. If only we had a light.'

'We just might have—only to be used in emergency, but this could be it.' And there was the sharp crack of glass being broken and a strip of paper had burst into flame. He held the flickering light aloft.

'You see, I managed to bring a light, but not a knife—that was a bad mistake.'

'What on earth...?'

'It's a new invention, though not ideal— a phosphoric candle. We had them in Spain, but they are expensive and dangerous. We must protect the flame as best we can.' Lizzie looked up, temporarily distracted. Candlelight revealed for the first time the enormity of the cavern. A huge domed ceiling swept down to jagged walls of white chalk, discoloured at intervals by great patches of green seepage. At floor level, chalk teeth guarded an abundance of small crevices, any of which might lead somewhere or nowhere.

Candle in hand, Justin waded to the far side of her. In the thin beam of light she caught a glimpse of blue, then a flash of white. They *were* clothes, she thought. How extraordinary.

'Oh, my God!' He was bending close to the water and peering intently.

'Whatever is it?'

'I cannot tell you. Look away, Lizzie.'

She could feel him trembling and grasped hold of him. 'Whatever it is, tell me. What have you seen?'

But somehow she knew what he had seen, knew that the mystery of Gil's disappearance was solved at last and in the most dreadful way.

He took her hand again and, with the candle to light their way, they waded through the deep water to dry rock beyond. Once there, they collapsed on the floor, both of them shaking and sick to the stomach.

'Justin, I am so sorry.' What could she say? No words of comfort could make this better.

He put his arms round her. 'I suppose I always knew deep down that I would never find him alive.

'But this…'

'It is too terrible to think of. And we should not think of it—not now. We must concentrate on saving ourselves, getting help. Gil must have a Christian burial and a grave for his parents to visit.'

He jumped to his feet, newly determined. 'We have to find a way out. The candle is still alight and we must search every inch of these walls.'

He began to move the light first up and down, then from left to right, his eyes anxiously scanning the rough surfaces of the cave. A large passage swam out of the darkness, but he made no move towards it. 'That is the route that Gil and I travelled, but it leads only to the sea. There must be another passage, one that runs upwards to the surface of the cliff.'

He began to feel along the walls in the hope that his fingers rather than his eyes might locate what he sought. Lizzie, standing a few feet back, gradually became aware of a darker smudge against the white chalk. 'It's there! I'm sure it's there', and she pointed to a hole in the rock no bigger than two feet high. 'But it is so small.'

'And may lead nowhere,' he warned. 'Hold the candle and I will explore. First, though, I need to rid myself of these wet clothes.'

And without a moment's hesitation he tore off his shirt and breeches and threw them to the ground. She stood mesmerised by the sight, his strong male body glowing nakedly in the faint light of the candle. The thought of his poor, dead friend rose unbidden to her mind—staying alive had never seemed more important.

'I'll travel as far along the passage as I can. Listen out for my call.'

He went to crouch down at the small aperture, then suddenly straightened up and walked back to her.

'Gil is no more, but we must try to live—for him and for each other. But if anything should happen to me, Lizzie, if anything should happen to either of us, know that I love you.'

He had said the words—words she had so wanted to hear—and joy, pure in its intensity, sang through her whole being. She wanted to clasp him to her, tell him not to risk his life alone. They would stay here together and face whatever fate had determined for them. But he was already bent double on hands and knees, and in a few seconds had disappeared from view.

For anxious moments Lizzie clutched the candle, the light seeming ever dimmer in the encroaching darkness. She heard him scrabbling along the rocky surface, but gradually the noise faded and she heard nothing. Her pulse was beating fast and she tried to still it. If the passage proved a dead end, Justin would

return, and if it did not he could go onwards
and find help. Surely the water from the river
did not come this far inland and she would
be safe until rescue arrived. But the thought
of staying for unknown hours in this dark,
echoing hole, and with a dead man floating
close by, was appalling.

A faint sound came from the aperture, Justin's voice seeming to come from a long distance. She bent down to hear and as she did
so, the candle dropped from her hand and
went out. Thick blackness engulfed her, for
not even the slightest sliver of moonlight
found its way this deep into the cliff. She felt
the beginnings of a new panic rising to take
her in its grip.

His voice sounded again and this time she
could make out several words. 'Come, long
passage, more light.'

There would need to be, she thought fear-
fully, but she followed his example and
stripped off her sodden gown and petticoat. Then, crouching down near to where
she thought the entrance to the passageway
should be located, she felt along the wall with
her hands. It took her some minutes to find
it, but then she was on her knees and crawl-
ing forwards, trying not to think of what she

was doing. She could see nothing, just feel the hot, close darkness. She moved slowly along the passage, shuffling forwards in an endless and unforgiving journey. The sharp flints bit into her soft flesh and the walls on either side seemed intent on crushing her between them. She must not think, she must keep her mind a blank, until she came out at the other side. She thought she must be travelling upwards and now she could hear Justin's voice growing louder, then just the glimmer of light, and at last the hazy outline of his form. She was through! She collapsed nervelessly on the floor and he had to scoop her into his arms to set her back on her feet.

'Are you hurt?'

'Not hurt—terrified. I cannot bear enclosed spaces.'

He smoothed her hair from her face and kissed each eyelid. 'My poor darling. What have I brought you to?'

'I brought myself,' she reminded him. 'But I find that, after all, I am a coward.'

'Dearest Lizzie, a coward is something you are not! But see—your courage is rewarded. There is more light here—it is very little, but it must be coming from somewhere. We have travelled nearer the surface.'

He took her hand again and together they began to work their way around the huge boulders of chalk that over the years had detached themselves from the walls. With bare feet, the terrain was rough and painful, but they managed to make good progress and within a quarter of an hour stood facing what appeared to be the end of the massive chamber. Justin moistened his finger and held it high.

'I thought so. There is a current of air here and it's quite strong. I wonder...it seems to be coming from that far corner.'

She looked to the left, to the spot he was indicating, and hoped he was wrong. 'It's very dark—it doesn't look too promising.'

'Yet I would bet my regimentals that that is the way out.'

And so it proved. Hidden in the depths of the darkness was the first of many steps which had been hewn from the rock by some unknown hand. One step at a time, they mounted the spiral staircase, winding round and round up the cavern face until Lizzie fell into a veritable stupor. The lack of sleep, the terror of being trapped and the dreadful moment when they had found Gil's body were combining to make her feel she was walking through a parallel world.

Justin had his arms around her waist and lifted her bodily up the last few steps, only for them to face once more a blank wall. Surely they could not have endured all this for nothing. But the faintest pencil of light was visible, light which traced the shape of a door. Justin put his shoulders to it and there was a loud cracking. A rush of fresh air hit them in the face. They were out, standing in moonlight, standing in the middle of the folly.

'I always wondered where that door led to.' There was a surprised look on his face. 'Whenever I came to tea as a child, I would play here and marvel at it—a door without a handle!'

She sank down on to cushions, body and mind exhausted, and when he followed her, they stayed locked in grateful silence. Then, without warning, tears began to fill her eyes and spill down her cheeks. He wiped them away as delicately as he could with the palm of his hand.

'No handkerchief, I fear,' he apologised.

She looked at him and shook her head. It was too ridiculous and she could not prevent a small giggle. The bandages around his wrist were dark with dirt and dried blood. His underwear was green with the slime of seaweed, his wonderful golden hair sticky with chalk and his naked feet cut and bruised.

'Laugh away, Miss Ingram! But consider—how elegant do you look right now?'

She knew that she must be the most frightful sight, but she cared not a jot. They were safe, they were alive and they were together. No matter that he would soon be packing to leave, he loved her. She would cherish that for the rest of her life.

He put his arms around her and gave her a gentle kiss. He tasted warm and salty and she kissed him back. He kissed her again, hugging her near-naked body to his, caressing her softness with his hands until they broke from each other in sudden dismay. The image of Gil, so lately left behind, haunted them. Yet the drive to live and love was so strong that within a minute they had begun to kiss again, more and more fiercely, until she shivered from the penetrating cold. The realisation that they were both soaked to the skin was a sobering thought.

'We should not be dallying here,' she managed breathlessly. 'We must get warm. And should we not alert the preventives?'

'I warned them there might be trouble to-night and their ship, *The Stag*, is waiting off the coast. I told them that the gang were due to make their run to France—presumably after they'd disposed of me.'

'And how did you come by that information?'

He smiled. 'Was I not a smuggler, too? I didn't admit to it, of course. I was suitably vague when I sent a message to the new excise man, but with luck he will have alerted his colleagues and they will catch the gang red-handed.'

'Then we are quite done with our adventuring.' She felt strangely empty. Justin loved her, she must hold on to that, and if this night were the beginning and the end of their love, then at least she would have the memory. But somehow that didn't make the emptiness go away.

'I wouldn't say quite,' he said enigmatically. 'But right now, it is a hot bath and warm sheets that we need.'

## Chapter Thirteen

Lizzie had never been so fussed over. Hester had heard her stumbling up the stairs before dawn and had taken the sight of a bedraggled, near-naked girl surprisingly well. Her first response was to boil cans of water and plunge Lizzie into a hot bath. Only when the young woman was wrapped in sheets warmed by a hot brick and sipping milk straight from the stove did she ask for an explanation. Lizzie told her story haltingly and even to her ears it sounded fantastical. The maid listened stolidly without passing comment and, when the last words had been murmured, said only, 'You should sleep now.' Lizzie thought that highly unlikely. She had passed the most terrifying night of her life and her mind was still vivid with fearful images. But as soon as her eyelids drooped, sheer exhaustion sent her into a deep sleep where she stayed until well into the afternoon.

It was her employer tiptoeing into the room that finally awoke her. A single beam of light was cutting a bright passage through the curtains and she glimpsed the hazy outline of Mrs Croft's figure. She blinked as the old lady came to hover at the foot of the bed.

'I had not meant to wake you, my dear, but we were growing anxious.'

Lizzie turned her head and glanced at her small timepiece. Startled by the late hour, she struggled to sit up.

'I am so sorry, Mrs Croft.' She was dry mouthed and her head was spinning. 'I should have been up and dressed hours ago.'

'You will not be working today, Elizabeth,' Mrs Croft said firmly. 'Hester has told me a story that I could hardly credit, but whatever the truth, it is evident that you have been through a dreadful ordeal and you need to rest. By all accounts, you will be lucky to escape pneumonia. Hester said you were soaked to the skin when she found you.'

'I was, but thanks to her I am sure I will

suffer no lasting ill. You have both been very kind, but I must get up.'

'Only if you are quite certain. Otherwise you must rest. Hester is bringing you chocolate and, once you have drunk it, you may rise and dress if you feel well enough. But no working, mind you.'

'But…'

'And no "buts". I want you fit and well. I have had a message from Chelwood and Sir Justin has asked to visit to see how you fare. He will be here within the hour.'

She paused, waiting, it seemed, for Lizzie to speak, but when her companion made no response, she continued, 'Justin did not feature excessively in Hester's account, yet he appears most anxious to talk with you.' She looked hopefully at Lizzie, then gave a small sigh. 'No doubt I shall eventually learn what has been happening beneath my nose. I have the feeling it is quite a story.'

At that moment Hester came in with a cup of steaming chocolate and the two older ladies went quietly downstairs together. What decadence, Lizzie thought wryly, as she sipped at her cup. Now if I were mistress of Chelwood, this would be commonplace. But at that point her thoughts slammed to a halt. Justin had said he loved her and with that she must be content. He had said it at a moment of the greatest danger and it was well known that people in desperate situations were liable to say things that they later regretted.

The terrible events of the night came back with crushing force; over the last few weeks she'd had sufficient adventure to last her a lifetime and imperceptibly she had begun to long for the settled existence she had always rejected. But not just any settled life. A married life—with a strong and loving man who could make her giddy with just one look from those beautiful, changeful eyes. If only…but it was no good daydreaming. Even if Justin truly loved her, he would never give up soldiering. From their very first meeting in the churchyard, he had made that clear. She swung her legs out of bed and her limbs felt tired and sore. Indeed, her whole being felt drained. If she was determined on that secure life, she thought unhappily, then her only course was to accept Piers Silchester. And that she could not do, for he was far too good a man to deceive in such a miserable fashion.

No, she would remain a companion, perching on the edge of someone else's world, never quite belonging, never quite at ease. Right

now, though, she could not think of the future.
She must concentrate on looking her best for
Justin's visit, for she knew that these were the
final precious moments she would have with
him. Mrs Croft had said that he was coming
to see how she fared, but her employer did
not know the whole truth. He was coming
for much more, she was certain: he was coming to say goodbye. He would not want last
night's declaration of love to beguile her into
thinking that there was a future for them. And
after all, there was nothing now to keep him
in Rye—Chelwood was once more flourish-
ing and he knew at last the dreadful truth of
his friend's disappearance.

She heard the murmur of voices below.
He was here already! Hastily she splashed
water on her face and dragged a comb
through untidy ringlets. In the stark winter
light her glass showed a pallid face with dark
smudges beneath the eyes. She would wear
her very best dress—a charming confection
of deep-peach sarsnet and creamy lace—and
hope its vibrant colour would compensate for
her pallor. Scrambling through the contents
of her chest drawer, she unearthed a ribbon
of the same deep peach which she threaded

through her curls. Another swift glance in the mirror and she was satisfied.

Justin rose as she walked through the door and his eyes rested on her trim figure just a moment too long.

'How are you feeling, Miss Ingram?'

'Ashamed that I have slept so long.'

'You should not be. You look charmingly for it.'

Mrs Croft's face registered surprise at the compliment, but she said nothing, merely making space for Lizzie beside her on the brown velvet sofa.

'I was telling Mrs Croft that I have this moment come from Five Oaks. I could not tell the Armitages everything they wanted— how Gil became caught up in Rosanna's net must always remain guesswork—but I think I managed to piece together the final details of his story accurately enough. It was the telling that was so difficult.'

Lizzie's face clouded with sympathy. 'I imagine your call on them must have been unbearable.'

He nodded. 'Gil's death was always going to be a dreadful thing for them to accept, no matter how gently I sought to break the news.

But it is done and at least they now have certainty. I have organised a work party from Five Oaks to retrieve his body at low tide and the Rector has agreed to a funeral date next week.'

And that is when you will go, she told herself, but aloud she replied as cheerfully as she could, 'You *have* been busy and all I have done is sleep.'

'I would have slept, too, but I could not rest until I had spoken to James and Caroline.'

There was a pained silence while each of them thought of the terrible death the young man had suffered. Then Justin said a little more brightly, 'You will be glad to know that the preventives caught the gang halfway to the French coast. They believe they have captured them all. And there is sufficient evidence to hang Thomas Chapman for the excise man's murder, if not for Gil's.'

'And Rosanna?' Even now she could not keep the note of uncertainty from her voice.

'She has turned King's evidence in order to save her skin and has agreed to incriminate Chapman in return for a lighter sentence. So much for love!'

The contempt in his voice made Lizzie's stomach twist and turn. His opinion of women had never been high and with good reason, but she'd hoped that his harsh judgment had been tempered by knowing and loving her. Not so, it seemed. No doubt he was readying himself to take back last night's declaration, as well as to say goodbye.

Mrs Croft rose unsteadily to her feet. 'I should not be glad to hear such a thing of a fellow human, but I have to confess that I am delighted that Chapman will hang. The more I think of it, the more convinced I am that he and his gang were responsible for poor, dear Susanna's untimely death and I can feel no regret at his fate.'

Justin had risen, too. 'Nor should you. He will be given justice, no more and no less.'

Then, turning to Lizzie, he offered his arm. 'I wonder, Miss Ingram, if you would be good enough to walk with me a while.'

Lizzie was about to demur when the old lady intervened. 'After last night, you will want to talk together, I'm sure. Be careful to wrap up warmly.'

Unwillingly Lizzie followed him into the hall. With all her might she wanted to push away the encounter that was coming, pack it tightly in a box and mark it 'not to be opened', but she had no choice—better, then, to get it over with as swiftly as possible.

Reaching up for her cloak, she brushed against a small posy of freesias that had been left lying on the rosewood console. 'They are for Gil.' Justin was beside her. 'They were his favourite flowers and fortunately Chelwood's succession house had sufficient blooms.'

She put her nose to them and breathed in their sweet, fresh scent. 'They are quite beautiful.'

'Would you object if we were to walk to the cove? The flowers are by way of a wreath.'

'No, I suppose not,' she said, but there was a tremor in her voice.

'It might be good to exorcise the demons,' he said gently.

The cove, the flowers…he was saying a last farewell to Gil. But a last goodbye to her, too. The cove had loomed large in the short drama of their love and would be a fitting backdrop to its final scene.

He unlatched the kitchen door and she passed through into the garden, quiet and still in the late-November afternoon. Slowly she walked beside him down the path towards the wicket gate, unable quite to stifle a returning fear. A group of rooks rose noisily into the air at their approach and then swirled southwards making circles against the darkening sky.

Their sudden flight startled her into speech. 'How is your mother? Does she know all that has happened?'

'I have told her some of it, but not all. I think it best that I do not feed the gossip machine too voraciously.'

'Is she likely then to spread the story to her friends in London?'

'Her "friends" are currently on her black list so I am hopeful that we will contain the terrible news here in Rye. But she was most definitely intrigued. She cannot quite believe that a small town can be every bit as exciting as London. I fear she is in for a disappointment if she stays too long.'

'And is she staying?'

'In the district, yes. At Chelwood, no.'

A small frown flitted across Lizzie's face. Seeing it, he made haste to say, 'It would never do. We are chalk and cheese and her constant presence at Chelwood would suit neither of us.'

'So where will she go?'

'An acquaintance of hers is selling a manor house towards Hawkhurst.' He grinned at her, surprisingly boyish. 'We are not like to upset each other, ten miles apart.'

They were just then passing the folly and she did not respond. The memory of the hours she had spent with him was threatening to unleash the tears.

Justin seemed not to notice either the folly or her silence. 'I have undertaken to drive my mother tomorrow and, if she likes what she sees, the Delacourt lawyers will start proceedings to buy. At least the duke seems to have come to his senses and is willing now to meet his obligations by setting aside a considerable sum of money. Of course, if she takes the property, you can be sure that she will spend every penny of his on its refurbishment.'

He swung the wicket gate to one side and in single file they made their way down the wooden steps to a deserted shore. In the muted light the cove stretched before them, bland, innocent, the river flowing calmly a few feet away. They crunched their way across the shingle to the water's edge. The tide was on the turn, but it would be several hours before the cave once more filled with its deathly freight. She resolutely faced away from the dark, gaping hole.

'The adventure is over, Lizzie,' he said softly, noticing her stiff shoulders and determined back.

A spiteful gust of wind rose out of nowhere and lifted the edges of the loose cloak she wore to toss it on to the pebbles below. Swiftly he bent to retrieve the garment and placed it gently around her shoulders again. She could bear this no longer, she must get this parting over and then she could cry alone. She would make it easy for him.

'*This* adventure is over,' she agreed, 'but you will be leaving for Spain very soon and I am sure that plenty more await you there.'

'There is only one,' he said carefully, 'one last adventure.'

'You anticipate a final battle, I collect? I hope the Duke of Wellington knows of it!'

'Not a battle, Lizzie, and not a war.'

What could he mean? Was he deliberately talking moonshine to confuse her?

'Marriage,' he said in response to her questioning look. The single word echoed and re-echoed across the beach, breaking apart its calm.

She hardly dared to ask the next question. 'Whose marriage?'

'Mine.'

If hearts could stop beating, then hers did, right there, at a stroke. Of course, he would have to marry and soon, despite his misgivings. He owed it to his family. His bride would be wealthy, elegant, a member of the *ton*, far more acceptable to the Delacourts and to society than she would ever be. It was not just to say a simple farewell that he had brought her to this cove, but to tell her as gently as he could what his future was to be. She wanted to turn and flee, back up the stairs, back along the path, back to her room. And never, ever come out.

'And your marriage, too, of course,' he was saying, his voice a little less confident, 'if you feel you can trust a soldier after all that has befallen. Can you, Lizzie? Can you entrust yourself to me?'

She felt the earth shift beneath her feet and her breath come quick and short. He could not mean it, he could not. She turned a deathly white face towards him. 'I cannot pretend to understand you. I can only imagine that you are jesting, but I should tell you that it is in very poor taste.'

'It would be in abominable taste, if I *were* jesting. How am I to convince you?' He fell on to one knee and fixed her with a hesitant smile. 'Elizabeth Ingram, will you marry me?'

'But…'

'Just say, yes, Lizzie, if you mean it. My knee is already cut to ribbons.'

'Yes,' she said, laughing and crying at the same time, 'yes, yes, Justin. And do get up or you will ruin another pair of breeches!'

In seconds he was on his feet and had his arms around her. He tipped her chin upwards and brought his warm mouth down on hers. She had thought not to feel those lips again and she clung to him as though she would never let him go, kissing him over and over, until they broke from each other, breathless and laughing.

An anxious expression crossed his face and he held her at arm's length. 'Are you sure you will not find life dull with me? You see, I remember what you said about marriage.'

'I was talking nonsense. It was other men that I found dull, not marriage. I had to meet you before I came to see that.'

'And you think you could be happy at Chelwood?'

'More than happy. I have loved it from the day you sat me down in the library and scolded me for trespassing!'

'Tried to, you mean. I doubt that anyone has managed to scold you successfully, unless it be your father.' He paused and then said more seriously, 'By rights, I should have asked his permission before I came to you, but circumstances being what they are...'

'You will soon have the chance. My father is coming home and will be with us in weeks.'

Justin looked astonished. 'But when did you learn this? You said nothing.'

'I heard only yesterday and there has hardly been a chance to speak of it. I am still finding it difficult to believe.'

Difficult but delighted, she thought, so very delighted. She could meet the Colonel with pleasure now, confide her love and know that he would approve her choice. He must always have wanted this, she found herself conceding. He had acted in her best interests, even when it appeared otherwise. Through the long years he had protected her in the only way he knew, so that one day she could enjoy this happiness without fear and without regret.

'It is excellent news, Lizzie. While he is here, he can help us plan our wedding. I know that you will want him beside you on the day.'

She did not answer immediately but walked a few steps along the beach and when she turned towards him, her smile was awry. 'Are you certain of this, Justin, certain that you wish to marry?' Some part of her mind was still telling her this had to be a fantasy.

'Why ever do you ask, my darling? Surely you can see that I am deranged with love for you. Unless I am to go through the rest of my life as blue as megrim, we will have to marry.'

She returned to his side and nestled her head against his shoulder, wondering if he had thoroughly considered the problems ahead. 'Will marriage mean you must sell out?'

'I have no intention of dragging my wife from battlefield to battlefield, so, yes, I must sell out.' He tickled her chin lovingly. 'Lizzie, such a great sadness for you! Your ambition to follow the drum will never be realised!'

'I have gained another ambition,' she said shyly, 'one that is like to prove far more satisfying. But the army, your regiment...have you considered?'

'How could I not? The army will go on without me—sad but true. Even my regiment will soon forget that I was ever part of it.'

'But you were so sure that you would never leave the military. You love the life dearly.'

'I have learned to love something else more dearly!' Then seeing the trouble in her eyes, he continued forcefully, 'I have been a fool, Lizzie. I joined the army as much for my father's sake as for mine. I felt I owed it to him after the wretched unhappiness my mother caused. He had sacrificed himself and it was my job to make that sacrifice count. Or so I thought. That was a burden that Gil and I shared—a parent who loved us a little too much. But husbanding Chelwood will be an even better means by which to honour him, and lately I have been talking to Lavinia in a way that I could not before. I don't like to admit it, but it seems that my father must share some of the blame for what happened between them.'

'But Sir Lucien was not the only reason that you became a soldier. You will still find it difficult to leave the army, I think.'

'Not so difficult. It's true that for years my father's tales of soldiering stirred my blood, but I had other less praiseworthy reasons for joining up. I needed to escape—from gossip, innuendo—I needed to be as far away from women and *ton* society as possible.'

'And now?'

'Now I have no need to escape. Not that I haven't tried—for weeks I've refused to see that I loved you, that you were far more important to me than any army career, no matter how illustrious. If ever the truth began to break through the lies I told myself, I would hound it from sight. But last night when we found Gil, when I thought that only death awaited us, too, I knew without a shadow of a doubt that I had to live—but it was for you that I had to live, only you!'

He bent his head towards her and once more found her lips. 'How good it is to be alive, Lizzie,' he murmured.

Then breaking reluctantly away, he retraced his steps and picked up the small bunch of freesias from the rock on which they had lain.

'I am sure that Gil would be happy for us,' he said slowly.

'I am sure, too. And we will be happy for him—always.'

Each placed a hand on the bouquet and threw the flowers into the river, watching as the posy bobbed happily on the water's surface, a small splash of colour amid an expanse of grey. Then very gradually the turning tide took the flowers in its clasp and sent them sailing towards freedom and the open sea.

* * * * *

*A sneaky peek at next month...*

# HISTORICAL

IGNITE YOUR IMAGINATION, STEP INTO THE PAST...

## *My wish list for next month's titles...*

In stores from 6th December 2013:

❑ Not Just a Wallflower – Carole Mortimer

❑ Courted by the Captain – Anne Herries

❑ Running from Scandal – Amanda McCabe

❑ The Knight's Fugitive Lady – Meriel Fuller

❑ Falling for the Highland Rogue – Ann Lethbridge

❑ The Texas Ranger's Heiress Wife – Kate Welsh

**Available at WHSmith, Tesco, Asda, Eason, Amazon and Apple**

## *Just can't wait?*

1113/04

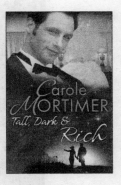

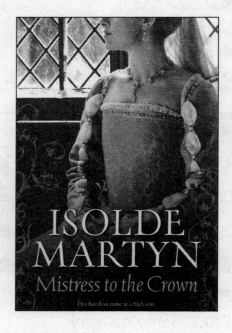